THE
JESUS CHRIST
CYPHER

SEBASTIAN KENTOR

ISBN: 9781650122090
www.sebastiankentor.com

📷 @sebastiankentorauthor

📘 www.facebook.com/sebastian.kentor.5

DEDICATION

I would like to dedicate this book to my family who supported my daily writing despite the problematic period of confinement, and to all COVID-19 outbreak victims, especially to the ones who still suffer the effects of this horrible virus. I hope that humanity will learn from its mistakes and focus on the future to rebuild and avoid more suffering of its most vulnerable people.

We are at a turning point in the history of our civilization, and we have the tremendous responsibility of shaping the future for our children. I hope that the scientific discoveries combined with the will to do good in this world will unite us all toward a common goal: the survival of our race and to improve our society's quality of life in a sustainable way. I also dedicate this book to my two favorite authors whose books inspired me to write mine (waiting for their next masterpiece was sometimes too long and painful).

This eagerness pushed me to write my book in the style of Dan Brown and J.K. Rowling. Thank you again for all the fantastic books you have written and for inspiring me to take this journey, which helped me to also pass the difficult moments of COVID-19 by quickly writing my first book after watching Dan's Masterclass. Special thanks to Josh and Heather for their amazing editorial work.

CONTENTS

§PREFACE§

For an augmented experience, you can access: *www.sebastiankentor.com/playlist* to listen to the songs adapted to each chapter matching the thrilling adventure you are about to embark on.

All of the artwork, scientific facts, historical places and figures described are real and based on evidence. The Order is an organization whose name I changed, but who is active across the globe preaching the word of Jesus. The European Union is governed by a mix of institutions that have at their heart the European Commission, whose President is one of the most powerful political figures in the world; her vision shaping the future of modern civilization. The Grand Egyptian Museum is almost completed. All characters in this book are fictional, and any resemblance to real people, living or dead, is purely coincidental.

§EPIGRAPH§

"History is opaque. You see what comes out, not the script that produces events, [...]

The generator of historical events is different from the events themselves, much as the minds of the gods cannot be read just by witnessing their deeds."

Nassim Nicholas Taleb, "The Black Swan: The Impact of the Highly Improbable"

§PROLOGUE§

19:23, OCTOBER 2ND
EGYPT, GIZA PLATEAU
SOMEWHERE
INSIDE THE
GREAT PYRAMID
OF KHUFU

LYDIA DEL BIONDO realized she only had a few minutes before she would choke to death.

The oxygen was being burned by a mysterious flame that engulfed the chamber's high ceiling in which she was a prisoner.

A myriad of thoughts flashed through her mind, adrenaline flooding her brain, as she began trying to find a way to extinguish the fire.

A familiar odor reached her nostrils, and the

glint of an ancient oil coating the stony surface of the ceiling struck her eye. *I must have triggered a spark which ignited that oil.*

She whirled about, desperately seeking a clue, but there was nothing besides the flickering of her shadow on the wall.

Damn clever Egyptians and their bloody traps perfectly hidden in this godforsaken place, Lydia muttered, trying to adapt her vision to the bright light of the flame.

Well done, Lydia, this is the end.

I came so far; this cannot be the way I die.

The answer must be just in front of me, but where?

Neo will have a solution, but of course, there is no satellite signal underneath of all these tons of solid rock.

She looked desperately around the room but could not find any marks or writing on the walls.

More strange shadows appeared before her eyes brought to life by the flames, which now had a blueish tone.

Where is the exit?

Think. Lydia; look carefully at "what lies beneath," as my dad would have said…

What lies beneath…

The entrance that closed behind her formed a

perfectly smooth surface. The wall was so well polished that she could see a faint reflection of herself in it.

The ancient basaltic stone was sucking all the light around like a dark mirror.

And then it struck her...*what lies beneath.*

I did not check the floor. What if the exit is below me?

"Activate light," Lydia bellowed, and her cell phone connected *XGlass* instantly activated the flashlight beaming it directly onto the floor.

The flame was quickly burning through the remaining oxygen. The lack of breathable air started a slow strangulation process.

I will choke in the next minute. She knew this from the medical symptoms her body was experiencing.

After carefully screening the floor, her gaze fell upon a set of hieroglyphs at the bottom of a wall.

That must be it, and at that moment, she remembered the experiments she was performing in her lab. At *Calico* as chief geneticist, she oversaw running the *Elysium* project on extending the life span of human beings.

Using the *CRISPR Cas9* gene-editing tool, she was trying to create human organs in animals to develop a genome transplantation tool for xenotransplantation.

Her experiments on nematode worms aimed to bring them to the limits of survival by using a senescence-related pattern.

Could I replicate the same life extension effects on human beings?

The irony was that now the roles were reversed. She was choking to death, and instead of focusing on the potential lifesaving hieroglyphs, old memories were playing tricks on her.

I do not want to end like my nematode worms.

Peering at the symbols, she could not read them, but something seemed off. *What was it?*

Then it hit her: the scarab symbol was carrying on his back an almost invisible variation of the *tree of life* in the center of a series of dots which could have been the pattern of a long-gone *flower of life.*

Zahawi, her Egyptian lab colleague, was always joking that she should have worked on scarabs, not on worms.

She vividly remembered his words. "Lydia, scarabs are a symbol of renewal, the endurance of the human soul, an amulet to unlock the gate to eternity."

And while looking at the strange scarab, she felt she could no longer breathe.

Acting on an impulse, she jabbed the scarab hard with her palm.

Suddenly, the floor opened, and she started to slide uncontrollably, as if she were on a roller coaster, descending towards a dark abyss leaving behind her the blue glimmer of the flames until nothingness surrounded her.

§CHAPTER 1§
07:23 AM, OCTOBER 1ST
VATICAN

THE POPE was breathing heavily, his body engulfed by the spasms of being strangled by an invisible oppressor.

He opened his eyes. Outside, the thundering noise was deafening. The staccato sound of the rain hitting his bedroom window reminded him of his childhood.

I'm just an old frail shell; I don't regret anything, my childhood…a distant memory.

He couldn't explain why the first thing that came to his mind was the dark history of the ground above the place he was now sleeping.

The entire land under *Vatican City* was a cemetery where were buried the bodies of many executed Christians for several years before the *Cir-*

cus of Nero was built in 65 AC.

This was a place of death, and now it is a place of hope. To mark this change, a first church was built in the 4$_{th}$ century AC by the *Roman emperor Constantine the Great,* where *Saint Peter's Basilica* now stands, completed in 1626 after 120 years of construction.

He could almost taste the humidity in the air, which, when combined with his Lonicera japonica essential oils—meticulously diffused by his staff before he retired to bed—generated a soothing environment calming his senses.

The creator is tormenting me; I failed Him. His followers don't believe in Him anymore.

"Give me a sign, as You gave me before. Help me to rebuild their faith in You," the Pope muttered faintly.

Deep inside, he knew that the notion of God had been altered across the centuries, and faith was at its lowest, the Church having lost all meaning.

Now there is a new digital God were everybody can ask a question, and the answer will be instantly revealed: a search engine, this insidious reality was tormenting him for the past several years.

The Pope was trying to find new, innovative ways to attract more followers to spread the Christian faith of goodness and helping those in need.

The present belonged to the rebellious new generation, the millennials who did not need any advice.

I have to help them find back their way to the creator, or I will be the last Pope, the last guardian of the Holy See.

My name is Peter; I symbolize the beginning; I cannot be the end; he continuously repeated these words as a mantra to calm his mind.

Despite the advice and criticism of the entire Cardinals' Conclave, he took the name of the first Pope.

Out of respect for Saint Peter, no Pope had ever adopted the name Peter II before. Many Popes had the Saint's name as their baptismal name, like *Pietro Orsini*, who became later *Pope Benedict XIII*.

"It cannot be, I do not believe the heretic prophecy," the Pope whispered to himself.

The Prophecy of the Popes was attributed to Saint Malachy, an 11_{th} century Irish Saint having as birth name: *Máel Máedóc Ua Morgair*.

Ever since his youth, the Pope was fascinated by the melodicity of the Saint's original Irish name.

Saint Malachy, during his life, served as the Archbishop of Armagh, to whom several miracles were attributed and an alleged vision which was written down and interpreted as a prophecy.

This text was insidiously circulating amidst the most influential Cardinals who would have wanted to take his place.

He believed that those heretic Cardinals were trying to undermine his authority by using the final passage of this Prophecy, which refers to a *Petrus Romanus.*

Peter the Roman, was considered to be the last Pope, whose pontificate would supposedly herald the destruction of the city of *Rome* and trigger the apocalypse.

The words of this text were giving him nightmares since he ascended in the ultimate position of power of the modern Christian Church.

I had a vision; I have chosen the righteous path…

His election was surrounded by controversy, as the Conclave was caught among a superstorm that evacuated the entire *Saint Peter's Square,* and *Rome* was in a state of emergency due to the natural disaster.

The Pope could still vividly remember the events that had unfolded eight years ago. The *Sistine Chapel* seemed like a maximum-security prison, surrounded by many security forces, the best of the *Pontifical Swiss Guard.*

The entire Vatican was under high alert and ready to have its entire population evacuated in case the storm compromised the integrity of its building complex.

For two days, several Cardinals tried scheming and forming coalitions to reach the majority needed to elect the new Pope.

The interminable bickering of the hundreds of voices of the Cardinals Conclave echoing in the Sistine Chapel was giving him a pounding headache. He wanted to make the excruciating noise stop.

Suddenly a loud clatter of a thunder, granted his wish, silencing for a few seconds the entire Conclave.

Trying to pinpoint the origin of the thunder, he looked up to *Michelangelo*'s *"Creation of Adam"* fresco painting, portraying the creation of humankind by God.

Just in between the gap of precisely $3/4_{\text{ths}}$ of an inch, which separated the two index fingers, he saw a strange blinding light.

Is this the unattainable divinity; is my mind playing tricks on me? For a moment, he was convinced that the sight had been merely a side effect of his excruciating migraine.

This was his favorite painting from the entire chapel. Michelangelo cleverly hid several symbols.

The background faces of the eleven unborn children of Adam and Eve, the future humanity depicted behind the figure of God, seemed to be an anatomically precise picture of the human brain, including the pituitary gland.

A metaphor of the things to come, a glimpse into the future, when Man will become God, and they will be one again.

Could this be the first portrayal of Divine Singularity?

These thoughts he always kept to himself. As progressive as his ideas were, they were close to heresy, and it might have cost him his position and even endangered his life.

Another round of thunder, even stronger than before, struck the Conclave, and then another.

"The voice of God is silencing the greed for power over a billion of faithful souls," he whispered to himself.

Another Cardinal sitting next to him noticed

he was unwell and asked him:

"Did you just say something?"

"You are very pale Pietro, is everything okay?"

The voice of the fellow Cardinal was fading like a distant echo, and the light coming from the gap above became blinding, forcing him to close his eyes.

Darkness became a dreamlike state, as if he were floating above the *Saint Peter's Square.*

The heavy rain seemed to pass directly through him.

Did I have a stroke? What is happening to me?

Oh Lord, please don't abandon me; help me find my way back.

And there in the middle of the square, he saw a little girl who seemed abandoned in the fierce winds of the storm, screaming for help.

He knew this was real, a premonition, a divine vision.

It was up to him to save the little girl.

§CHAPTER 2§

OPENING HIS EYES, he stood up and left his place in an unnatural haste.

It was as if someone gave him an extra boost of energy, making him feel young again.

He broke the Conclave, despite the Cardinals' desperate looks and started to bang on the locked doors screaming that there was a medical emergency.

Once the guards opened the doors, he sped off outside, ignoring all their attempts to stop him.

The rain was pouring down, and there was absolute darkness projected by black clouds.

A mini-tornado was swirling through the *Piazza San Pietro* dangerously close to the ancient pink granite Egyptian obelisk located at the center of the square, which seemed to be moving.

His red robes were all wet and his vision blurred.

I will be crushed by the falling obelisk, which was initially erected at Heliopolis 4500 years ago by a long-forgotten Pharaoh.

Such irony. I need to save the child; it is my destiny.

The child was dressed in white with dark hair, and he could hear her whimpering for help, clutching the stone surface of the obelisk to protect herself against the forces of nature.

Could it be an angel?

Am I being tested?

Since he was a child, he was fascinated with the story of the *Vatican Obelisk.*

He remembered from his high-school history lessons that it was the only obelisk in *Rome* that had not collapsed since ancient Roman times.

He was particularly intrigued by the myth that in the past, it even possessed on its top, a golden ball that supposedly contained the ashes of *Julius Caesar.*

The *piazza*'s pavement was submerged underwater, with the deluge covering its radiating lines in travertine, the smooth surface of its cobblestones giving it a faint glitter.

He approached the *Capricorn* signs of the zodiac, which made the obelisk a gigantic sundial's *gnomon*, aligned to the summer solstice, which would accurately show the time under a perfect blue Roman sky, with the pearly dome of the *Saint Peter's Church* in the back. The scion of all churches stretching out the long arms of its colonnade to embrace God's Catholic flock.

He was also fascinated by the twelve Zodiac signs. The shadow of the obelisk's tip hit each stone sign on the day that the sun moved above it.

Today he knew it was a special day. Nobody was aware that in his youth, he passionately studied astrology.

Today the sun will fringe Chiron, the wounded healer, and precisely sextile Pluto in Capricorn, the planet of demise and alteration in the sign of the creation.

Is this a sign, oh God, what is your plan for me?

Why did you bring me here under my zodiac sign?

As he approached the child, he felt a sudden and overwhelming warmth. A light sunburst blinded him again.

The light transformed into darkness, and he collapsed on the wet pavement; while in the back, the Vatican staff were running to reach him.

Everyone thought he was dead. Who could survive at such an age, after being struck by lightning?

The next day the entire press was raging:

"A miracle. The first Cardinal struck by lightning to survive."

"A miraculous vision; the Cardinal is alive."

While the Cardinals thought he was dead, he simply fainted, inexplicably having quickly recovered the next day.

The Cardinals and the entire Vatican took this sign as a divine omen; he was genuinely protected by God.

The Conclave and his opponents had no other choice than to elect him as Pope.

This made him determined to keep his first name, *Pietro di Monti* born in Rome, or *Peter II.*

The entire event was surrounded by a shroud of mystery, *was this a vision, a prophecy, or an omen of the things to come*?

After being elected as Pope, he opened an inquiry regarding the little girl. Everyone was baffled.

"Your Holiness, nobody had any recollection of finding a lost little girl."

The Pope thought: *A vision from the Holy Spirit?*

The prophecy's words were churning in his mind:

"he would feed his sheep in many tribulations and in the days of the final persecution…"

Malachy should have never been proclaimed a Saint, and his prophecy should have been declared a blasphemy, a forgery at best, the Pope thought.

His vision was to stop creating fake saints and focus on helping humanity. He wanted to give meaning and purpose to religion, to calm the soul and meditate toward positive energy.

A long time ago, Time magazine asked on its front cover, "Is God Dead?" A shy young boy was contemplating this shocking title by the press shop window.

"Mama, why is God dead? Can he be killed?"

His mother gave him a worried but equally sweet look.

"No, my son. God cannot be killed as long as people have Him in their hearts."

She was a religious person who was an orphan and grew up being taken care of by an orphanage run by nuns near the outskirts of Rome.

The Pope remembered the magazine and wondered whether religion was relevant to modern life in the post-atomic age and when science was explaining more about our natural world than ever before.

Scientific advancement is not just making people question God; it is also connecting those who doubt.

It is easy to find atheist and agnostic discussion groups online, even if you come from a religious family or community.

Each day I am trying to find a way to tackle the past ten years worrying statistics.

One-third of the world's spiritual population is Christian; however, Christians in Europe were dying faster than new ones being born.

Each year there was a staggering number of

Christians losing their faith in God.

Oh, Father, show me the light, to bring humanity back to their one true God.

I'll use the new tool you have bestowed on us: technology and access to information.

I'll purge the unfaithful and usher a new era for our Church.

As I have done my entire life and until the dawn of time. Amen.

And with this thought, he closed his eyes and fell asleep.

§CHAPTER 3§
22:10, OCTOBER 1_{ST}
BELGIUM, BRUSSELS, BERLAYMONT BUILDING

BRUSSELS' GLOOMY skies were illuminated by rapid lightning. A heavy rain washed over the empty streets of the European Union's administrative capital.

Ranking as one of the most depressing places to live in Europe, it wasn't widely embraced even by the sudden warmth brought by climate change.

Helene de Moncler, a tall woman in her late sixties, was at her desk, which gave a stunning view over the European Union's institutional center.

It was not easy being the first female President of the powerful European Commission, which managed to make even the most dominant corporation in big data bow before its legislative power.

But today she canceled her agenda as The Order's fate was lying in her hands. *All these centuries The Order survived trying to preserve Jesus' forgotten teachings, the guardians of his secrets*, she thought as she gazed at the dark stormy clouds.

At the top of the well-guarded 13_{th} floor of the iconic Berlaymont building, she was sitting in front of an immaculate desk that had an interactive Microsoft Surface Studio.

She was frantically shaking while activating her biometric credentials.

"Security identification: alpha, beta 238978 lambda, voice recognition pattern: I am Helene de Moncler, the guardian of light, the last sister of the Berlaymont."

The warm female voice from her A.I. virtual assistant answered: "security identification verified."

"Add the profile stored for Lydia del Biondo and use her biomarkers for the security database to access my office."

"Send the encrypted message to XGlass code number *AT23XV912*," Helene ordered with sadness trickling through her voice.

"Profile stored and biomarkers added for Lydia del Biondo, the message was sent Madame President," her A.I. confirmed.

"I have to defend the vault of my Berlaymont Sisters, the legacy of my Order. I'm its last guardian, the only one who can make a difference."

Her security perimeter was almost impenetrable. Each person present was identified by his weight, pulse, and iris through the security system, which used a multitude of invisible micro cameras.

Her *Zaha Hadid* jewelry also influenced the minimalistic design of her office adorned with different screens, which were projecting a synthesis of news across the world.

The financial markets were crashing in Asia because of a pandemic flu outbreak on which the standard antiviral treatments were not effective.

It originally started in the city of *Wuhan*, in China which boasted more than 11 million people; an important transport hub that was now basically an isolated city. Railway stations were closed, flights were suspended, and the road routes of entry and exit to the city were now heavily secured checkpoints. The neighboring city of *Huanggang*, which had a population of about 7 million people, announced similar measures.

"Incredible," she shouted. "We are planning to send the first humans to Mars, and we still did not agree to tackle the effects of climate change at a planetary level."

Now the superpowers around the world were suffering due to erratic outbreaks, which were decimating their populations.

"Increase volume to 50%," Helene instructed. CNN was presenting the breaking news.

China had extended travel restrictions to eleven cities, affecting more than 36 million people, as it raced to contain a SARS-like virus that has overwhelmed local hospitals and sparked global alarm.

The novel coronavirus denoted 2019-nCoV by the World Health Organization saw mass victims across Asia.

After the first reported cases in the United States, together with the European Union, they were joining forces to increase airport scans to detect the travelers, who were coming from one of the affected areas, exhibiting fever and other symptoms specific to this aggressive virus.

Helene felt a chill running down her spine, thinking about the casualties of the 1918 influenza virus.

I need to accelerate my plan; otherwise, it will be too late.

"Call Neo Moore on a secure channel," she commanded.

In a matter of seconds, the calm voice of her virtual assistant announced, "patching through on the EU top-secret channel."

"Neo, I need your help. You remember that we discussed the *Omega* protocol. Now it's time to activate it."

"I count on you, my child. Please do not disappoint me. The faith of all humanity rests in your hands."

"I understand perfectly Madame President. One is always glad to be of service."

"I granted you all the necessary access rights."

"Good luck Neo Moore; I hope we'll meet one day again."

Neo knew what he had to do; he never believed this day would come so soon.

His eyes were fixated on the dark screen, which replaced Helene's kind face when the call ended.

On top, I am just a cripple with nothing to lose.

I do not want to end up like Stephen Hawking, completely paralyzed with an artificial voice, Neo's dark thoughts were slowly creeping back.

Despite all the breakthroughs in gene therapy the past few years, the mortality rate of people touched by *amyotrophic lateral sclerosis* (ALS) was still extremely high.

I have a mission to accomplish, and I need to hurry up, because tomorrow I might not be able to use my hands anymore.

Neo believed in her and thought that destiny brought him to this phase in his life for a reason

Helene instructed him that as soon as possible, he should contact the best scientists in the world who study life-long debilitating diseases. Hopefully, they would be able to find a cure using gene therapy.

If someone could deactivate or block my defective ALS genes and replace them with healthy versions, I might stand a chance.

Will she help me, that is the real question. Will she take a break from her research work as a molecular biologist?

Neo knew she was absorbed into discovering the secrets of the presence of mysterious sequences: *Clustered Regularly Interspaced Short Palindromic Repeats (CRISPR)* and using the scientific work of previous researchers redesigning the enzyme called *Cas9* to extend the lifespan of humans.

She was continuing the work of the researchers who discovered that CRISPR segments could be manipulated to navigate Cas9 to locations on the genome, where it would then cut like scissors.

Together, CRISPR and Cas9 could slice out genes or change their function to render their negative impact obsolete, tackling rare diseases which until then were untreatable while discovering new methods to alter a genome to avoid any future complications.

§CHAPTER 12§
23:32, OCTOBER 1ST
BRUSSELS
THE CINQUANTENAIRE TUNNEL

LYDIA REMEMBERED her dad was once the chief of security for the entire Commission and had to reinforce the monitoring in one of the weakest potential penetration points of the Berlaymont's security perimeter.

After the horrendous terrorist attacks of 2016, they decided to create a new visitor center, which would more effectively deter any ill-intended attempts.

Previously the visitors were only allowed to access the inner space of the building's reception prior to security checks.

She also remembered her dad was angry due to the lack of funding, which allowed one spot to remain vulnerable: the *Cinquantenaire* tunnel car's access to the building.

To facilitate the building's staff access to parking, a car entry point was built via the tunnel underneath the *Arcades du Cinquantenaire*, a monumental triple arch in the center of the *Cinquantenaire Park* in Brussels.

Still in her pajamas, she quickly took her cell phone, which was fully charged and summoned an UBER driver.

Anthony:*4.93 stars* was going to be downstairs in 5 minutes.

Hmm, he is rather handsome, and I will ride in a Tesla.

She loved technology and especially liked not having to go through the hassle of parking a car.

I need to tell Anthony to drop me just before the Berlaymont tunnel entrance because no vehicle is allowed without a full check-up.

I will have to avoid detection by the security cameras, hoping the guards and motion sensors will not be alerted.

To tackle the detection issue, she packed up her black stretchable sport-training suit with a comfortable hoodie, which would also protect her face.

She also took a silicon face mask of an elderly lady, forgotten in one of her drawers from an old Halloween party.

Last year she became addicted to CrossFit to cope with her research related stress.

It was paying off; her slim athletic figure was looked upon with desire or envy by friends and strangers alike.

A smart and sharp scientific mind with an almost perfectly sculpted body; it was an irresistible combination.

Her XGlass popped-up in her field of vision with a notification: *your UBER driver is almost here.*

The storm was wreaking havoc on the poorly illuminated street, where halogen lights were peering through the darkness, as two lighthouses illuminated the path to a mysterious adventure.

"Hi Anthony, do you have the destination?"

"Yes, ma'am, the *Schuman Square* is not far from here," the driver responded in excellent English with a Flemish accent. His voice quickly grew angry as the car's leather interior was splashed by the heavy rain while Lydia hurried inside.

When Lydia lifted her wet hood, the driver saw her beauty, stylish hair, and sweet dark eyes. He was mesmerized and realized that his luck had quickly turned.

"Madame Lydia, how are you tonight?" he asked.

Lydia, rather surprised, answered, "I'm in a bit of a hurry to visit a sick friend."

The driver gave her a compassionate look, "no worries, ma'am, we'll be there in no time."

She was worried; *I have to help Helene and find out if she is okay.*

Lydia hoped that the electromagnetic charge from the storm interfered with Helene's phone signal. On the other hand, something like this could not happen in a building like Berlaymont.

While trying to order the UBER, her 5G connection dropped several times, and the home's Wi-Fi was not working...

She has to be okay. She is the only one I've got.

Approaching the Cinquantenaire tunnel, a message was flickering at the entrance.

TUNNEL INONDÉ APPROCHEZ-VOUS AVEC PRÉCAUTION

Damn it, the tunnel is flooded. Will the electric car manage?

Or we'll sink, and the car will stop functioning.

Hopefully, Elon Musk's claims of the Tesla being waterproof are true, Lydia thought while frowning.

Even at this late hour, there was a long queue of cars.

"The GPS app says we'll exit this traffic blockage in a few minutes," Anthony kindly announced.

She suddenly felt her cell phone vibrating and lifted the screen, full of hope.

Lydia took a deep breath of relief: *incoming call from Helene de Moncler, accept encryption yes or no?*

She quickly clicked on yes: "Helene, are you okay," Lydia bellowed. For one second, there was no answer.

From the other end, a man's perfectly pitched voice said: "Lydia, I'm Neo Moore, and Helene de Moncler asked me to contact you."

"Listen carefully. We don't have much time. In a few minutes, the traffic will be free, and you have to ask your driver to drop you directly in the tunnel.

Lydia did not know what to say.

"Where is Helene? Is she okay?"

"I am afraid Helene was killed, you are in terrible danger. Tell your driver to drop you in two hundred meters."

"Helene told me you'd not be able to trust me from the beginning."

"Remember what she told you once: 'In dark times you should always look within, the Universe will help you solve the mystery. Trust your instinct and the One who is always glad to be of service.'"

The driver accelerated, and they managed to pass the flooded segment, reassured that the tunnel was relatively dry.

Lydia suddenly asked the driver: "Anthony, please excuse me! Actually, can you please drop me here, at this Berlaymont tunnel entrance? I just remembered forgetting something in my office. I am working in the Berlaymont building."

The driver was taken by surprise but did not comment as he was mesmerized by her beauty.

"Are you sure you want me to stop here?" I can drop you in front of the building."

"Here is perfect. It will even be faster. Many thanks for this perfect drive, and I will punch in a hefty tip for all your effort."

"Thank you, ma'am."

In the next second, Lydia was already out of the car, and the driver hurried away to pick up his next customer.

§CHAPTER 4§
23:12, OCTOBER 1$_{ST}$
BRUSSELS

LYDIA WAS COVERED in sweat; haunted by the same terrible nightmare that plagued her since childhood.

"Mummy, daddy, where are you?"

"I am so cold, please don't leave me here."

"Take me in your arms; cover me with your warm kisses."

She was abandoned again in absolute darkness with her little feet trembling uncontrollably on the white marble. A vulnerable three-year-old Lydia became almost paralyzed by the freezing surface.

In their desperation, the kindergarten employees forgot her during the evacuation of the building.

An emergency power cut triggered by a terrorist attack at one of Brussels' nuclear power plants left most of the city with no electricity. The backup generators were never tested to comply with such an apocalyptic scenario.

Lydia was still trembling in her sleep and was jolted back to reality by the loud rain tapping against her glass ceiling.

She always found solace in the sound of raindrops or by watching the starry sky with the clouds being carried away by invisible winds.

It reminded her of the stormy days from the relaxing exotic trips her parents organized a few times each year.

This was an opportunity for them to explore another archeological museum and unravel the secrets of lost civilizations, with her mom and dad organizing quizzing contests.

Another damn nightmare, but you are still gone… you simply vanished from my life.

Mom, dad, wherever you might be, I love you…I want to embrace you so much…even if it would be for one last time.

She was beginning to acknowledge the hypothesis that dreams are like the pages of a book where one's lifeforce is writing about its destiny.

All of the sad memories were melting away as raindrops intertwined with her thoughts about the future.

While the figures of her parents were slowly dissolving into the dark sky, her A.I. assistant, Alexa, announced an urgent call.

"Lydia, you have a priority call from Helene de Moncler. Can I connect you to her?"

It is almost past 01h00 AM. Why would the President of the European Commission be calling me at this hour?

It must be something very urgent.

I never recall her ever calling my parents at such an hour...

"Yes, connect me and activate the encryption protocol."

Helene always had a determined voice, speaking with an eerie calm, but tonight she seemed terrified.

"Lydia, I am deeply sorry for everything."

"There are so many things I would like to tell you, but there is no time."

"We are in grave danger."

§CHAPTER 5§
23:20, BRUSSELS
"THE ONE" BUILDING

THE ASSASSIN was on his way to the rooftop of Brussels' tallest skyscraper.

He strategically chose this roof for its proximity to Berlaymont: the emblematic building that represented the administrative heart of the European Union.

"My Master will be proud of me," he whispered with absolute certainty.

"I'll finally become worthy of the Phoenix's blessing; he will welcome me among his kin."

He could not spot anyone in the streets emptied by the heavy rain.

The building resembled a giant domino castle with its windows in black and white, some fluttering uncontrollably in the fierce winds.

"These Europeans have such strange taste in design."

On top, they called it the ONE, the Assassin thought and could not stop his lips from curling into a grin.

Modern art adorned the lobby's walls made of dark granite and teak, making for a perfect synergy of cold and warm, which, together with the scent of fresh roses and freesia, were invading his senses.

The skyscraper had a mix of offices and apartments, which gave a stunning view across Brussels. A variety of advanced video cameras were scrutinizing all angles.

The Assassin already knew this, and his cloak discreetly hid his face.

With a simple hacking app, he managed to open the unguarded main entrance, simulating the magnetic card of an apartment owner and then unlocked the elevator to the building's roof-top.

Inside the elevator, he activated the restricted access to the rooftop. The elevator acknowledged his command with a warm voice specially designed to complement the modern design.

"Welcome, Mister Sutherland, doors are closing …lift going up. I wish you a pleasant evening."

At the same time, the clever security algorithms were trying to process his facial features to match his identity to open the door of his penthouse, …but his face was still perfectly hidden.

It was too late. The moment the security system tried to block the elevator, the doors swung open. The Assassin exited in the nick of time.

The building's alarm was activated, producing an infernal noise, and he knew he had precisely ten minutes until the security forces invaded the rooftop.

His target was in range, and he had to flawlessly navigate the stormy weather to be able to arrive on the other side safely.

I have to gain enough speed; otherwise, I'll not succeed.

He already calculated the distance between the two buildings, and from the 22_{nd} floor, he was absolutely sure that he would safely make it to the other side.

Within seconds, he started to sprint and leaped into the void.

For a moment, he floated in the air, supported by the weight of the heavy drops.

He was flying at high speed, experiencing a fantastic sensation being propelled by his paragliding suit, which activated when the proper velocity was reached.

In time he learned to master and perfect his flying technique using it when he had to eliminate well-secured targets from above.

I'll carry out my orders, and the Phoenix will bless me with his immortality.

Berlaymont had a strange shape of a crooked cross, reminding him of a proto-Christian cross.

A glorious symbol for some, ready to sacrifice everything across millennia, for others marking their eternal tomb, he thought, trying aftward to empty his mind and focus on the path ahead.

The flight was thrilling, but for a second, he felt he would not manage to cross over, as the gust of an aggressive wind began to slow his perfectly calculated jump.

His dark Batman-like military-grade suit was doing its job perfectly. His training made his body adaptable to any type of environment including severe conditions.

Soon my Master will bring me close to my enlightenment.

The excitement of these thoughts filled his mind.

I just need to resist a few more seconds.

The shape of Berlaymont was getting closer; however, the crosswind was also getting stronger.

With great precision, while skillfully maneuvering the current, he landed softly on the metallic rooftop by rolling in a methodical manner.

This was nothing compared to all the jumps he had to do over the years; however, he was feeling old and fragile for the first time.

I need to be reborn.

I need to get back my strength, and I will succeed, he repeated over and over in his mind.

The building's metallic structure was engulfed by the darkness of the clouds reflected in the solar panels, and the noise of the rain began to claw at his sensitive ears to a deafening pace.

It was like the sound of infinite torture, a repetitive noise of the storm to come.

§CHAPTER 6§

23:25

THE PRESIDENT of the European Commission felt a heavy responsibility on her shoulders.

She sensed that after all this time, something dark would happen.

Her security was impeccable, surrounded by guardians who were perfectly trained. The building had the latest upgrade with the addition of a new A.I. driven interface that would manage to identify any intruders.

I must quickly put my plan in motion.

However, they were never prepared for an intrusion from above.

The rooftop did not have any security sensors, due to a cut in the European Union's budget because its member states had complained that it was overly inflated.

Hearing Lydia's calm voice was always so soothing, and she had so many things to tell her. While talking to Lydia, Helene thought about next steps. Her body began to shake under the tremendous psychological pressure...

There will not be enough time to explain everything to her. Where should I start?

I need to protect her; she is the daughter I never had.

I made a promise...

I need to tell her how proud I am of her achievements, as a renowned geneticist pioneering new paths in gene editing, and not seeking any fame.

There is so much goodness in her.

I need to help her succeed where I failed.

"Lydia, please listen carefully. It's about your parents; you need to go to your dad's office and find an access card."

"The Fibonacci code will show you the way; you have to..."

Her voice abruptly ended with a muffled sound.

"Helene, are you okay? Talk to me." There was no answer.

"Alexa, is the connection still active?"

"Yes, Lydia, the network has full signal; maybe

Madame de Moncler fainted?"

"Should I call the emergency number?"

Lydia did not answer. She had a gut feeling that something terrible happened, and nobody could help.

She had to find a way to talk to her again and find the access card Helene mentioned.

"Alexa, try to re-establish the secure connection."

§CHAPTER 7§

THE ASSASSIN was getting closer, recalling the plans he simply downloaded from the internet; he just had to find the location of the President's office, which was positioned on the northern part of the cruciform.

"My target has to be there. I have to end this and fulfill my destiny."

His eyes were protected by a special augmentation XGlass, offering a real-time data feed of the weather parameters. A stronger storm was coming.

In recent years, the climate of the country abruptly changed; severe thunderstorms and even hurricanes sweeping every corner of the European Union.

He quickly traversed the rooftop and headed towards the west wing.

On the horizon, he noticed another oddly-shaped spherical structure illuminated from inside.

It could have been a dragon egg pulsating with energy, the perfect example of the deep symbolism around the city. Yet so many were blind and ignorant of the mystic arts.

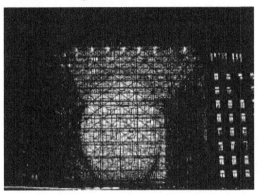

A strange wind started blowing, and his face was being hit by ice-cold droplets of water, a much welcome shower preparing him for his target.

His XGlass was reviewing details about the building he was staring at. Its name was the EUROPA building, the main seat of the European Council.

Interestingly, the dragon egg was encased in a wooden cage joined together by glass windows; a transparent frame simulating the fragility of an eggshell.

The facade consisted of a patchwork of restored wooden window frames recovered from restoration or demolition locations all over the European Union.

The facade stood as a reminder of the EU motto: "united in diversity" as all the windows were distinct.

The darkness was playing tricks on his eyes. He detached a cord and gently leaped to the level of the so-called 13_{th} floor of the building.

He used the rain to dampen any noise and carefully hide from the motion cameras, which were a part of one of the most sophisticated security systems in the world.

The sensors on the outside of the building were blinded and not designed to cope with such a massive amount of rain.

Supporting himself on the building's glass exoskeleton, he took out his weapon.

I hope the glass structure will not move; it should not.

His prior research stated that Berlaymont was refurbished some decades ago, and the glass structure made it one of the most environmentally friendly buildings in the world.

The glass structure on which he was standing was protecting the building from the sun by closing the panels and opening them when there was no light.

Today he was also lucky because as it was such a chilly night, the automatic system should have closed the protective frame.

However, the surreal darkness overwrote the system and kept the frames open to get any possible outside light.

The silencer on the gun was specially designed to help penetrate the safest bulletproof glass in the world.

Each bullet carried a mini radioactive payload coated with artificial diamond powder.

His target was visible as her office was among the few still illuminated at that late hour.

He aimed, and Helene fell struck by the silenced bullet, which in a millisecond went through the glass straight to its target.

She dropped motionless onto the floor, while from the office speaker, Lydia's desperate voice could still be heard.

"Helene, Helene, talk to me...what happened? Goddammit, please say something..."

The Assassin understood that he had just interrupted a conversation. He began to wonder who she was talking to...

§CHAPTER 8§

AFTER TRYING several times to reach Helene over the phone, Lydia again felt abandoned in the world.

Why do I have to endure this fate and all this suffering? First, my parents vanish and now Helene.

What could have happened to her? I need to go and check on her. Or should I call the police?

Her body started to shake, being engulfed by memories from her childhood.

It is like I am dreaming again; wake up Lydia, you have to focus now.

Helene trusted me; I should not disappoint her.

Moving swiftly, she ran across the apartment, a modern design motif that gave a splendid view across Brussels' skyline where on the near horizon, you could clearly spot several of its main landmarks like the golden dome of the *Palais de Justice* and the bizarre *Atomium* structure.

Her dad's desk was facing this strange monument symbolizing the carbon atom, erected by the Belgians, to match the French on their *Eiffel Tower*.

She looked around, and nothing was displaced; the grey marble desk had only a minimalistic screen, nothing else.

Behind the desk, her dad placed with pride, all of her diplomas from the University of Washington in Seattle.

She was one of the world's leading experts in genetics, specifically in gene editing using CRISPR technology.

Humanity was just scratching the surface of the true potential of this innovative technology that allowed the use of a protein to cut and replace faulty segments in human DNA.

Lydia remembered one of the last discussions she had with her dad before his disappearance.

"Lydia, do you think an ancient civilization could already have possessed this technology? I think it is highly possible," her dad said excitedly, waving a hand through his dark hair. "This civilization would have already been buried for millions of years beyond our reach. Perhaps under the ocean bedrock or covered by massive lava layers."

"Do you hear mom?"

"Our daughter will find a cure for all the diseases by simply activating our immune system to perpetually regenerate our bodies," her dad shouted towards the kitchen where her mom was preparing Lydia's favorite plate, smoked onion soup.

Lydia was jolted back to reality by the feeling that this entire story was related to why her parents disappeared.

On the left side of the wall, he also hung her Doctoral diploma in Archeology.

This was one of her other passions. She could never make up her mind which field she should focus on and oscillated between them from time to time.

Her dad and mom were both convinced that the *Silurian hypothesis* was true.

They believed that modern science's capacity to detect proof of a prior advanced civilization, perhaps several million years ago, was quite limited.

Humans have existed in current morphology only for the past 300,000 years, with modern technology for only the last few centuries.

Next to her diplomas, there was a framed schematic of the lost city of Atlantis.

She was always fascinated by how her parents had as a hobby watching documentaries on how to discover the mysteries of lost civilizations while trying to keep up with their busy schedules working long hours for the European Commission.

I just need to find the clue Helene was mentioning. Something related to the Fibonacci Sequence.

She remembered from some of her dad's books that Fibonacci, an Italian mathematician, calculated each number as the sum of the previous two numbers and discovered an infinite string of numbers.

It was later used in Renaissance paintings, and modern architecture. Based on its natural occurrence in the universe, it can also take the shape of galaxies and the structure of flowers.

Looking around the room, her childhood memories started to overwhelm her...the fragrance of her dad still lingered.

The entire room had a deep sadness without the jovial and charismatic presence of her dad.

She gazed down, and her eyes glittered with hope.

The object she was seeking lay on the coffee table made of a white asymmetric marble mosaic that imitated the white sea waves. It was her dad's black fossilized ammonite shell, another natural occurrence of the Fibonacci sequence.

The perfectly polished ammonite reflected the moon's light, an invisible bond between this world and the heavenly one.

It was difficult to believe that 160 million years ago, this creature graciously swam the oceans of the Jurassic world and suddenly became extinct along with the dinosaurs.

I remember dad; all the stories you were telling me about the previous races.

I could only imagine what this ammonite might have thought all those eons ago.

She grabbed the ammonite and tried to look for an inscription, checking it on all sides. There was nothing.

Is there something else I'm missing?

Why the Fibonacci reference? What if I try to rotate it in the sequence's direction?

She started to rotate it gently, and the ammonite separated into two parts.

Inside it revealed an empty inner space out of which a silver metallic card fell on the floor.

When lifting it, she noticed the metallic card displayed an intricate pattern, and underneath it the following marking:

13/001

While flipping it over in her hand, she noticed that on its back, a long sentence was engraved.

Tears flooded her eyes and spilled down her cheeks, as she understood that her dad left this clue for her, much like he used to do when they were playing their favorite game together: "find the mystery gift by tracing the clues" or "The Escape" board game.

§CHAPTER 9§

LYDIA STARTED to quickly read the engraving on the backside:

> ### "The seed of life is planted underneath the number of the infinite. Make it vanish from the height of the cruciform, and it will reveal the way to the underground path."

She was wondering what the number of the infinite was.

I think I have discussed this with my mom once.

Lydia, you have to remember it quickly.

Her mom was well versed in symbology and an avid reader of religious history and mysticism.

And then she remembered...

The number of the infinite is eight. When you rotate it 90 degrees, it becomes ∞, the symbol of infinity.

That was too easy...now 13/001, this was more difficult.

It does not make sense. If you divide 13 by 0.01, you will obtain 13.000; what is this?

Carefully looking at the metallic card, she realized that in its middle, there was a whitish plastic frame.

What if this is an access card?

She realized that inside the two metallic sides, there must be a magnetic card.

A magnetic card to open what...?

To the cruciform, maybe?

And it struck her: *It's not a number but an office address, like her parents' office.*

The cruciform was Berlaymont; 13/001 was the office on the 13$_{th}$ floor.

It belonged to Helene de Moncler. Her office was the first one.

Her memory was flooded with images of when she first visited her dad's office. He gave her a tour of the building and told her:

"Here is the office of the President of the European Commission, one of the most prominent people in the world; one day, it might be yours."

"Silly daddy, I'll be an archaeologist exploring

distant worlds, searching for alien civilizations. I'll not be bored to death sitting in an office."

Her dad gave her an unsatisfied smirk.

"This is not any office; it is the place where you coordinate the center of power of the European Union."

"You'll have a say on what the European Union's future space policy will be, and the world will follow."

"Why risk your life when you can explore the solar system and the galaxy from the safety of your desk?"

Her dad just wanted to protect her; she was their only child, the apple of his eye. He would have done anything to keep her safe.

She did not want to disappoint him, so she gave him the answer he was hoping for:

"We'll see dad; I'm sure I'll make you very proud one day" …

A mighty thunder nudged her back from the past…

I have to go to Berlaymont and check on her.

How will I do that?

I do not think the guardians will simply let me in.

She knew the heightened level of security in the building but also realized this must be a master card, which could unlock any door in the building.

After pondering for a few moments, she started putting together a plan to enter one of the most secured places on the planet, maybe after the *White House* or the *Pentagon.*

I have to be extra careful and not be detected.

I think I can manage that, for Helene and my mom and dad; my dear lost parents.

§CHAPTER 10§
11:25, OCTOBER 1ST
CASTEL GANDOLFO

THE POPE felt like he was suffocating. He needed to breathe but his asthma started to aggravate him.

Was it caused by the stress of the latest news or merely pollution engulfing the streets of Rome (despite the limited traffic and the strict confinement rules)? he wondered, almost bursting into tears when thinking of the current situation.

His smartwatch had an app installed, which showed the pollution level.

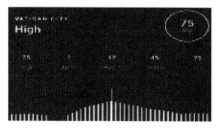

Vatican City was not spared; he could not summon a protective shield against pollution or to kill the virus. He chuckled at the idea: *His Holiness protected, while the population was suffering.*

The technology was not yet there, and he could not hope for any Divine intervention.

He craved the soothing panorama of the crystal-clear water of Lake Albano, remembering its name was based on its location in the splendid Alban Hills of Lazio.

His black Tesla car was taking him there, and he felt delighted with the choice he made; the electric car almost soundlessly traversing the winding cobblestone road.

The ride was so smooth that he was able to relax and admire the Mediterranean vegetation, still green despite it being the beginning of October.

With the push of a button, he opened the intercom to his driver.

"Per favore aprire la finestra, ho bisogno di un po 'd'aria fresca."

He took out his Ventolin spray and inhaled several puffs to open his bronchi to be able to fully enjoy the freshness of the country air.

You could smell the fall in the breeze; it reminded him of his childhood, so far away, like another life.

"Tutto bene your Holiness?"

Avoiding the driver's question, the Pope asked him, "Silvestro, you were born in Lazio if I remember well?"

Silvestro was taken by surprise, and after a few moments, he opened his mouth:

"Indeed, your Holiness," he was astonished that the Pope would know such a detail.

This was no surprise. Pope Peter II took no risks in choosing his staff; he had personally and secretly evaluated the files of everyone who worked closely with him.

"Tell me then, have you ever bathed in Lake Albano?" the Pope inquired.

Now the driver almost seemed terrified of the strange question.

"No, your Holiness, but I know that the lake formed in a previous small volcanic crater."

"My grandma once told me a story: that in ancient times the volcanic activity made it flood the entire area," the driver said, happy he could dig up in his memory a potential satisfactory answer for the Pope.

"Excellent Silvestro, I see you know the history of the lake well. In fact, several hundreds of years before our *Savior Jesus Christ* was born, during the wars between Rome and Veii, a discharge tunnel was built crossing the crater walls to avoid any further flooding."

"The tunnel was prophesied by the *Oracle of Delphi*, as the Roman victory against Veii would only be possible when *Albanus Lacus'* water would be controlled by the Romans and used for the good of the people."

"Did you know that this tunnel still exists, and it ends at a place named "*Le Mole*," below our summer residence? Maybe the former Popes were using it as an exit tunnel," the Pope said with a hint of mischief in his voice.

Silvestro was confused, his mind trying to understand the purpose of this discussion.

He could not focus on his driving, and at a turn, he almost lost the control of the car, slightly steering it towards the end of the road.

"Just joking Silvestro, I would not need the tunnel; I am too well protected."

"Your Holiness, we are approaching our destination. I will always protect you with my life," the driver said sincerely.

The Pope nodded and added: "I know my son, I know…"

"God bless you!"

The security agents were using a small drone to scan the perimeter, and the aerial sight offered by the livestreaming video directed to their XGlasses was breathtaking.

"Your Holiness, welcome," said a young priest who was in charge of the Pope's secretariat while visiting his residence.

"I am afraid there is an urgent call that you need to answer," the priest announced with a trembling voice almost afraid to spoil the Pope's arrival.

The Pope seemed worried, *what could it be now? Can I not even enjoy the sight of the lake for a few minutes?*

"Enzio, please transfer it to the secure line in my office."

He quickly stormed into the castle and pretended to ignore the opulent paintings, which adorned many of the walls. He did not care for the portraits of the previous Popes.

The Pope picked up the phone, "yes, please talk

now; the line is secured."

After several minutes of a monologue from the person on the other line, the Pope started to tremble.

The walls of the Papal Palace of Castel Gandolfo were painted into a blend of white and cream to keep the premises cooler during scorching hot summers.

Castel Gandolfo also boasted three beautifully preserved domes, and with its perfect location at the pinnacle of the hill, it offered a splendid view of the lake.

Its arched garden touched by the sun most of the day had a perfectly trimmed lawn traversed by several stone lines; meridians of an unknown symbol that always baffled high-profile visitors.

Few knew that one of the domes hosted the Vatican Observatory.

He was particularly fond of it, spending many nights inside it trying to understand the mysteries of Astronomy.

Was God speaking to us through science?

Is this the Universe's way of communicating with us?

Can a black hole be a gateway to Him; to another plane of existence?

"So many mysteries to discover and not much time for me to solve them," he liked to say to the scientific staff who were substantially reduced in number to please the conservative Cardinals, who deemed the Observatory useless.

§CHAPTER 11§

HIS HOLINESS was sitting on a brown leather couch watching the news with great fascination.

CNN was presenting a short simulation of the newly discovered potentially habitable planet, 110 light-years away from Earth, and what it would look like.

Salvatore d'Umbria entered the Gandolfo's main papal office, which boasted a sizeable 4K plasma TV on an entire wall.

"Your Holiness I am afraid I…" he did not manage to finish his sentence, as the Pope made a hush sign with this finger.

"Salvatore, it can wait. Please come and sit next to me."

"Incredible… people are not speaking any more about miracles on Earth; they are showing us God's miracles far away.

"Your Holiness, I didn't know you were passionate about Astronomy."

"Do you think it could host life?" Salvatore asked, looking at the bluish tone of the planet with doubt.

"This question no one can answer yet. It is certainly possible. There is a remote chance," the Pope said with a hint of worry in his voice. "I am afraid…" he said, stopping abruptly, not wanting to show any sign of weakness.

"What are you afraid your Holiness?"

"Salvatore, I am afraid this would be too far for us."

"The closest Earth-sized exoplanet orbiting a star is in Alpha Centauri, just 4.3 light-years from Earth."

"On top of that, this one is inhabitable for humans, with just a faint chance to have any life."

"Do you know how much time it would take us to get there with the fastest space propulsion system available?"

"Your Holiness, I am afraid I do not know," Salvatore said, startled.

"Seventy thousand years Salvatore." the Pope quickly answered.

Salvatore took a few moments to reply. "That would be a very long voyage, your Holiness. One would need to live forever to make this trip."

His face had a strange grimace as the numbers were still swirling in his mind; he always had a keen eye for details but was never good at math.

"It would not even help if we sent Methuselah on this voyage," the Pope said, laughing.

"After more than five thousand years, he still holds the highest recorded lifespan of a human on this planet, he was nine hundred sixty-nine years old as recorded in Genesis 5:21–27," the Pope said, still chuckling.

"However, my son, until now, astronomers have found more than five hundred solar systems, and presently scientists estimate we might have one hundred billion solar systems in our galaxy and if we multiply this with the two hundred billion galaxies in the universe…"

"I guess there is a good chance we find life in space and maybe one day reach God in a material form, rather than in a spiritual one," Salvatore said, his voice full of faith.

"We have to remain faithful that God will guide us, Salvatore, towards the light of hope."

"What I am afraid of is that most people have lost hope. Scientists do not even believe in God anymore."

"Salvatore, I called you here because I have to share some vital information with you."

Salvatore's face suddenly changed at the

thought that something terrible might have happened.

"I need to return to Rome urgently. Would you prefer to take a walk in the garden?" the Pope asked.

"Come, my son, I'll explain it all. I think some more fresh air. It would do me well."

The Pope made Salvatore understand that he wanted to discuss some secretive information to avoid any interception by one of his zealous conservative Cardinals.

The garden was teeming with different spices like daphne and oregano. That, combined with the scent from the roses, was giving a unique, pleasant odor to the place occupying the site of the Roman Emperor Domitian's former residence.

There was even a small fountain in the middle of several column structures that resembled an improvised Stonehenge temple—the difference being that its top was wooden and its base was surrounded by ivy and roses.

"Salvatore, I need you to go on a special mission."

"I am afraid that someone who appeared in one of my early visions will destroy everything we built."

"She must be stopped, or there will be no

Christian Church in the next decade," the Pope said with anger in his voice.

The sounds of crickets and of frogs ribbiting made for a pleasant walk.

The Pope began again to tremble, clutching his fists.

"Are you feeling well, your Holiness? May I bring you a glass of water?" a worried Salvatore asked.

"*Grazie* Salvatore, but there is no need for that."

"I want you to prepare my return to the Vatican using our chopper."

"There is no time to waste. I am afraid calamity is upon us."

One hour later, a white helicopter with blue stripes bearing the papal flag landed. On its side were the words *Republica Italiana*, a sign that the Italian state was gracefully providing the Papal rapid means of transport.

Was the emergency justified? What is the carbon footprint of this helicopter ride? the Pope thought.

A young activist would have believed differently; only adding to the rift between the lavish Vatican lifestyle and poverty that its Church followers were still living in during the pandemic crisis.

But if Hollywood celebrities afforded to do this and were allowed, why should his Holiness be any different?

Young people had stopped believing anyway … and if the Pope did not act, catastrophe would fall upon the entire Catholic Church and most of the other world's religions.

§CHAPTER 13§

"I AM OUT of the car, Neo. I cannot believe she is dead. I recognized her words and believe you. When did it happen?"

"Lydia, there is no time now. I'll explain everything later. I am afraid your life is also in danger, and Helene's killers might still be lurking in the building. You need to be extra careful to avoid the security system and not be detected."

Neo knew it would not be so easy, but he did not want to cause her further panic.

She wanted so badly to understand why someone would hurt Helene.

I will find her killers and get revenge. She remembered what her dad had always told her: "do not let revenge blind you; instead, let it fuel you to do the right thing."

She wanted justice, and she needed answers.

"I know from my dad that the underground

tunnel garage entrance had a security flaw. But how am I going to make it inside?"

Lydia's worries were clouding her reasoning.

"No worries Lydia, I have a plan, and it will work. You just need to follow my instructions very closely."

The odor from the rain was embedded in the tunnel's walls as cars passed by. For the moment, she felt safe under cover of the tunnel's shadows.

"You'll have to synchronize your movements with one of the incoming cars to avoid detection. Use the cover of incoming car's lights, which will temporarily blind the video cameras, to get past them."

"Unfortunately, I cannot hack into the video camera's system as it is isolated from the main-frame."

"You need to time your moves and go underneath them."

Her face was now covered by the mask, and she looked like an older woman wearing a sport outfit.

Lydia did not know why she trusted this stranger; *did he extract the words from Helene?*

She wanted to trust him; his soothing voice made her feel safe.

She was in; she managed to avoid being detected by the security cameras.

In front of her, there was a small shack with a guard inside it, fiddling with his cell phone.

The entrance to the inner parking was heavily protected by a metallic bar door that only opened once you scanned your identification badge.

It was also equipped with a special protective elevated ramp that would block the passage of any intruder who might attempt to force their way in.

"I managed to find a way to open the metallic doors."

"They will only stay open for three seconds."

"You have to be very quick, as I'll not be able to activate them again," Neo said. "Tell me when you are ready and use the outside noise to distract the guard."

She crouched and gently moved underneath the guard's window.

A car was approaching, and Lydia gave the order. "Now, Neo."

As he executed the command, the metallic door swung open.

The guard was monitoring the various cameras, and with the noise from the passing car, he did not notice Lydia.

She carefully crawled past the barrier and then

inside the building through the revolving doors.

"Gosh that was close," Neo said, relieved.

"Now you have to run. Avoid the light…"

Lydia started running, and after a few hundred meters, she was in, at -4, the lowest floor of Berlaymont's underground parking structure.

It was still a long path from there to the 13_{th} floor.

"You'll have to keep a low profile and avoid the video cameras installed on the top of the pillars. Have a look around. They're easy to spot."

"I have to be a shadow; this was not taught in any of my classes…"

"Now, you have to go on the right side. You'll see a set of doors that will take you to the ground floor."

She quickly avoided video cameras and entered a small corridor with rolling escalators.

"Lydia, you need to run up; there is no time to lose."

She started to jump the stairs passing through the -3, -2, and -1 floors at a rapid pace.

Now she was finally in front of a glass door next to the building's main reception.

Several guards were discussing the risks of the COVID-19 virus, and she could clearly hear their voices. They were worried because in a few hours, Belgium was entering into a full lockdown due to the rapid spread of the virus across the globe.

"I cannot believe I have to cancel all my holidays; I'll not be able to leave this rainy country for a little while," a disappointed guard complained to his colleagues.

"I'll create an incident to distract the guards and clear a path for you," Neo informed her with a sense of urgency in his voice.

"Wait, I have the card that Helene gave to my dad. I think it can open any door."

She hastily swiped it, and the green light indicated she could pass.

"No… Lydia, now there is a trace that you're in the building! I don't know if I'll be able to delete this from the access log," Neo said and sounded quite worried.

§CHAPTER 14§

"I DIDN'T HAVE time to explain the entire plan; I still have to find a way for you to pass undetected. I need to distract the guards while they are monitoring all the video cameras; I'll trigger an alarm now. Be ready to run."

Lydia understood and acted instinctively. She was still hoping Helene might be alive.

In the next second, an alarm started to sound at the main entrance of the building.

*"Intrusion porte principale,
alerte d'intrusion…"*

The message triggered the guards to leave their office and head towards the noise.

"Now Lydia, go scan your badge and head towards the main elevators. I'll scramble the rest of the video cameras."

Running, she passed the dimly lit windowed

corridor, which on the right side boasted a stony esplanade with perfectly trimmed trees that unnaturally sprung from the asymmetrical concrete.

"I have ordered an elevator for you. It will arrive in two seconds. Elevator *B*," Neo quickly announced.

Lydia looked above, and indeed the six elevators were each labeled with one letter. You could not simply push the button on the floor you wanted from inside the elevator. You had to enter the floor number on the outside panel, and a computerized system would indicate which elevator you'd have to take.

"Thank you, Neo. I don't know how I would have managed to pull this off without your help."

Inside the elevator, Neo made sure to deactivate the security cameras. Lydia was looking at herself in the wall mirror.

You need to pull yourself together and stay focused. You cannot fail Helene!

She took off the mask because the latex was almost suffocating her. Her reflection revealed she was shaking.

She could not pinpoint what was happening to her body, *was it anger, or fatigue, or perhaps both?*

§CHAPTER 15§
00:18
BERLAYMONT
13_{TH} FLOOR

THE DOORS of the elevator suddenly swung open.

"Now pay attention. You'll have to outsmart the security guards on this floor and then make your way to Helene's office on the right."

The Berlaymont's 13_{th} floor boasted an elegant yellowish parquet with leather couches.

The security system was mostly A.I. driven, instantly recognizing the biometrics of visitors or employees.

As instructed by Helene, Neo was first notified of her death, and he managed to block the security system in triggering the alarm, which would have made Lydia's attempt to enter the building impossible.

After exiting the elevator, she quickly swiped her badge to open a set of glass doors.

Two guards, both well into their sixties, were sitting on opposite corners of an asymmetrically shaped lobby.

"Alfonso, I'll come back in a minute; I need to use the toilet," informed one of them via a walkie-talkie lying on his desk.

After he left the walkie-talkie informed:

"All stations be alerted of the fire alarm activated at the ground floor. Please remain vigilant as we don't know what triggered it. A team is now investigating the fire sensors."

"Good news, Lydia. Our job just got easier," Neo said with an optimistic tone.

Alfonso chuckled when hearing the alert over his walkie-talkie. *At least I don't have to worry about a fire here on this floor; we'll just crack the ceiling and let all the rainwater extinguish it...*"

Via the Wi-Fi hotspot, Neo managed to hack into Alfonso's cell phone.

Suddenly, Alphonso received a text message from his wife: "There is an emergency at home, please call me now."

He knew that the internal security protocol did not allow any phone calls.

What should I do? I cannot leave my post. The President is still working in her office.

My wife will kill me; I will just move away from the cameras and make a quick call.

"Lydia, you have precisely forty-five seconds to swipe your badge on the door and enter Helene's office."

She quickly ran along the windows while the guard was distracted with calling his wife.

Lydia became distracted by the grandiosity of the opposite building; the strange multi-floored lantern-shaped sphere inside a wooden box made of windows—the Europa building.

The architect had such a wild idea, but at least it's seen as a beacon of light and hope in this godforsaken night, Lydia thought with a sigh.

At that moment, people were coming out of another meeting. *The European Commission seems to be working around the clock*, Lydia thought, also recalling the long hours her parents dedicated to their jobs.

Lydia was lucky as Helene de Moncler's assistant was sick. His replacement left earlier as well, too tired to cover the night shift.

She swiped, and the sliding doors silently opened. She had a strange feeling she knew this place...

"Neo, I think I was here before when I was a little girl."

The wooden corridor was adorned with pictures of all the previous European Commission Presidents. It gave her the chills.

The office of the President had a waiting room with heavy black leather armchairs and minimalistic furniture, including several red pots with green plants for a splash of color.

Lydia quickly passed through the secretariat, and now she was in front of a heavy wooden door with a discrete card reader on the right side.

The flickering red light indicated that the President was busy and should not be disturbed under any circumstance.

After swiping her card again, she finally arrived inside Helene's office.

Looking around, she gasped...Helene was collapsed on the floor in a pool of blood, her eyes still open.

"I am so sorry, Helene, if only I could have saved you..."

"Lydia, there is no time now."

"The alarm from downstairs made the security system reboot their firewall."

"They will be alerted of the President's status at any moment."

"And be careful. The killers might still be watching you. They must have used a military-grade weapon that managed to penetrate the thick glass."

§CHAPTER 16§

LYDIA LOOKED around at the stylishly decorated office, with pictures hanging on the wall of various world leaders posing together with Helene.

"The magnetic card mentioned *the seed of life ...will reveal the way to the underground path.*"

"Where can I find this symbol?" Lydia asked.

"Neo, can you help to scan the office visually? I'll rotate 360 degrees to give you a panoramic view."

"Yes, I am setting up a search algorithm now to scan all the visual data to match this symbol."

"I have it; it's in the library on the side cover of a purple book," Neo roared.

"Yes, there it is!" Lydia quickly took out the book, which had a golden flower of life, barely visible on its thick spine.

Inside the flower of life, there was a faint stylized seed of life, almost invisible to the naked eye.

Peering through the space left by the book, she could spot a secret badge reader pad.

Holding Helene's card, she put her hand inside the bookshelf, and after swiping it, a loud alarm was triggered through the entire building.

At the same time, from the library, a hidden door popped open made from the bookshelves, a cleverly hidden secret door accessible only with Helene's card.

A narrow tunnel revealed itself in front of her,

with metallic walls that reflected a faint light coming from the ceiling.

The air seemed damp; *clearly, this passage has not been used for a long time*, Lydia thought while slightly hesitating to step in.

"Lydia, you need to hurry. People are approaching the President's office," Neo warned.

She returned into the office and replaced the flower of life book. As she stepped back inside the metallic corridor, the secret door began to close behind her.

She glanced back one last time towards the office and spotted Helene's face. Her kind eyes, still open, strangely seemed to be fixated on the secret entrance or Lydia. It was hard to tell.

One last goodbye beyond death. Helene seemed to have anticipated this moment. May your soul rest in peace, Helene.

Lydia was heartbroken. With her eyes in tears, she turned and headed deeper inside the tunnel, the door closing silently behind her.

"I know it is difficult, Lydia. Helene loved you like the daughter she never had," Neo said, consoling her while also profoundly affected by what he saw through Lydia's XGlass: "We'll find her murderers and make them pay. I promise you, Lydia!"

§CHAPTER 17§

THE ASSASSIN WAS CLIMBING back to the rooftop, drenched from the heavy rains, but it did not bother him.

It was a cathartic cold shower, washing all his thoughts and worries away.

Immense satisfaction colored his face. *My Master will be proud of me.*

His mission was accomplished as Helene's lips were frozen by the kiss of sudden death.

He knew he had to vanish as quickly as possible.

The Assassin carefully grasped the glasslike surface using his special anti-slip gloves.

The force and precision of his hands were almost inhuman.

Guided by instinct, he turned his gaze to have one last look at his trophy. His protective glasses zoomed in on the office of the President, and to his surprise, a tall, slender brunette woman was standing in front of the library. Startled by what he just witnessed, he wondered: *How is this possible? Who is she?*

My Master did not warn me of such an encounter. Did she sound the alarm?

I need to climb back to check from a closer angle.

His satisfaction was soon replaced with fury, and he started his descent again towards his shooting point, hoping to catch a better glimpse of the stranger.

The rain pounded even harder.

The wrath of the creator is punishing me. Who is this woman?

The rain clouded his vision, and even with the filter algorithms embedded into his XGlass, he could not accurately see the face of the young woman.

His frustration grew at not being able to identify her. He would not be able to find a name match with her via the internet.

His anger reached its peak as the sound of the alarm grew louder. The glass shielding panels on the building began to close, triggered by a protective mechanism within the building's security system.

He had to go back. He couldn't let her escape

alive. While making his way down, he caught a glimpse of Lydia just before she vanished inside the library.

This baffled him even more.

Now it's too late; they must have already discovered the dead body; I need to hurry.

I only have to make one more leap of faith, and with that, he plunged again, vanishing into the darkness of the storm.

§CHAPTER 18§

AT THE END of the corridor, she could spot her reflection. *Is this a mirror?* For a moment, Lydia was scared of her reflection, thinking that it was somebody else.

It was just another elevator from the same metallic composite as the walls of the tunnel.

"Neo, do you know where this elevator is going?"

There was no answer through the headphones, just a crackling sound.

"Oh no, there is no signal here, our direct link must have gotten interrupted. XGlass, try again to establish the connection with Neo Moore!"

"There is no network coverage for the moment, should I try again later?" the A.I. assistant asked.

I am on my own.

I just have to find the underground path Helene mentioned. How hard could it be?

Inside the elevator, there was no card reader; instead, a pad with the floor numbers was gently pulsating.

What now? Which floor should I go to? Lydia wondered.

13 12

11 10

9 8

7 6

5 4

3 2

1 G

-1 -2

-3 -4

I need to read the card again; maybe I missed something...

"The seed of life is planted underneath the number of the infinite. Make it vanish from the height of the cruciform, and it will reveal the way to the underground path."

The building has thirteen floors, so if we deduct the number of the infinity, eight, we get five.

Could it be on the 5$_{th}$ floor?

She pushed the 5$_{th}$ floor button, but nothing happened.

But if it's an underground passage, could it be located at the bottom floor; the -4 level? She pushed it and again, nothing happened.

There must be something I am missing.

Looking more carefully at the elevator numbers pad, she noticed there was a little protrusion, a small hole below -4.

Reaching into her back pocket, from the space behind her cell phone's protective shell, she took the metallic sim card needle kept for emergency and pushed it inside the hole.

Instantly the metallic plate sprung on the elevator's floor, revealing another floor mark, which was now pulsating: -5.

13 12

11 10

9 8

7 6

5 4

3 2

10

-1 -2

-3 -4

-5

It must have been all along -5, and with her hand shaking, she pushed it.

The doors of the elevator silently closed, and her descent began.

§CHAPTER 19§

LYDIA COULD SEE the floors rapidly passing by, and then after -4, her descent continued for several minutes towards -5.

The elevator began to slow down but didn't seem to stop its advance into what almost felt like a bottomless pit.

Helene, where are you sending me? Lydia wondered, her eyes still in tears while an immense rage ravaged her mind.

She crouched down on the floor and cupped her hands over her face with tears running down her cheeks.

Suddenly, Lydia's gaze fell on the metallic plate she had detached from the elevator's floor pad.

She picked it up and noticed that engraved on its back was the tree of life inside the flower of life symbol.

While carefully studying the drawing, she noticed it was showing a double helix DNA structure, but something wasn't quite right.

In the typical structure of DNA, there are ten base pairs in one helical turn. However, in simplified models, four base pairs are used. The major groove occurs where the backbones are far apart, the first visual twist; the minor groove occurring where they are closer together.

Looking at the base pairs instead of four after the first major groove, there were only three base pairs, then two, and for the last one again three.

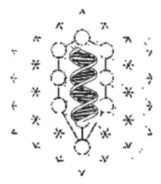

Is this another clue, 4 3 2 3? I should maybe remember this sequence for later.

The elevator finally stopped with a rather aggressive jolt.

I must be in the depths of Berlaymont. But why are the doors not unlocking?

In the next moment, a section of the mirror opened, revealing a pulsating card reader.

Lydia swiped her card, and the doors opened, revealing a dark tunnel with a faint light at the end.

Suddenly the elevator's doors closed, and she had the impression it was going back up.

No, this cannot be a one-way ticket, but there is no button to call it back. How am I going to return?

Or maybe this is for the best. By now, Helene's office must be swarming with security forces. Deep inside, she knew there was no turning back.

She had to face her deepest fear again and go through the darkness to reach the other side.

Unfortunately, her cell phone had no more charge and could not be used as a flashlight.

I have to stay strong for my parents and Helene. They are counting on me.

Deep inside, Lydia felt that there was a powerful link behind her parents' disappearance and Helene's murder. But how could she connect the dots?

The thought that this place could hold the answers she sought for so long gave her an energy boost to continue her journey.

What was Helene hiding here, and did my parents know about this place? Most importantly, what role did she have to play?

All these questions floated through her mind

as she advanced into the suffocating darkness.

There was a strange smell in the air, a slightly salty marine breeze that had a soothing effect on her.

The more she advanced into the darkness, the saltier the air became, so much so that she could almost taste it on the tip of her tongue.

And suddenly she was out. In front of her, a gigantic cavernous opening revealed itself, and Lydia could not help but gasp in surprise.

Looking around, she realized that she was inside an incredible cave-like structure, with the ceiling illuminated by strange phosphorous luminescent symbols.

Who could have built this structure?

Lydia was left wondering while mesmerized by the sight above. From the ceiling, gigantic stalactites peered down like a monstrous dragon's teeth.

§CHAPTER 20§
VATICAN, SISTINE CHAPEL

I NEED a sign from You!

Oh, why did You choose me, God?

Who is this girl haunting my dreams? Why will she destroy everything we build? The Pope's mind was swirling with so many questions, stalking him throughout the day.

I saved her once, but how can I find her again?

Am I losing my mind?

What if someone is poisoning me? I trust my team of doctors; all tests were perfect for my age.

I have to go back to where it all started.

The Pope lifted himself from the bed; it was already late, but he felt the same urge he did twenty-five years ago.

He wanted to reach the Sistine Chapel but suddenly collapsed.

He gradually opened his eyes and saw Salvatore next to him.

"Your Holiness, you collapsed but continually repeated that you need to reach the Sistine Chapel. We brought you here."

The papal doctor was extremely worried. "However, your Holiness, your vitals are normal."

"It's okay. Don't worry. When God communicates with you, it leaves you drained of all your energy. An epiphanic experience is not a walk in the park."

"The altar Salvatore, I had a vision... look at the black marble on the wall; it forms a cross on each side, both of them connected."

"I am connected to her as well, but what is this symbol?" the Pope asked.

Salvatore was puzzled because he didn't understand a word the Pope was saying.

"A cross with its center made of black marble, a mirror of darkness," the Pope continued looking at the cross, almost hypnotized by it.

He could see something in the stone which was beyond any human perception.

"I need to find her," the Pope muttered, almost collapsing in Salvatore's hands.

"Your Holiness, who is she? To whom are you referring?" Salvatore asked the Pope in an attempt to calm him because he seemed even more worried than before.

The doctor began making desperate gestures to Salvatore, trying to get him to understand the Pope needed to rest.

Was the Pope losing his mind? Salvatore and the Doctor were both bewildered.

"Your Holiness, you need to save your strength. Please, your Holiness," his Doctor pleaded, taking care not to insult him.

The pope collapsed again.

§CHAPTER 21§
01:30

THE MUST be a reason for these symbols: a double set of crosses inserted in two circles, a pentagram, the face of a person with one eye, and several others. But one, in particular, caught her eye.

"I think I have seen one of them before."

Looking above at the millions of tiny glittering green lights, she matched one with the representation of the tree of life, depicted inside of a giant flower of life.

What if this is a map, and I need to use the symbols to orient myself?

Looking above, she knew she had to continue and find a way through the darkness to reach this symbol.

Her parents were fascinated with the mythical legends of the tree of life, which holds the power to make its essence's drinker immortal.

She remembered the story her dad told her when she was just a little girl while visiting one of his favorite museums, the *British Museum*.

They were passing in front of a stone relief depicting King *Ashurnasirpal*:

"Do you see Lydia, in front of the king with the impossible name to read, there is a sacred tree, possibly symbolizing life, the one making a gesture of worship to the sun god *Shamas* in a winged disc?"

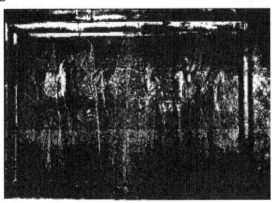

"Again, in Mesopotamian mythology, *Etana* looks for the plant of birth to be able to get a son. This was found inscribed on the sacred cylinder seals of ancient Akkad 2390–2249 BC."

"The tree of life was also a central mystic element in the ancient Assyrian city of Nimrud."

"Then in ancient Iran *Amordad* was a goddess and the guardian of trees and immortality and most importantly of *the Haoma* a sacred plant at the center of the *Zoroastrian* ritual."

"Daddy, will we ever find the tree of life?" Lydia asked naively.

Her dad smiled. "I don't think I will Lydia, but you certainly have a good chance of finding it if you do all your research and homework properly."

As she grew up, she also remembered reading an article written by her dad on how various ancient cultures worshipped this symbol.

The Urartian tree of life is depicted in the quest of Gilgamesh to find immortality.

But her favorite part was the ancient Taoist story speaking of a tree that makes the peach of immortality every three thousand years, and anyone who eats it becomes immortal.

Lydia knew that there must be a kernel of truth in all these mythical stories. There were too many occurrences across so many civilizations to simply be a lost ancient symbol.

Her parents' interest in this symbol convinced her to teach a class on the "The Flower of Life's Origins." Lydia's students at the University of Washington were captivated not only with her fascinating presentation but also with her sex appeal.

She always started her lecture with the tree of life and its reference from the Book of Genesis as the source of eternal life.

"It is distinct from the tree of knowledge of good and evil in the Garden of Eden. This was where human access to God was revoked and Adam and Eve were driven out from the garden."

"The Book of Enoch prophesied that during the great judgment God will give to all the names enshrined in the Book of Life the power to taste the tree of life's fruit."

"It resurfaces within the Bible's last book, the Book of Revelation, and mainly in the last chapter as a part of the new paradise's garden. Entry is then no longer banned for those *worthy* of tasting from the tree of life."

"The tree of life is also evoked in the Norse religion as Yggdrasil, the world tree."

"Then the Quran speaks of the Tree of Immortality, the only one tree in Eden."

"*Etz Chaim* is the Hebrew version for the tree of life, a common term used in Judaism."

"Depictions of world trees are also found in the art and mythological traditions of cultures such as the Aztec and Olmec. For the Mayans, the central world tree of life was by a ceiba tree, the *wacah chan,* and *yax imix che.*"

Lydia dedicated her life to the research of senescence, to finally understand what makes human cells die so fast.

She was trying to grasp the secrets of nature's evolutionary mechanism, which makes the cells wither instead of letting them evolve more, giving our species more time.

In a way, I was searching for the genetic tree of life for myself. And here I found it, to guide me through the darkness. Is it a coincidence of just my fate?

Heading towards its marking on the ceiling, she spotted several entrances in the shape of very narrow crevasses in the rocky northern part of the wall.

Which one should I take?

Damn it!

I hate labyrinths, and I do not want to be a living version of Ariadne looking for her Minotaur.

Turning around, she noticed that from a specific angle, some of the entrances had a different symbol engraved on their edges.

After several minutes of searching, she stumbled on a flower of life engraving.

This must be it; the flower of life has always guided me until now, I have a feeling I should follow it again.

The words of her dad were still echoing in her mind.

Lydia recalled her students really enjoyed the lecture part on the flower of life's global occurrence.

She was highlighting its global importance as it could be traced in almost all cultures, which had a crucial role in shaping present modern society. Moreover, these cultures were spread around the entire world, with some of them being remotely isolated and having no contact with each other.

From the temples within the Forbidden City of China, and ancient synagogues in Israel, the Buddhist temples of India and Japan to the *City of Ephesus* in Turkey and *Cordoba*, in *la Mezquita* Spain.

Lydia had a strange feeling, and while entering the tunnel, she could feel tremors shaking the ground.

What could be causing these vibrations?

I do not recall having any earthquakes in Belgium.

I have to find the exit quickly. Otherwise, I will be squashed like a trapped mouse.

The walls started to move faster and faster; she had to be quick in order to not get caught.

The tree of life kept shining light over her path. Suddenly the last wall closed so fast that it managed to catch the end of her blouse ripping off a part of the tissue.

This structure seemed ancient. *I cannot believe that underneath the modern architecture of Berlaymont, such a complex labyrinth could have been built.*

What kind of mechanism could be putting the walls in motion like this?

I am sure there was a hydraulic system cleverly designed millennia ago.

But who did it, and with what purpose?

Helene's death left so many unanswered questions and left Lydia wondering above all: *Why me, Helene? Why me…?*

§CHAPTER 22§
NEW YORK, 111 WEST 57TH STREET

SIMON LIGHTGOOD was gazing towards *Central Park* from his ultramodern penthouse located on the 73_{rd} floor of 111 West 57_{th} Street—a brand-new skyscraper with fourteen-foot ceilings, a private elevator, and luxurious touches of *Crystallo* quartzite, gray onyx, and white *Macauba* stone.

He felt at home along the walls ornated with artifacts, each with its own story.

But his most treasured item was a simple piece of wood with two thorny spikes encased in glass. He could almost feel the power of the artifact and went to great lengths to procure it.

Getting closer to it, he remembered all the efforts he made to detect a DNA trace of the holy blood, all of his attempts being unsuccessful.

He could only imagine the suffering they inflicted as a part of the fabled *Crown of Thornes,* which Jesus carried on his head during the crucifixion.

The view at the top of the tall building adorned with curved, wavy shapes of earthly terracotta framed by bronze, directly facing *Central Park,* was simply breathtaking. A green oasis at the feet of the second most powerful man on the planet, the Vice President of the United States.

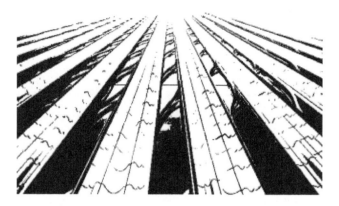

So many thoughts crossed his mind while sipping a cocktail of his daily supplements, as his doctors prescribed.

I am the Vice President of this nation. I have to be resilient and endure like a modern Prometheus chained in Paradise, he said, putting one of his hands on the window frame.

He cackled at the idea that no vultures could reach the height of his penthouse to devour his liver.

Suddenly, his personal A.I. assistant disturbed him from his thoughts.

"Sir, you have a call on the emergency line, code *alpha* from The Order's Grand Master. Should I put it through?

With a calm voice, he said, "Yes, activate general signal jamming protocol two."

The Vice President was also a high-tech fan, spending unlimited funds for his security and privacy; this was the highest level of protection he could access.

What could be the reason for this unexpected call? the Vice President wondered.

"Mr. Vice President, we need to act urgently! Helene de Moncler was murdered, and our location in Brussels is now compromised," the Grand Master exclaimed with panic in his voice, trying to speak as quickly as possible as if he had only a few seconds left.

"We cannot access any of the video footage. However, de Moncler made an encrypted phone call to a young researcher Lydia del Biondo. She is famous for writing several scientific articles on senescence."

"Hm, I never heard the name. Who is she? What is her real role in this entire disaster? Why senescence...?" the Vice President seemed to be more intrigued than puzzled.

"Mr. Vice President, it is a rather new area of anti-aging. Senescence is a process of cellular aging that appears naturally in a living organism. Instead of dying off over time, senescent cells hang around, phantom-like. The scientists' nicknamed them *zombie cells*. These cells become toxic around the healthy ones, triggering inflammation in the body, an impaired immune system, and set the stage for most of the diseases linked to aging," the Grand Master stated passionately.

"Thank you, that will be enough!" the Vice-President announced. "You sound fascinated by her. You could have just said she is trying to find a cure for death!" the Vice President roared with impatience.

"I don't know why de Moncler would contact her just before she died."

"This is such a mess; it is now everywhere in the news. A perfect combination with the global coronavirus outbreak."

Most of his plasma screens were now projecting the red-flagged "breaking news" with various titles: "Murder in Berlaymont, the European Commission's President dead."

"Helene de Moncler murdered, a tragedy for EU in Brussels."

"The EU leadership shattered and plunged into the COVID-19 crisis."

"Vice President, what are your instructions?" the Grand Master asked. "I think we should…"

Simon did not wait for the Grand Master to end his sentence, and he whispered: "end call."

I'll have to fly back to Washington. I need to take charge of this situation, which is now out of control.

"Ask the agents to prepare my flight and wait for my instructions. We are going to central quarters," and then he closed his eyes and re-opened them peering down and focusing on his favorite spot in *Central Park*: The Obelisk.

§CHAPTER 23§
01:46, BERLAYMONT'S UNDERGROUND CAVE

THE WALLS continued moving, and their pace began to increase. Their basaltic structure seemed to suck in all the light emanated by the ceiling.

I have to stay alert and keep going. I am almost there.

Looking above, she was guided by the tree of life symbol.

The air seemed to change; Lydia could smell a sweet honeysuckle fragrance.

I must be dreaming. How am I smelling honeysuckle here?

There is no light here for a tree to photosynthesize.

She remembered that in some cultures, this

was a sacred plant; some even calling it God's Mother hand.

Her biology teacher told her a story once when they were visiting the Brussels' botanical garden.

Of all her teachers, Madame Carmen was her favorite.

"Isn't it wonderful my child? Nature has made such a miracle, an amazing perfume. My grandma told me once that the smell is as close as you can get to the divine, hence its name *God's Mother hand*."

"I am sure it's more than a local legend of *Mary, the mother of Jesus* who found refuge under this plant while she was pursued by *King Herod's* soldiers."

"Afterwards, she blessed the plant giving it curative properties; in fact, it does not only have a special perfume, but it also acts as anti-bacterial and anti-coagulant."

The words were reverberating so clearly in Lydia's mind; she could almost hear the soft voice of her beloved teacher.

The cave must be acting as a sort of emotion amplifier. Lydia had a gut feeling that she was very close to her goal.

It is almost inconceivable that a group of nuns built all the parts of this ingenious mechanism.

Lydia was left baffled. Who could have actually

built this?

The Sisters of Berlaymont covenant could not have done it alone.

Lydia recalled from her European School history lessons that the sisters' covenant was created in 1625 by the *Countess Lalaing,* who was married to the *Count de Berlaymont.*

Their order must have protected this secret cavern for almost four hundred years.

Or was this a coverup for an even more ancient organization?

This cavern seemed to predate any existing culture, and their covenant must have inherited its protection.

What I see here goes beyond anything I could have imagined.

A powerful force went to great lengths to construct this intricate structure for a crucial purpose.

She quickly turned left with one black basaltic wall almost catching her foot, and there it was... a sight that left her breathless.

§CHAPTER 24§

IN FRONT of her, a golden pyramid floated in the air between the floor and a giant stalactite, which seemed unnaturally well-polished and made from a gold-like metal.

The pyramid was also surrounded by four basins of the same basaltic material filled with a dark oily liquid, which was spreading a thick and warm scent filled with hints of honey and ripe citrus, her favorite honeysuckle fragrance.

She suddenly started blushing while she closed her eyes to process the unexpected explosion of memories.

All these long-forgotten feelings generated a tremor that shook her from head to toe.

She was back in the botanical garden.

"The Latin name of your favorite honeysuckle is Lonicera Japonica," her teacher gently explained.

"After *Adam Lonicer*, a Renaissance botanist. This species originated in Japan."

"The vine will slowly suffocate everything around as an invasive species but will mesmerize you with its perfume."

"We all need to learn the lessons nature gives us. Its link with Christianity is still a mystery to me Lydia. Maybe one day, you'll solve it," madame Carmen said to thirteen-year-old Lydia.

Lydia stepped forward and was abruptly jolted back to the present as an unexpected flame ignited all four basins at the same time, engulfing the pyramid with a strange glowing bluish light.

Another pressure point activated mechanism; she was glad that at least she didn't trigger a deadly spiked trap on the floor.

She could not keep herself from grinning, and her heart started to pulsate faster while overwhelmed by a wave of adrenaline.

Getting closer to the floating pyramid, she could not help but wonder how the magnetic field was being generated to keep such a massive metallic object afloat.

She knew that gold didn't have magnetic properties. The only explanation was that it was coated and that inside there was another material with magnetic properties.

The floor and ceiling must also be a magnet—a

system of magnets in perfect equilibrium...

Looking closer, she realized that it was, in fact, a model of the Great Pyramid.

The flickering of the bluish flame revealed a shiny red precious stone.

The ruby highlighted the fabled King's chamber. All the Great Pyramid's chambers were faintly stylized, including the one of the Queen and the Grand Gallery.

Strangely from the ruby, there was another passage to an unknown chamber marked with a flower of life symbol.

The first thing that came to mind was that her students were particularly fascinated by her favorite lecture part, when she talked about the most ancient flower of life symbols from around 4.000 BC discovered at the Temple of Osiris in Abydos, Egypt.

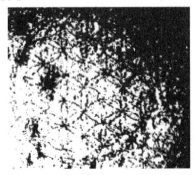

The oddest feature of the flower of life in Abydos was that it was not carved into the granite, but instead, it seemed to be burned or somehow drawn on with incredible precision.

Her colleagues in archaeology believed it could have represented the *Eye of RA*, a symbol of the Pharaoh's authority.

Was the ruby a marker point showing the path to the entrance of the secret chamber?

She felt pulled towards it, and when approaching her hand, the ruby started to pulsate faintly.

Without thinking, she pushed the precious stone down.

For a few seconds, nothing happened, and then on the surface of the golden pyramid, several letters started to emerge, written in a language she could not understand.

The letters seemed to have been pushed forward by a strange force from the previously perfect smooth surface.

"XGlass activate flash and start taking pictures every three seconds."

Using her XGlass, she took photos from all the pyramid's sides.

If I manage to escape this place alive, I am sure Neo will help me find a solution in translating the letters.

A few seconds later, Lydia heard a faint noise coming from the pyramid.

"Oh no, here it comes. I am sure I activated another damn trap."

However, nothing happened besides the top of the pyramid detaching from the main body and starting to float above it.

It's like an invitation to grab it, Lydia thought with a feeling of fear permeating her mind.

This mini-pyramidion seemed familiar to her...

Suddenly, as in the case of the previous markings, several symbols started to materialize on it, which looked to be Egyptian hieroglyphs.

Where did I see this pyramid model before?

Oh, Yes. I think I saw a similar one with my parents when we went to Egypt to celebrate my fourteenth birthday on a Nile cruise.

Indeed, it resembles to a Benben stone if I could only remember precisely where I spotted it.

A Benben stone, which, at its center, is a variation of the flower of life.

She felt the urge to take the mini-pyramid with her because it might prove useful in the future, despite all the risks and her mind saying: *don't do it; it will trigger a trap.*

When touching the smooth surface, it detached effortlessly, and it seemed to be much lighter than it appeared.

She quickly put it in one of her coat pockets and closed the invisible zipper.

A subtle breeze suddenly began stroking her hair.

This is not good. Where would the breeze be coming from?

The flames reduced in intensity, and the honeysuckle perfume became suffocating.

Immediately after, the breeze was replaced by a faint tremor, which started to increase in intensity. Then a howling noise came. The stalactites began falling one by one, and while this was happening, the illuminated ceiling began to go dark.

Oh no, this cannot be happening; I'll be squashed and die here in the dark.

Looking above for any falling rocks, she noticed that just two of the symbols remained active on the ceiling but in opposite directions.

Which one should I take? I am sure one of them will show me the exit.

I cannot make my mind. Think Lydia. Which one is it?

She knew the symbology of both luminescent drawings. The Caduceus, resembling a winged DNA structure, was an ancient Greco-Roman relic, thousands of years old.

She was fascinated by the shape of this mysterious object, and once she asked her mother what it was when she stumbled upon it in one of her visits to the Louvre Museum in Paris.

"Ahh, my child, it's a supernaturally powerful staff, composed of two serpents directly opposite one another, which are both coiled upwards on a rod."

"It was said to be used by the Greek Gods *Hermes* and *Asclepios* in unknown ways to both control and heal their human worshipers," her beautiful mom said with a soft voice.

"One day, maybe you'll discover one and use its powers, but please, only for good, my dear daughter," her mom said, showing a big smile.

This was a difficult and challenging problem for Lydia.

She never liked to make quick decisions. She always preferred to analyze every option thoroughly, as well as the impact her decision could have.

But now she had no choice; another leap of faith was required.

I miss you so much, mom. If only you could be here right now.

I knew you would have made a swift and logical decision.

With this in mind, she started running as fast as she could, trying to avoid the falling rocks.

The symbol was shining above her, and deep inside, she knew that she could have made the wrong choice.

§CHAPTER 25§
NEW YORK

THE VICE PRESIDENT of the United States was fixing a tiny structure lost in the green mass in front of him. The Obelisk had a name: "Cleopatra's Needle," not related in any way with the historical person.

Like most of the great cities around the world which owned similar Egyptian heritages, gifted or stolen, this one, in particular, was an antique, 3500-years-old, and perfectly preserved.

The two-hundred-ton Obelisk was a reminder of Egypt's glorious past.

He enjoyed diving into its symbolism as it reminded him of the Pharaoh *Thutmose III*'s story, one of the most powerful Pharaohs in history.

In 1450 BC, to commemorate his thirty-year reign, he ordered memorabilia to be created that would endure across millennia and etched from a single slab of precious rose granite.

This one had a twin, and they faced fifteen hundred years of turbulent times before collapsing under the sandstorms and conflict, being left to oblivion.

Its twin ended up in London in 1879 and was placed on the banks of the Thames. Two obelisks on different continents; two nations united by the same origin.

With Simon's mind wandering to the past; he could not understand why the scent of his first wife was invading his mind after such a long time.

Why are you haunting me?

She was standing in front of him, a mesmerizing ghost of the past.

Remember my love; nothing is forever. Was it really worth it? All this time, all the power you wanted, away from my embrace.

Simon knew the answer; his consciousness was projecting her ghost.

I'll never have the answer to this question.

I still believe that I made the right choices, and I'll endure the present-day hardships the same way the Pharaoh's obelisk survived for millennia.

For a moment, he glanced back at the flickering screens. All over the world, the pandemic was becoming catastrophic.

Even the remotest corner of the world was affected by COVID-19, with most of the victims located in developed Central European countries. The United States was becoming the second epicenter after China with scores of dead and its medical system overwhelmed.

Could this be divine justice?

We all knew this moment would arrive when overpopulation and our lack of respect towards the planet would backfire on us.

This is the moment when we need to mobilize and rebuild.

Our Order has protected this nation for so long. We will not wither in front of this challenge, Simon thought with unnerving self-control.

"Vice-President, I detected an incident in our vault," his A.I. informed in a perfectly calm voice. "Someone has broken in, and the underground structure collapsed. The drones cannot descend to assess the damage."

"How could this be possible in one of the most secured buildings in the world?" the Vice-President inquired with anger in his voice.

"Vice President, I am afraid all our data related to the event was mysteriously deleted. There is no way to trace back who has done this …"

"I am re-checking the residual memory of our servers. Maybe there are still some fragments which I can recover."

I have to find who is responsible for this breach or otherwise everything will be lost.

"I need an update on President Blackmoore's health status."

"The United States President's status remains unchanged. He is still in mechanical ventilation, and he doesn't seem to respond to the latest trial antiviral therapy he was enrolled in."

"A new study was just published, and the survival rate for patients over 65, who were placed on a machine, was just 3%. Furthermore, men had a higher mortality rate than women," the A.I. reported.

"Do you want to hear more statistics?"

"No, that will be enough. I am ready to take my flight to Washington."

The A.I. assistant instantly opened a communication channel with his security team, which was on standby for his order.

"Sir, your chopper is waiting for you on the helipad."

The Vice President whisked away with an eerie calm. He took one last glimpse at *Central Park*, fixating on the Obelisk again while whispering to himself:

"I will find you again, my love, and we'll be reunited."

§CHAPTER 26§

THE SYMBOL of the Egyptian ankh was growing closer on the horizon. She could now see a faint glittering light.

Could it be that I reached the exit?

For the moment, the tremors calmed, and she knew that, indeed, she made the right choice.

The Egyptians thought the ankh symbolized the gate to eternal life; a token of protection to open the path to the afterlife, the first symbol of a cross.

The ancient mystics' symbol of the circularity between life and death.

The early Christians knew its power and adopted it as their faith's symbol with the culmination of Jesus being crucified, an unfortunate coincidence for such a powerful symbol to be correlated with such a cruel way to die.

The stone walls of the cave became darker

as the two luminescent symbols' light became fainter, projecting just a dim glitter from the high ceiling.

Will I be soon surrounded by absolute darkness? Lydia's phobia was gradually beginning to take a toll on her, especially as she began to have difficulty breathing.

Will I die here alone in pure darkness with my greatest fear? Now she was feeling almost suffocated by the darkness. It was engulfing her slowly, choking her bronchia, nearly triggering an asthma attack.

Hello, my fear. It has been such a long time. Where have you been?

While breathing heavily, she noticed the air seemed impure; a strange foul smell seemed to ooze from all directions.

What a difference compared with the honeysuckle perfume, she thought.

And when the last faint glitter vanished from above, and all hope seemed lost...

"XGlass activate light."

"Light cannot be activated as the battery levels are to 2%, please recharge your..." the device said as it switched off.

In the absolute darkness, a whitish light began to shine not far from her on the upper part of one of the walls.

A beacon of hope in absolute darkness, Lydia said to herself with a dash of optimism.

She realized that there was an ascending path she had to take until reaching the light.

The path was extremely narrow, and she had to be careful not to stumble and fall to her death, as there was no protective border to prevent her plunge.

She felt incredibly tired. Going up a slope in almost complete darkness took a toll on her energy level.

I am going up, but where?

Small tremors were still coming and going, and she knew the sooner she was out of the underground cave, the better.

Time seemed to pass at a snail's pace. After what seemed like endless climbing, there it was.

The shining white light was, in fact, a giant rock crystal, which was receiving light via a mirror system only now visible.

Looking back, it seemed to have reached the top of the cave, and at its center, the four burning honeysuckle oil flames were just four faint dots but still burning.

As she approached the hanging crystal, its light was becoming stronger, and again a tremor started to shake the ground underneath her.

The path in front of her was blocked, but the wall above the crystal began to crack open.

A secret exit, maybe, Lydia thought with a glimmer of hope.

Now big chunks of stone were detaching and rolling down in the chasm behind her.

While Lydia tried to avoid being taken down by a chunk of stone which almost crushed her shoulder, the wall in front of her crumbled revealing the structure of an ancient gate.

Instantaneously, to her surprise, in a soundless explosion, the rock crystal shattered into a fine powder which almost generated fake sparkly snow falling in front of the newly formed gateway; a carpet of crystal dust and an invitation to the unknown.

§CHAPTER 27§

THE ORDER WAS forced to relocate several times. However, they always kept a guardian of their secrets to protect the entrance and exit to their vault.

Lydia found herself in a small room looking for an opening, a way out of the catacombs. Her XGlass and cell phone were now depleted.

The darkness once again began to slowly choke her to death.

Desperate and barely breathing, she came up with one final idea. *What if I try to reopen my cell phone again? Maybe there is still some residual battery left.*

Switching it on, she felt beyond lucky, seeing a 3% battery.

She quickly activated its light with trembling hands and projected it onto the walls full of roots and earth.

She quickly picked up a moldy, rotten leaf smell emanating from every corner.

In one of the walls, she noticed a polished stone, covered with dirt and roots.

I know the exit is so close, but where am I?

Lydia started to pull out all the roots and cleaned the stone with her elbow.

The stone revealed a pattern; the flower of life, which seemed to be sculpted inside the stone.

It appears that somebody was obsessed with this ancient pattern. The flower of life is everywhere...

Touching it, she realized the flower of life was composed of several metallic rings, but some seemed to be missing.

She rotated one of the rings, and suddenly a strong current of air began to blow. It came from above and below and from all sides.

So strange...I guess no flame would have survived here.

My fire torch would have been immediately extinguished; luckily, I still have a bit of battery.

Lydia knew she had to be extremely fast. Her battery was now at 1% and would switch off at any moment.

"I'll never manage to find the rest of the chains to form the pattern. Where are the rest?" she muttered nervously.

Looking down at the soft muddy earth, she dug her feet in.

She could not help but gasp in excitement, as she noticed a faint shimmer coming from several chains that had been buried shallowly.

Quickly digging them out one by one, she matched the empty spaces, keeping in mind how the flower of life was formed.

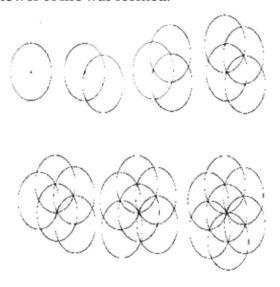

And what now? Why is nothing happening? Have I done something wrong? There must be a secret mechanism behind it. I can't seem to rotate the stone.

What if I push it again?

Using all her might she hit the stone with her elbow, but it barely budged.

Remembering her tai chi lessons, she took a deep breath and focused all her energy on one last kick.

And as the light of her phone switched off, she kicked it as hard as she could.

In that moment, a centuries-old mechanism, long-dormant, sprang back, opening a spiral staircase. To her great relief, she could see a faint natural light peering down on her.

The staircase unfurled for several long moments.

Afraid that the mechanism could trigger another trap, she quickly began to climb the stairs.

After several minutes of a rapid ascent, she was almost out of breath. But soon she felt some fresh air; a good sign that she was approaching the surface.

Her phone started to pop on the screen dozens of notifications from missed calls and messages.

Finally, a signal, Neo must have tried to contact me so many times.

"Are you okay?"

"What happened?"

"Call me back…"

And the last one:

"I geolocated you."

"Go the nearest exit on Rue Nerviene 41; there is an UBER Mercedes-Benz limousine with the plate TLAN 219 B."

"It's going to pick you up in five minutes."

"Just confirm you received the message."

Neo understood that my battery was nearly depleted.

While climbing the last step, she found herself locked in a small stony cylinder-shaped structure.

She quickly typed: "all ok, heading to UBER," and hit the "send" button.

Her face was both relieved and terrified. Her muscles began to give up one after the other, generating a tingling feeling throughout her exhausted body.

Looking above, she noticed that the ceiling was made of red bricks ingeniously forming a simplified flower of life pattern.

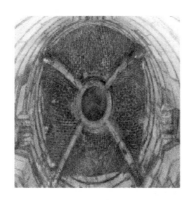

I guess the Sisters of Berlaymont must have set up this cleverly hidden secret passage in plain sight.

Behind her, she could hear the mechanism retracting the stairs. The cracked square stone lid was gradually closing behind her.

She managed to escape the labyrinth, and now she knew that whatever mission laid ahead, it will only get more complicated.

She could see some vegetation outside through a freshly painted transparent metallic gate.

This is the Cinquantenaire Park, but where exactly?

The stairs vanished, and the mechanism closed the exit with the massive square in the middle of the cylindric room.

Trying to open the metallic door, Lydia realized that it was locked.

Oh, this cannot be true. The door had a lock with a four-digit cypher.

"I cannot believe that after all I had to endure; I am stuck here like this?" Lydia whispered angrily.

What could the combination be? Think Lydia; there is no time.

And then it came to her: *what if is the sequence I found on the elevator's metallic card in the abnormal DNA structure represents the code?*

I think the sequence was 4 3 2 3, and when moving the rotative metallic disks of the lock to match this combination, the lock mechanism opened.

Ah Helene, you carefully thought through every-thing...

Leaving the structure, she realized the exit was located in the peculiar little tower that, as a child, she always wondered why it was placed in the middle of the park.

Next to the metallic door, Lydia noticed a small descriptive panel explaining in several languages, for lost tourists, the history of the tower.

She could not hold back her curiosity and took a glance while running towards her UBER meeting point:

"*The Tournai* tower or *Beyaert* tower, a curious building, designed by the architect *Henri Beyaert* on the occasion of the national *Jubilee exhibition* of 1880 to celebrate the fiftieth anniversary of Belgian independence.

Erected in 1880 in a pseudo-medieval style resembling a Lily flower, a heraldic symbol of the noble houses, it was intended to demonstrate the qualities of Tournai stone."

This architect must have been a part of The Order, an agent of the Berlaymont sisters, entrusted to design the tower to hide their secret, Lydia thought while hurrying towards the meeting point.

Leaving behind the shadow of the tower, she noticed its protective gargoyles on the roof.

A clever distraction for people not to notice the architect's perfectly symmetric anagram which she kept in her mind, Lydia thought.

Lydia grasped that by turning upside down, the anagram could have perfectly stood for HdM, Helene de Moncler.

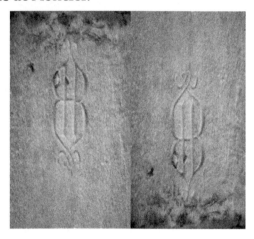

Helene and Henri Beyaert could have been related...everything is connected.

I guess today was my lucky day, Lydia said to herself.

This small victory gave her the extra energy she needed to leave the park and catch her UBER.

§CHAPTER 28§

THE PARK was a hidden green breathing oasis engulfed in an eerie silence. Symbols were hiding everywhere in this part of Brussels, and the tower was the last symbol of the ancient history that marked this place.

Trees were fretting in the brisk wind, and little tornadoes were causing leaves to fall in all directions, creating a bizarre picture.

The Order came here for hundreds of years to embrace nature and pray for Jesus' blessings.

What almost nobody knew was that below this green park, a labyrinth of catacombs was built to preserve their legacy together with their most treasured artifact.

Lydia always loved to come here as its trees were planted in a harmonious mix to match the obsessive geometry of this place.

She quickly passed by the collapsed ruin of a

barely known wooden chapel wherein the Sisters of Berlaymont, one of The Order's most devoted factions, came to get the blessing of the divine.

The trees had origins from all over the globe, forming a mosaic of shapes and colors like Horse-chestnut, European beech, Sycamore, Silver maple, Oaks with hairy cups, American white ash, and Corded alder.

Lydia almost fainted when she reached her meeting point at *Rue Nerviene 41.* She noticed that her UBER ride was approaching.

The black limo stopped next to her. She opened the door and crawled inside.

"Good evening ma'am. Mister Xavier ordered this trip for you, and he instructed me to give you this package."

Hm, mister Xavier, this must be an alias for Neo, Lydia thought.

"Thank you, sir. Do you have any water? I am extremely thirsty," Lydia said, her throat dry like sandpaper.

"Certainly, ma'am, there are several bottles in the door compartment," the driver said politely in a Flemish accent.

She was so dehydrated that she managed to guzzle down two bottles one after the other.

"I am sorry, I had to train myself for a marathon this evening," Lydia said, embarrassed.

"Do not worry, ma'am, there is more water if you want," the driver said kindly.

On the radio, worrying news was emerging: "The COVID-19 infections and the death rate in Belgium are skyrocketing, being one of the countries with the highest mortality rate. The virus can mutate, and it can be transmitted through the breathing of an infected person. The entire population is advised to respect social distancing rules."

"Our destination is the Zaventem airport, and mister Xavier indicated you'd need to charge your devices. Next to you there are all the cables you need.

Lydia connected her XGlass and cell phone, and after a few seconds, they switched on again.

Neo was trying to reach her. Gently touching the frames, she activated the call.

"I am so happy to hear your voice, mister Xavier," Lydia said with excitement in her voice.

"Me too, it was incredible you managed to escape. What an adventure. For a while, I thought I'd never be able to see you again." Neo's voice sounded relieved. "Listen, carefully, Lydia; I have downloaded all the data you stored. What an amazing discovery you made; it's unbelievable."

"The box given by the driver contains an XGlass prototype having an enhanced satellite coverage, powered with a special micro hydrogen-based fuel cell, giving it power for two full days. On top of that, you don't need to connect it to your cell phone."

Neo's voice sounded extremely happy and comforted that Lydia made it out alive.

"Please put the new XGlass next to the old one to synchronize their profiles; and one more thing, Lydia, this is a gift from Helene. A courier came to me with a strange note."

"If you receive this Neo then I am dead, please give this package to Lydia, I have an important message for her. Helene de Moncler."

§CHAPTER 29§

THE PHOENIX was looking at his hand, and only the protruded veins betrayed his real age.

I had to endure for so long, and now my mission will come to an end.

The Assassin called his Master to report back.

"The mission was accomplished Master. Helene de Moncler is dead. However, I am afraid there was someone who entered her office; a young woman who mysteriously vanished," the Assassin said, trying to control his voice.

His heart was pounding faster, and his vision was blurred. He knew that if his Master could sense he failed, it would be the end of him.

"I know my son," the Phoenix said in a somber tone.

"She will be your next mission."

The Phoenix's voice gave off an air of authority. Over the years, he was called many names, but this one, he believed was destined for him.

Every ancient afterlife symbol was concentrated within this mythological creature, which after burning, could regenerate herself and re-emerge from the ashes. All its memories were preserved, and it was constantly evolving.

The ancient Greeks and Egyptians were fascinated with this fabled creature's myth. The historian of antiquity, Herodotus, described it as a sacred creature locked in an eternal five-hundred-year cycle of regeneration.

"Her name is Lydia del Biondo, a family acquaintance of de Moncler."

"You'll have to follow each movement she makes."

"I feel she has a vital role to play in the events to come."

"De Moncler must have entrusted her with a mission, and to overturn her devious plot; we need to follow this girl and discover what de Moncler was up to. Then, I'll let you know when the right time is to terminate her."

The Assassin listened carefully to each instruction given by his Master so as not to miss any detail.

"Your wish is my command, Master. It shall be done."

The Assassin knew she could not be far away;

only two hours passed since he last saw her.

I will start with her apartment; maybe she left some traces there.

My Master will inform me if she attempts to cross the border. Hopefully, she will try to board a plane.

With a few clicks on his cell phone, the Assassin succeeded in breaking into Lydia's official administrative records and found the location of her house.

The Phoenix was looking through the window of his luxury car, telling his driver.

"Prepare my jet; we need to turn around; we need to head towards the airport. I have a feeling I will need to travel for a few days. Tell the pilots to be on standby."

The time has come to take my destiny into my own hands.

§CHAPTER 30§

LYDIA KNEW she only had twenty more minutes until reaching the airport. She never felt so tired in her life, yet there was no time for a nap.

"Neo, please talk to me. Otherwise, I'll fall asleep," Lydia whispered with a faint voice.

"I have something important to tell you. After analyzing several ancient language data-bases to cross-reference the pyramid's symbols you discovered below Berlaymont, it appears they belong to the Assyrians. This was one of the earliest civilizations emerging in the Middle East, having a history spanning over 6760 years."

"The Assyrian kingdom was one of the first in Mesopotamia until its collapse in 612 BC, and their language was Aramaic, the actual language spoken by Jesus. As a Semitic language, the Aramaic language is related to Hebrew and Arabic but predates both."

"In addition, whereas most Arabs are Muslim, Assyrians are essentially Christian," Neo stated.

"Fascinating story Professor Neo, did you also manage to translate the text?" Lydia asked impatiently.

"There are many versions of Aramaic words, and most of them are cross-referenced to different chapters of the Bible, depending on which Apostle wrote which part."

"The phonetic readout of your text would be":

OHaB'oBo,AB'KHaYeA,D'TS-aB,eAD'aB,RaA

ܟܬܒܐ ܚܝܐ ܪܥܝܐ ܢܛܪܐ ܐܘܪܚܟ

With the approximate translation:

"The flower of life under the protection of Bennu will guide your path."

"Yes, we know the flower of life appeared everywhere while I was underground. Is there nothing else?" Lydia asked worriedly.

"Hang on a moment. I recalled in the cave having seen the same pattern on a pyramid during one of my childhood trips to Egypt…"

"Can you search the internet database and

cross-reference the picture of the mini-pyramid?" Lydia asked, her eyes glittering with hope and curiosity.

"Already did it, Lydia. We have a match for a very similar object, with the flower of life adorned on top. Early Egyptian priests thought that *RA* came to Earth in a strange mystic object called *Akka*. That object was given later in history, the name Benben, a term originating from an Egyptian word signifying *essence.* It is frequently recorded in traditional Egyptian history that the Benben landed from the sky, and it became the most cherished object of the time. Legend continues to state that Benben was the mound that arose from the primordial waters *Nu* upon which the creator deity *Atum* settled in the creation myth."

Lydia knew the Benben stone or the pyramidion became the capstone of Pyramids and Obelisks.

In ancient Egypt, these were probably gold-plated, so they would have gloriously sparkled in the sunlight, serving as a beacon for its followers and for the creator himself, the power of *RA*.

"And here it is your pyramid," Neo exclaimed, projecting on Lydia's XGlass the image of the Benben stone.

"It's, in fact, the Benben stone from the Pyramid of *Amenemhat III*, 12_{th} Dynasty, exhibited now in the recently opened Grand Egyptian Museum in Cairo."

"From the picture, it seems to also have in its center, a flower of life or the solar disk pattern."

"I think it has a strong link with the ruby indicating the King's chamber and the secret room," Neo said almost without taking a breath.

"The bird deity you can see is indeed Bennu evoked by the Aramaic inscription."

"*Bennu* had its origin in the phoenix myth and was initially worshiped in *Heliopolis*, The City of the Sun or the House of RA, nesting on top of the Benben stone."

"*Heliopolis* was one of the wonders of the ancient Egyptian world and one of its oldest cities."

Today it lays largely in ruins with its structures scavenged by the poor and used as construction material for medieval Cairo.

"We need to go to the Grand Egyptian Museum to check the Benben stone. If only my parents could see me now," Lydia said with a wistful tone after taking a deep sigh.

"I can hear the fatigue in your voice, Lydia. There will be time to rest during the flight," Neo said with compassion.

"Good news, I just found a flight leaving in two hours to Cairo. I have booked you a business class ticket," Neo said.

"If I could, I would come myself to pick you up and hold you while you rest, Neo added.

"Is this a proposal or a promise?" Lydia asked. Despite having never seen him, she felt an intense attraction for his voice.

"Helene not only left you a message that you need to listen now but also a hefty bank account in your name."

"Okay, but first, I want to see your picture Neo. It is not fair that you know everything about me, and I don't even know what you look like."

"That's only fair. This is me now," Neo said. And to Lydia's surprise, a picture appeared on her XGlass.

§CHAPTER 31§

LYDIA GASPED because Neo was incredibly handsome. He had long blond hair and piercing blue eyes that emanated a genuine kindness.

"Is this really you or a fake avatar?" Lydia asked in a cheeky tone.

"It's me for the moment, but not for long. I'll tell you more, but now you need to listen to Helene's message. I am afraid we are running out of time," Neo said hastily.

Lydia quickly put on the new XGlass prototype, which felt even lighter, and it self-activated instantaneously.

Her display was showing the setup was almost finalized:

"biomarker parameters loading;"

"27% of data is being processed; please wait;"

"biomarker parameters loading 83% profile is being established."

A soft female voice spoke through the bone conduction technology.

"Welcome, Lydia del Biondo. I am the XGlass' latest generation of A.I. assistant. All your data has been synchronized with your new profile."

A new classified message was coming in from President Helene de Moncler:

"My child, if you receive this message it means that I am dead, and you have successfully accessed The Order's secret vault."

"It's time to learn a secret that unfortunately, I had to keep too long from you," the former President of the European Commission said in a calm voice that showed a tinge of sorrow and regret.

"Your parents and I have always tried to protect you and to preserve The Order."

"We are the last descendants of Mary, Mother of Jesus, and the last blood of Atlantis."

"You see, my child, Jesus Christ, was not just the child of God. This was just an alleged myth to justify his tremendous power and knowledge."

"He thought that by preaching inner healing and goodness, he would peacefully convince large masses of people; ultimately, generating a perpetual peacefulness that would spread across the planet."

"But he could not be more wrong; he made a

grave mistake, one that I must have also made... he underestimated his enemies and their determination to control the masses."

"One of the real elements depicted in the Bible was that he was immortal, and that's true."

"The Atlanteans possessed such an advanced technology that they managed to find a cure for death, rendering them practically immortal. Their world was the true paradise until the devastating cataclysm destroyed it, and only a handful managed to escape so many millennia ago and then became worshiped for a time as the Greek Gods."

"Jesus wanted to share the secret of eternal life with the entire humanity, only when he thought they would be prepared for such a heavy responsibility and burden."

"However, he was killed before he could reveal his secret Atlantean knowledge, and the betrayal of some of his followers and disciples convinced him to pass the knowledge to a few worthy ones in order to carry out his mission."

"Nobody knows what actually happened. However, he left a trail of clues and entrusted their protection to his mother Mary and Peter, the most faithful among his Apostles."

"Mary simply vanished, never to be found. She was so affected by her son's death that she considered the entire humanity unworthy of his gift."

"Peter was killed by Emperor Nero, and thus became the founding 'stone' of the modern Church."

"Both left a legacy to few trustful followers, who then created The Order."

"We tried over the millennia to put together all the clues and find the path to Jesus' Grail, but we utterly failed."

"All our efforts withered into oblivion, and we were slowly consumed by a hidden enemy, the Phoenix."

"In time, our order faded, and the Grail's quest was abandoned. We simply became its guardians, known as *The Order*, while waiting for someone worthy and capable to solve its mystery."

"I can only hope that what you discovered in our vault will show you the righteous path."

"I'll also give you a final clue left in our possession:"

Ο παγανιστικός ιερός κύκλος θα σας δείξει το δρόμο και κάτω από την τελειότητα του αριστερού χεριού του Κόσμου όταν χαθεί στο σκοτάδι ο σταυρός θα σας δείξει το φως.

"I am sure my child, you'll find what your destiny foretold."

"I deeply regret I'll not be able to accompany you on this perilous journey where you cannot trust anyone other than Simon Lightgood."

"He will offer all the support you'll need. Seek his advice, and never doubt him as his heart is pure."

"And please take care of Neo. He needs your help and has been in love with you for many years. He was your protector during your earlier years, watching and making sure nothing bad happened to you."

"He's like my child. You are the children I never had. Lydia, please help him find a cure, he's dying..."

"End of transmission, would you like to play the message again," her XGlass announced.

I'll help you, Neo, and I'll accomplish my mission for my parents and you, Helene.

I cannot believe what I've seen and heard today.

Could Jesus really have been an Atlantean?

Maybe this is the explanation of the technology's origin used to set up the intricate system of caves underneath the Berlaymont, Lydia wondered.

"Alexa, please connect me to Neo."

The dark clouds were making the night even heavier. The limo was now on the highway heading towards the Zaventem airport. Lydia finally grasped the importance of her mission.

I can fulfill my dream to find a cure for death.

"Lydia, now you know the whole truth, and no, it was not a deepfake video of Helene. This is the reality; believe it or not."

"Neo, you omitted to tell me the most important fact; that you are dying... when were you planning to tell me? I have so many questions, but first, tell me why you are dying? What happened to you?" Lydia asked, feeling both sad and worried.

§CHAPTER 32§

"I HAVE ALS, and it is progressing very quickly. I think you know this disease very well," Neo said, his voice trembling.

Lydia was taken by surprise and tried her best to control her emotions.

She knew this merciless disease well and even remembered writing a long scientific article during her first year in university on the genetic risk of the children inheriting this disease.

"I am deeply sorry, Neo. Please hang on in there."

"I think that Helene wanted us to continue her mission. Did you hear her message as well?"

"If we find the clues Jesus left, we might be able to cure your disease."

"It doesn't matter anymore…"

"My dream, to just talk to you, has been accomplished. I just hope I'll also meet you in person someday," Neo confessed with a little shyness in his voice.

The car was on the last bit of highway before the airport and approaching fast. There was no moon or stars, just deep darkness. Lydia knew the path ahead would be full of peril.

"Neo, our destiny brought us here, now at this moment. Together we have a purpose, and I am confident we'll find a way to get through," Lydia said, though, in her mind, she was unsure...

Was I too cold? she wondered.

I have to admit, I find a deep, inexplicable attraction for Neo, but right now we need to focus on our mission.

"Helene left me an additional clue written in Greek. I am not sure that my rusty ancient Greek is good enough... Would you be able to use the translation algorithm to translate it?" Lydia asked timidly.

§CHAPTER 33§

THE POPE was full of anger. The situation at the global level was getting out of control.

The liturgical services and Holy Masses were being canceled in all corners of the world. Governments were closing the churches' doors, with fear now creeping everywhere.

"Brother Cardinals, the COVID-19 virus is destroying our communities," the Pope started with dread in his voice.

"Christianity is in decline. Each year we have fewer and fewer faithful in our Church."

"Infant baptism is steadily dropping around the globe. Countless churches are shutting down or uniting due to the lack of congregants."

"We are risking being the last generation of the Church, which will take us down the path to oblivion."

"We need now to reform; you must all be aware

of the Saint Malachy prophecy."

"We shouldn't repeat the same mistakes of the past. Previous pandemic outbreaks like the Black Death killed more than half of Europe eight hundred years ago."

"Brothers, look deep inside your soul and ask yourselves, where was the Holy Church back then. We have to leave behind the mentality of the Dark Ages that flourished under the Inquisition."

"The Black Death killed 200 million people in Eurasia, and then we had the 1918 influenza pandemic."

"The 1918 flu—which was erroneously named the Spanish flu in order to deflect attention from the center of the outbreaks and put the blame on neutral Spain—infected 500 million people around the world. It may have killed more than 100 million people. This flu killed more people in two years than AIDS killed in twenty years. Politics should never be involved when peoples' lives are at stake."

"But your Holiness, we cannot compare it to the Black Death, which lasted much longer and had a much more violent impact on a smaller population," said an elderly Cardinal with a strong Italian accent."

Another Cardinal took the floor with panic in his voice, "I am reading very worrying news from China:

"It has extended travel restrictions to eleven cities as it races to contain the SARS-like virus that has overwhelmed local hospitals and sparked global alarm. The coronavirus COVID-19 outbreak has already killed a record number of people. An additional 10,072 cases are suspected in twenty provinces, while cases have been confirmed in the U.S., Japan, South Korea, Thailand, Macau, Taiwan, Singapore, Vietnam, and Hong Kong."

"I have a bad feeling about this virus. It has already spread outside its ground zero, and could also potentially further mutate."

"The College needs to make a decision. We have to act and save our followers. I am afraid that this will only make things worse," the Pope concluded while his Cardinals stared on with unpleasant grimaces on their faces.

§CHAPTER 34§

THE CORONAVIRUS OUTBREAK was spreading around the world, generating panic in even the most developed countries. Special filters were also installed in the Brussels airport with staff scanning the temperature of incoming passengers, mostly from non-European countries.

"Ma'am, we've arrived. Thank you for riding with me, and I hope you'll give me five stars," the UBER driver said, not even daring to ask for Lydia's final destination.

"Absolutely, and you'll also get a very generous tip," Lydia reassured him while she exited the car, getting soaked almost instantly by a cold shower of rain.

The airport was still recovering from the 2016 Daesh\ISIS terrorist attacks that killed dozens of people and left many wounded.

As a precautionary measure, the UBER or other passenger drop-off point was fixed twenty meters outside of one of the main entrances, which was heavily guarded.

It was also a way to make the life of the other drivers more difficult in favor of taxi drivers, who managed to set up one of the most influential syndicates around the world, resisting the challenges brought on by the new trends of the gig economy and ride-sharing services.

As she entered the airport, almost everybody was wearing protective masks which were given at the entrance by the airport staff.

"It's not enough that this airport was almost completely shattered by the 2017 terrorist attacks, now it has to endure more sorrow and panic," Lydia thought as she saw several families who had to catch a flight to Beijing, panicking and speaking in Mandarin.

"**BREAKING NEWS**: China's coronavirus to spread."

Beijing cautioned that it expects the spread of the deadly coronavirus to hasten, as the death toll skyrocketed, and the number of confirmed cases reached 20,732.

In the epicenter of Wuhan, more than 5 million citizens who supposedly were under lockdown, managed to exit the city and the Mayor offered his resignation.

"Did you hear that, Lydia?" Neo asked.

"I activated for you the translation function, which could come very handy in the near future. We have the flight 734TM operated by Egypt air."

"I booked you a first-class ticket with Egypt Air. It is the fastest option now."

"The good part is that you are not on the Interpol blacklist, and you can still safely travel. We managed to keep your escape from Berlaymont secret."

"That's great Neo, if they catch me, I'll write you some charming letters from prison," Lydia said with a big smile on her face.

Entering the airport, she took out her now soaked leather hoodie and realized that she had the mini-pyramidion in her possession.

"What if they confiscate it after going through the metal detector Neo? It has magnetic properties," Lydia worried aloud.

"I have a solution. Why don't you go to one of the airport's souvenir shops and buy some metal replicas of the *Atomium, Manneken Pis* figurines and most importantly some kitchen magnets? If you put them together with the mini-pyramidion in a backpack, it will look less suspicious, and maybe they will let it pass being mistaken for some worthless trinkets."

"You should also buy the Samsonite backpack in front of you. It may come handy and seems very light."

"You'll need to get some summer clothes because we expect 30^0C during the day but 18^0C or lower during the night."

"When it comes to the Great Pyramid, you should not worry since one of its greatest mysteries resides in its innate capacity to stay at 20^0C all year. Oddly enough, this is also the average temperature across the planet." Neo said, fascinated at the thought that he would be able to explore it together with Lydia.

"You have precisely fifty-four minutes until the boarding gate is closed."

Lydia listened carefully to Neo and quickly went to the first souvenir shop before going through security and bought a bag packed with souvenirs.

"Could I please have an extra wrapping?" Lydia gently asked the seller.

"*Bien sûr Madame, voici*," the young blue-eyed seller said but could not take his eyes off Lydia.

"Where are you traveling to?" inquired the seller.

Lydia paused for a moment; "actually, it's a secret," she said, smiling.

"Well done, Lydia, but I think the poor guy has to follow the standard procedure."

"Okay, I understand. Have a pleasant trip Madame and please come more often to shop with us," the seller said, smiling.

Neo chuckled, and wrote a message, which appeared, on the display of her XGlass:

"LOL, everyone wants to flirt with you."

Lydia grabbed the bag and whisked herself off to the security gates, feeling confident and hoping everything would be fine.

§CHAPTER 35§

SEVERAL IMAGES were running through Lydia's mind. She could see the desert with golden dunes and far on the horizon, she could spot a person dressed in white.

Was this person, Jesus?

He didn't have a beard, just long brown hair. His face radiated kindness and wisdom. Lydia seemed to have a gut feeling it was Jesus Christ.

Next to him, there was a figure who seemed to be wearing the traditional clothes of a Pharaoh with his *pschent*, the conventional golden double crown reflecting the powerful sun and his leopard-skin fluttering over his shoulders.

And who was this Pharaoh?

Suddenly the sky darkened with the arrival of a gigantic wall of sand that was rapidly approaching the two figures.

Several other men riding on mighty horses

were advancing from the opposite direction, trying to warn them of the massive sandstorm.

The men gave them horses, and the two figures started to ride towards the Great Pyramid, which wasn't far from their current location.

Its golden Benben stone shone in the darkness with the last rays of the sun reflected on the metallic surface, transforming the Great Pyramid into a tower of light beaming into the approaching inferno of sand.

Lydia felt pulled towards the men traveling through the sandstorm, which had no impact on her. It was as if she were a ghost floating through the atmosphere.

She was rapidly approaching the pyramid, and below, she saw the Pharaoh's men trying to escape their sandy death.

But it was too late for them. The storm engulfed and obliterated everything in its path.

And then everything went black for Lydia. The darkness was suffocating her. She could not breathe anymore.

She was falling into a black abyss when suddenly she found herself inside the pyramid next to Jesus.

She was so close to him that she could not resist the temptation to touch him, but her hand passed directly through him.

Am I a ghost? What is this? Did I travel through time? It all seems so real. Lydia was fascinated by what was happening to her.

Then Jesus gave the Pharaoh a mini-pyramidion similar to the one she found underneath Berlaymont.

He was speaking Egyptian, but Lydia was surprised to understand every word:

"Protect this key with your life. Together with its twin, it will one day open the gates of the future."

§CHAPTER 36§
10:30, OCTOBER 2_{ND}
EGYPT, CAIRO

"MA'AM WE ARE SORRY to wake you. We are landing soon. You asked to be served your meal now," the flight attendant said while gently trying to bring Lydia back from the dream world.

"Today we have *canard confit* with *truffle parsnip* mash and a mousseline of *wild raspberries* and *morel mushrooms*. What would you like to drink?"

"Thank you, I would like a strong double espresso. I have a terribly busy day ahead of me," Lydia said, almost ready to yawn in front of the flight attendant.

Several notifications on her XGlass had caught her attention. "Coronavirus deaths surge."

"The death toll from the coronavirus outbreak

rose beyond predictions as foreign governments prepared to evacuate their nationals from China. Markets from all over the world are collapsing as the outbreak rattled sectors from travel to manufacturing."

"Can I bring you anything else?"

"I also have to say that you look ravishing even when you just wake up," the flight attendant said.

Lydia was a bit surprised by this sudden compliment. She was not used to strangers approaching her like this.

"I have to confess something to you, ma'am. You look very much like the love of my life," the female flight attendant said. She was tall and blonde with perfect skin and piercing aquamarine eyes.

"I know I could lose my job, but I had to tell you. If I can do anything else to make your flight more enjoyable, do let me know, it would be my pleasure," she said and then winked at Lydia.

Lydia didn't know how to answer for a moment. Reading her nametag, she said, "no, thank you... Sophie, I am still a bit tired, but if you are based in Cairo, I would be glad to buy you a drink."

She quickly thought that it would be best to simply indulge the pushy flight attendant.

Her eyes flickered, and Sophie, who must have been in her mid-twenties, began to babble.

"I am staying at the Kempinski Nile Hotel, and this is my cell phone number," the flight attendant said, full of excitement while giving Lydia a handwritten napkin.

While the flight attendant left to bring her a meal, Lydia tapped the XGlass, which she kept on just in case Neo had to alert her with any news and said, "did you listen to the conversation? I hope you are in your bed still sleeping."

"Of course, I listened."

"I think your beauty is going to get us into trouble. It seems that women are attracted to you as much as men. Why did you offer to buy her a drink?" Neo asked with a slight yawn.

"Well, aren't you a curious cat, but you know what happened at the end with the kitty?" Lydia said playfully.

"I just wanted to get rid of her. I gave her a little false hope, so she'd leave me in peace. You don't have to remind me to stay away from that hotel."

"I hope I'll have the time to rest when all this ordeal is behind us."

"Any trace of Helen's killers?"

"I wonder if they managed to somehow tap into the airport security surveillance and trace me."

"The investigation is still ongoing; it was a bullet shot from outside. But nothing to worry about at the moment, Lydia. No one can place you inside Berlaymont when it happened. I made sure of it…"

The Phoenix was boiling with anger, "so you managed to lose her again?"

"Master, I didn't have any option. By the time I traced her, she already boarded a plane."

"I have taken a private charter, and I'll arrive immediately after her. I might be able to intercept her at the airport because I'll be skipping all the security checks."

"Master, do you know why she is going to Egypt?" the Assassin asked, his voice indicating he felt humiliated.

"I do not know, but it must be related to what she found in de Moncler's office. The stakes are incredibly high now."

"What baffles me is that she managed to exit our vault, despite all the security measures put in place."

"I'll personally come to Cairo and, together, will find the underlying cause of this."

The Assassin's voice started to tremble, and he uttered: "Master, I have done everything I could in order not to fail you, but this girl has managed to elude me. She clearly has some help. She is not acting alone."

"One of de Moncler's henchmen must be offering her logistical support. I'll find out who it is and eliminate him soon."

"End transmission," the Phoenix roared. Twenty-five minutes later, he was boarding his private jet.

"Pass me the phone and get me the President of Egypt," he ordered his valet.

"Yes, your eminence. It shall be done."

§CHAPTER 37§

LYDIA HAD a very smooth landing. The coffee, in addition to the several hours of sleep, helped reinvigorate her mind. The dream she had was still with her and she couldn't shake it.

Could it be possible that this secret remained hidden for more than two millennia? Did I see glimpses of the past? What could have caused this vision?

She touched the inner pocket of her jacket and felt the surface of the mini-pyramidion artifact, which was slightly vibrating.

Could it be that the dream was, in fact, a distant memory of Jesus somehow embedded into it?

Maybe I should tell Neo, or perhaps he should not worry about me. He has to worry about his ASL.

This will be my burden to carry.

The brand-new Cairo Sphinx International Airport was just open some months ago. It was specially designed to serve masses of tourists, who were flooding into Egypt again.

A global frenzy began because Egypt would be displaying new archeological wonders for the first time ever inside the world's largest museum dedicated to one civilization—the Grand Egyptian Museum, or GEM.

Lydia was fascinated with this project since its construction began several years ago.

She knew that GEM hosted more than 100,000 artifacts from Egypt and beyond, out of which 20,000 would be shown to the public at large for the very first time.

"Lydia, I am a bit jealous. I would have liked to be there with you on this part of the journey," Neo said with a sad voice.

"The flight attendant was gorgeous. Are you sure you don't want to visit her? If you change your mind, please leave the XGlass active."

"You naughty boy. You would like to watch, wouldn't you? I am afraid there won't be time to fool around," Lydia said playfully.

"Your driver will be Mostafa," Neo said. "He doesn't speak any English, but he seems exceptionally reliable. You can use the XGlass live Arabic translator.

"I have more good news," Neo said with excitement.

Apparently, Helene's clue was in ancient Greek, with the approximate translation:

"The pagan holy circle will show you the way, and under the perfection of the right hand of Kosmos when lost in darkness, the cruciform will show you the light."

"What could it mean, Neo? Could this be located in Greece?

"Maybe your research skills will prove extremely useful again," Lydia said with hope in her voice.

"You might be right, Lydia. I can't think of anything at the moment. But I am sure I'll find a plausible answer."

After passing a relaxed security check, nobody asked her what the mini-pyramidion was doing in her pocket.

The moment Lydia exited the airport, she was hit by a wave of warmth, a welcome feeling after the horrendous gray Brussels' weather.

Lydia always loved to be caressed by the sun's rays. She was impressed by the outside area of the airport adorned with modern glass and brownish colored stone slabs that imitated the color of sand dunes.

The entrance and exit were guarded by several well-armed soldiers in case any intruders attempted an attack.

There was no time to lose, and she knew that this would be a race against the clock.

§CHAPTER 38§

MOSTAFA WAS ALREADY parked in front of the main entrance, waiting with a tablet: *Madame del Biondo.*

Lydia went straight to him, and the short, round driver quickly opened the passenger door, with surprising agility for a man his size.

"Welcome to Egypt madame del Biondo. No luggage?" the driver asked, slightly puzzled.

"No luggage. I am traveling light."

"I am rather in a hurry. Is our destination far away?" Lydia asked, knowing that for her plan to succeed, she would have to quickly time all her movements.

"Not far, Madame, we have a thirty-minute drive to the Grand Egyptian Museum via the beautiful Alexandria Desert Road."

"We have the largest Archaeological museum in the world. I want to see it myself," the driver said in broken English.

For Lydia, it was clear that this was a line he learned for all his customers.

Neo started to whisper into her XGlass:

"A symbol of Egypt's new ruling class and to bring to life a new wave of tourism which would not have been possible with the security and infrastructure of the old Egyptian Museum in Tahrir Square."

"This legendary museum also had to be re-vamped and transformed from practically a storehouse to a new museum."

"There were so many artifacts still deposited in the old museum's archives that even GEM would not have been able to exhibit all of them. They were discovered over the last two hundred years by several generations of archaeologists."

"The GEM, a $1 billion state-of-the-art, glass, and concrete display space had at its heart the most precious Egyptian treasures taking its visitors on the same quest as the explorer Howard Carter made when discovering Tutankhamun, a century ago."

"It sounds exciting," Lydia said, and after some more minutes of driving, a magnificent view appeared: the shining structure of the GEM overlooking the Giza plateau's famous pyramid complex.

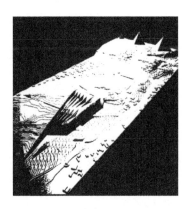

It was built on the slope between the Nile valley, where the main entrance was, and the Giza plateau.

Above Lydia's limo, the Assassin was following her closely by watching a live video feed on his XGlass from the drone, which he programmed to follow the license plate of the car Lydia was in.

The Egyptian weather was still scorching in October, and he could not stand the heat of the sun. "I hate the bloody desert. The faster I accomplish this mission the better," he muttered with displeasure.

"This time, there is no escape."

He drove a black BMW SUV and carefully monitored the trajectory of Lydia's car.

At the main entrance, Lydia was admiring the fountains and the palm trees among the white limestone, arranged in perfectly triangular green and white formations.

"I am afraid we have a problem that we can use to our advantage. The increase in cases of COVID-19 in Egypt will soon trigger the closure of all tourist sites," Neo announced worried.

"The GEM has advanced security systems in case of a terrorist attack. I think I can hack into their system and issue an alert to have it evacuated for you so you can access the Benben stone."

From the highway, they passed a modern building labeled: CONSERVATION CENTER. After a couple of minutes of driving, she caught her first glimpse of the museum's immaculate entrance.

Its gigantic translucent façade was designed to subtly mirror the nearby pyramids.

The driver stopped, and Lydia exited quickly, muttering: "*shukran.*"

On a plasma screen, she could see the various zones of the impressive complex. There was also a palm-fringed "Nile Park," honoring the personification of the life-giving river using serene fountains with solar panels powering the innovative architecture.

§CHAPTER 39§
14:00, GRAND EGYPTIAN MUSEUM

THE MASSIVE MUSEUM spanned more than 500,000 square meters; its surrounding totally revamped to accommodate everything from hotels to fancy restaurants.

In front of it, there were scores of tourists waiting and wearing various protection masks. Their allotted tour guides were nervously standing by.

"Lydia, underneath the museum there is a complex web of networks that will take you to a secret lab which restores the most precious artifacts. One of the tunnels will take us directly to the Benben stone."

"We are lucky the museum has yet to open today due to the government-mandated safety precaution to sanitize everything inside."

"I created a false alert about several tourists having Coronavirus and being hospitalized. It didn't take long for the authorities to panic."

"Worldwide, the global panic is taking apocalyptic proportions with more than 120,000 cases of COVID-19 and at least 4,400 deaths."

"Iran is now reporting 9.000 cases and 354 deaths. Spain has 2020 cases and 45 deaths. Even more cases have ravaged in Italy. The authorities there have decreed a countrywide quarantine," Neo said worriedly.

"I also have some good news; the algorithm found a potential match for our destination in Greece."

"The *pagan circle* could be an ancient circular building called the Galerius' Rotunda, and it's located in Thessaloniki."

"I don't remember if I visited this city with my parents, but I vividly recall that my mom was fascinated with Greece and the history of Thessaloniki."

"It cannot be a coincidence; everything is connected, my dear Neo," Lydia said in a positive tone.

"Do you have any more good news?"

"As a matter of fact, yes."

"I found our way in."

"You'll need to take an emergency evacuation exit located on the right side of the main entrance."

"From there, you'll find a staircase to the -2 underground floor that has a direct connection to the main galleries."

§CHAPTER 40§

LYDIA HEADED towards the entrance that Neo had directed her to. It was embedded directly into the museum's wall, hidden entirely in plain sight. Suddenly a door swung open after being activated by Neo.

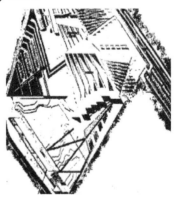

The Assassin was just behind her after parking his car into the crowded visitors' parking spaces.

I'll have to follow her and see why she is going to the museum.

Just then, he received a notification on his XGlass that startled him. *An incoming call from the Phoenix.*

He answered: "Master, I am in pursuit of del Biondo."

"Good, I will watch from very close. We must not fail again," the Phoenix whispered, his voice cold and distant.

With that, he took off running with almost inhuman speed in pursuit of Lydia, who vanished behind the door.

It took him a few seconds to crack the security code and followed Lydia's steps.

After several turns, guided by Neo, Lydia emerged behind a tall escalator, which generated a noise similar to water falling from a cascade.

At the bottom of the staircase, there was an enormous asymmetric room made of a mix of glass and stone, designed to imitate the colors of a sand dune.

It also had several water ponds to cool the heat of the desert sun. The rooftop in different pyramid shapes helped with better air circulation.

In front of her, she had one of the most magnificent views she had ever seen: the museum's grand staircase, adorned with twenty-two massive artifacts in chronological order.

She instantly spotted the statue of the god Ptah weighing a staggering six tons. There was also a pink granite statue of *King Ramses II* in addition to *King Thutmose III*'s black statue along with a quartzite box protecting its canopic jars.

The Benben stone was installed on a pedestal, just in front of her. She had to climb more stairs to reach it.

As she approached it, she noticed somebody was following her.

Maybe it was one of the cleaning workers. Looking above, she noticed two parallel glass passages that acted as connecting bridges so tourists could walk through the various museum zones.

But strangely, she could not see anyone, despite having the sensation of being watched.

§CHAPTER 41§

LYDIA WAS climbing the grand staircase adorned with the sculptures of Egyptian Pharaohs dating back almost five thousand years.

These were symbols of supreme divine power frozen in stone, each of them accompanied by one of their representative tokens.

The grand staircase led from valley level to the plateau, a historical path guarded by eighty-seven statues of kings and gods.

She was looking specifically for *Amenemhat III*, a Pharaoh from the 12_{th} dynasty, who was blessed with a forty-six-year reign beginning in 1860 BC.

He ruled eight dynasties after Khufu, the alleged builder of the Great Pyramid.

After passing the first builders of Egypt, she finally came face to face with the figure of the Pharaoh, towering over the Benben stone.

"I found him Neo. What a strange face he had…"

Lydia tried to compare it with the other faces of the Pharaohs she encountered.

"I can read sadness and so many worries on the Pharaoh's face, frozen for eternity in the cold stone."

"Lydia, his reign is considered to be the golden age of the Middle Kingdom."

"He was also famous for the maze he built in *God Sobek's* honor, which was depicted with the head of a crocodile."

"Even the ancient Greek historians *Strabo* and *Herodotus* talked about a gigantic temple maze designed with intricated tunnels and three thousand rooms."

"In this maze, the Egyptian priests were feeding a crocodile, which was believed to be *God Sobek*'s incarnation on earth."

"The maze was built in front of his Black Pyramid, which had our Benben as a capstone, one of the five enduring pyramids of the initial eleven complex pyramids situated in Dahshur."

"The Black or the dark pyramid term originates from its deplorable state of decay because after more than seven hundred years, the techniques of building pyramids like the ones on the Giza plateau were clearly lost."

"It was thought that the maze represented a funerary temple for the Pharaoh."

"Interesting Neo, I see a connection with the labyrinth of Berlaymont, and with the one at Knossos, too. I wonder if we'll also end up there. We have to go to Greece afterward, anyway," Lydia said boldly.

"Two labyrinths serving the same mystic purpose…"

"The Benben capstone symbolized the primordial mountain that first emerged at the creation of the world."

"It sat next to the Pharaoh's sorrowful bust, and its hieroglyphs described him as being the messenger of *God RA* and the ruler of upper and lower Egypt into eternal life," Neo continued his quick lecture while Lydia inspected the Benben stone admiring each detail.

"The open eyes gazing outwards have an almost hypnotizing effect."

"One last message of the Pharaoh towards his people: *even if my eyes are closed by death on Earth, they are forever opened into eternity*," Lydia recited these lines as if she knew them from another life.

Behind Lydia, the Assassin emerged, and using the shadows of the various statues, he approached her silently.

He made every gesture with absolute precision. His training made him a perfect killing machine.

§CHAPTER 42§

I NEED TO UNDERSTAND what she is seeking before ending her once and for all, the Assassin said to himself, grinning while his eyes glittered with malevolence and anger.

The beautiful carved Benben stone, which once gloriously sat on top of *Amenemhat III*'s pyramid, was cracked on one side. However, the black basaltic rock still emanated a strange energy.

Lydia remembered the words inscribed on the

floating mini-pyramidion underneath the Berlaymont:

> *"The flower of life under the protection
> of Bennu will guide your path."*

"Neo, do you see a flower of life on the Benben stone?" Lydia asked in a worried tone.

"When I went around it, I could not spot anything."

"I cannot see the pattern either, but there is a central circle that symbolizes the sun disk, *RA*, which in the pictures resembled the flower of life. Maybe it was just an optic illusion."

Lydia took out the metallic mini-pyramidion from her pocket and directed it towards the Benben stone.

There was an instant reaction, and the mini-pyramidion started to vibrate in her hand. The closer she got, the stronger the vibration grew.

Touching the circle with mini-pyramidion's base made the vibration stop, and a golden stylization of the flower of life pattern started to appear on its surface.

A kind of mechanism seemed to have been activated and pushed up the newly formed pattern, ejecting a cylindrical piece from the stone mass.

"Such an incredible mechanism. This must be Atlantean technology again," Neo said with excitement.

"It's astonishing how they managed to harness magnetic energy and were able to design such an intricate mechanism."

The cylindrical basalt piece, in which the flower of life was still pulsating, made a faint click and started to rotate on its left side, revealing a dark hole from which another mini-pyramidion began to rise.

To her surprise, the mini-pyramidion she was holding clasped onto the other forming a perfect match which now pulsated in her hand.

It resembled a strange shard and was illuminated by a golden light. It almost seemed alive. A heart of antiquity brought to life again after millennia of slumber.

"The question is, Neo, why someone would go to all this trouble to hide the different pieces in such a way. Do you think this could have been Jesus' doing?"

"He was trying to protect his legacy until humanity was ready to cope with the new reality he tried to unveil to the masses."

§CHAPTER 43§

LYDIA'S HAND shook with the vibration of the double mini-pyramidion. She then saw the Assassin's shadow out of the corner of her eye.

Her senses seemed to have been heightened for a few seconds. She could hear every little noise around her perfectly.

She understood immediately that in a matter of moments, he would kill her.

And in that instant, she came up with an idea. She pushed a Pharaoh statue that sat on the edge of the stairs, dislodging it easily, and it began to roll down.

The Assassin skillfully dodged it, avoiding being crushed by the massive object.

This gave Lydia enough time to leap towards the end of the staircase. She ran, pushing down priceless artifacts to slow down the menacing killer.

She caught a glimpse of the metallic plate describing her next victim, *Thutmose III,* the sixth Pharaoh of the 18$_{th}$ Dynasty.

She felt overwhelming guilt doing this, but she had to stay alive.

"Lydia, be careful; this could be Helene's killer," Neo said, fearing for her life.

The Assassin, despite his incredible agility, had not anticipated the domino effect of the rolling statues.

Lydia's actions triggered havoc, and the security sensors triggered a deafening alarm system.

He could already hear security forces running towards them, and he could not be caught.

Now everything, including his fate, lay in the hands of his Master.

§CHAPTER 44§

THE ASSASSIN scrambled and started to scale the walls of the great staircase. He resembled a real-life Spiderman and would do anything to avoid being caught.

He had the necessary information, *she will have to exit the museum somehow. If she is not caught by the guards then I will make my next move.* With this thought, he vanished into one of the aeration tubes.

Lydia now found herself on top of the staircase, "Neo, which direction should I go in? I need to exit as soon as possible. I can hear the security guards."

"I tapped into the security system. They are coming from downstairs. You can only go up now."

"I am in the process of wiping clean all the video footage. Your face is everywhere. Otherwise, you'll end up in an Egyptian prison, and believe me, that's not a very pleasant experience."

"You need to head to the main galleries which are located left of the staircase and are organized into different zones based on Beliefs and Eternity, Kingship and Power, and the last one Commoners and Society."

"There is also a zone that goes in chronological order from pre-dynastic (until 3100 BC) and Old Kingdom (the pyramid dwellers), to Middle Kingdom, then New Kingdom (the famous Tutankhamun), and finally, the Greco-Roman."

"You need to head towards the King Tut exhibit," Neo rapidly said.

Lydia didn't waste any time. She sprinted to the tall glass windows, which offered a panoramic view on the Giza pyramids' complex, the last token of the magnificent accomplishments of the Egyptian civilization.

And for a fraction of second, this fantastic view left her breathless. It was a worthy finale at the end of the epic staircase.

"Next to the Tutankhamun funerary mask, I'll guide you on how to find the path to a passage underneath the museum."

"It will take you to a network of tunnels, and from the plans, I see a gigantic space that is used as a laboratory."

"I think that this place was strategically selected. It must sit in an ancient location similar to the one you discovered in Berlaymont."

"The Order must also be very active here, but I think they remain unaware of the clues you received."

"There could be several antagonistic factions inside The Order, and for the moment, we just need to trust Helene de Moncler' s instinct," Neo instructed sadness in his voice.

Turning left, she entered the dark halls of the galleries filled with precious artifacts.

"Neo, is he following me, or was he caught by security?" Lydia asked with panic in her voice.

"I cannot see him anymore, but security is climbing the staircase quickly. In two minutes, they will have caught up with you."

Lydia stopped for a second from her sprint and spotted a strange whitish silhouette moving behind her from the right-side corridor.

When she turned to look, she almost gasped in shock. A white hooded figure was just a few meters away from her moving fast, and not running but floating.

Its hands extended like the tentacles of an evil sea monster who wanted to grasp its prey and shatter it into pieces.

Lydia managed to escape its clutch and leaped further towards the end of the corridor.

The hooded figure silently continued its pursuit.

Its white silk hooded robe not only protected her chaser's face from the myriad of video cameras embedded in the towering structure but also transformed his silhouette into a shadow using the latest military-grade scrambling material.

For the first time, the Phoenix was afraid that everything he accomplished would be lost.

"Lydia, quickly; at the end of the corridor, there is a locked security exit."

"I'll open the door to you."

Lydia ran as fast as she could with the pursuer rapidly approaching.

And there it was ...the mortuary mask of the boy King, with his tranquil face, the personification of the god Osiris, and the mesmerizing blue semiprecious stones that started to play tricks on Lydia's eyes with strange reflections.

Lydia could see in the protective glass cage the Phoenix's reflection, which was getting dangerously close. In an instant, her eyes connected with those of the boy King.

Such craftsmanship to be able to capture the soul of a person in the expression of its eyes made of lapis lazuli stones.

The eyes seemed for one moment to be talking to her: *run, run, save yourself, I will help you.*

"Neo what should I do next, he almost got me," Lydia frantically whispered, but there was no answer.

She began to scream uncontrollably, her body aching of anger:

"What do you want from me? Why are you attacking me?" her eyes were blinded with tears and fury.

No answer came from the hooded figure, who continued to rapidly approach her without uttering a word.

Behind the golden mask, a white light appeared from one wall that now had a wide-open door,

This must be it; I have to make a last-ditch effort.

And while Lydia sprinted desperately, Neo managed to reconnect, "that's it, Lydia," Neo said. "You are almost there."

The Phoenix's hands had almost grabbed her by the hair.

It was too late. Lydia quickly gave a nudge to the door and closed it in front of him without being able to have a good look at his hooded face.

"He cannot come after you, Lydia. I blocked

this door for good. You'll have to go down to the lower level preservation laboratory, and from there, I'll indicate to you which is the exit door."

"In fact, it's another emergency door that is masked from the outside. It will take you directly to the main entrance."

"It will be already packed with tourists, so this will hopefully give you the necessary decoy, to help you avoid those who are following you."

"From there, you'll have to take the new two-kilometer special walkway from the museum to the Great Pyramid of Giza."

"What a freakish hooded figure. I think they were both working together…"

"Tuck the shard into your inner jacket pocket. And prepare for a quick run," Neo said.

§CHAPTER 45§

THE PHOENIX'S BLUE eyes were becoming reddish and inflamed.

She was so close; how could I have failed?

Even my Assassin, who never failed me before, became overwhelmed by this woman.

His mind was on fire, and the security was almost there.

I cannot be compromised. I have to disappear, and he then vanished into the darkness behind one of the security doors using a silvery badge, which made the door swing open. While he exited, he swore to himself:

I will destroy you with my own hands, puny creature. I am not going to waste any more energy on this.

"Destiny has spoken," the Phoenix screamed in anger.

He gently touched his cloak, activating the communicator: "Prepare my drive. I am exiting the building now."

Another vibration notified him of an incoming call: "Master, I failed you once more."

"Should I terminate my life now?" the Assassin asked with an apotheotic lamenting voice.

"Do you think you can forfeit your destiny so easily?" the Phoenix whispered. His voice was without emotion.

"You'll have to suffer for your failures, but for now, there is a chance to redeem yourself. I met her myself. This is not a normal woman. She must have strong outside support, but I also sensed her aura, and I am afraid fate favors her."

"I failed myself because she unexpectedly eluded me. She was always one step in front of us."

"Only contact me when she is dead. Recover the artifacts she has stolen from the museum and the Berlaymont vault. I want them back!"

"If you fail me again, terminate your life, because if I do it, I will not be so merciful," the Phoenix roared with an almost inhuman tone.

The Assassin clenched his fists in anger.

You will wish to have died inside this museum...

§CHAPTER 46§

LYDIA'S HEART was pounding, and the thought she had been so close to death flooded her system with adrenaline.

She exited the museum at the right time, blending with the last wave of tourists who were making their way to the main entrance and mesmerized by the gigantic sculpture in the front park.

Rays of light danced their way through the translucent wavy roof and had an almost a hypnotic effect.

They also reflected on the colossal statue of *Ramses II*, which greeted the scores of tourists with its frozen face several millennia-old, a worthy guardian for the entry to the main atrium.

People wearing protective masks were gazing at it, and Lydia could hear one of the tourist audio guides explaining the history of the gigantic statue.

"The almost twelve-meter tall red-granite statue was unearthed at the beginning of the 19$_{th}$ century in Memphis. Afterward, it was restored in Cairo and then displayed in the central Bab el-Hadid Square, towering over it for fifty-two years.

Finally, it was moved to Giza for safekeeping in 2006 before its final resting place under the GEM's steel and glass roof shade."

§CHAPTER 47§

"LYDIA, WE HAVE an issue. We need to enter the Great Pyramid, but now it is rush hour. I'll have to create a diversion.

I'll tell them there is a bomb in the pyramid, and they need to evacuate the tourists; hopefully, you'll take advantage of the COVID-19 virus panic and manage to enter the King's chamber undisturbed," Neo announced calmly.

"Hm… you are full of great ideas; lately, I wonder what you plan next," Lydia said, amused by the thrill of a new and dangerous adventure.

Lydia approached the Giza plateau, and while running at high speed, the XGlass gently whispered, stopping the musing she was listening to: "You have run 1.3 kilometers, your pulse is one hundred twenty beats per minute."

Now she could spot the Giza plateau; the Great Pyramid was surrounded by a complex of much smaller pyramids, known as the Queens' Pyramids.

Three of them choose to remain defiant, witnessing the rise and fall of different empires. However, the fourth was so devastated that it remained hidden under sand dunes until the recent discovery of pieces from its capstone and base stones.

Their only remaining protector, the Sphinx with its face mutilated by weather and the withering passage of time, was also starting to appear in her field of vision as she approached her target.

The connecting esplanade was not so populated with a few people slowly walking through.

She was pleasantly surprised by the desert's sweet, dry air; the sun scorching the Giza plateau as it did for the last millennia.

The Great Pyramid's Temple was barely visible except for black basalt paving, a gateway of darkness towards the sandy ocean of silence.

Hundreds of tourists were waiting in line to see and explore one of the seven wonders of the ancient world, with dozens of busses that were already starting to clutter her view.

Lydia had several thoughts crossing through her mind.

The Great Pyramid of Giza was the oldest and

largest of the four pyramids in the Giza complex. It was not only the last of antiquity's Seven Wonders still standing but also the oldest.

It endured the passage of time, with its structure almost intact as in the first glorious years when its pyramidion, the Benben stone was shining and reflecting from the top of the divine light of the god *RA* from the Pharaoh's last resting place.

The historians thought its Benben stone must have been made of gold-plated rose granite or diorite.

Neo, who stayed silent until now, said, "the pyramids still impress me after all the virtual trips I've made here. I never believed I'd actually explore it with you, though."

"I am still baffled how the casing-stones and inner chamber blocks of the Great Pyramid were combined with such accuracy—approximately 0.05 centimeters of joint space."

"Imagine what we could have achieved if this technology was used on a global scale, millennia ago. Buildings would have been made resistant to earthquakes and storms."

Lydia looked again at the Great Pyramid, "Hm, I thought it would have been taller," she said.

"It's an optical illusion. It is so massive you have to really be at the right angle to admire its greatness. It's just shy of 138-meters-tall, due to the erosion and the missing capstone."

"For millennia, this pyramid was the tallest man-made structure in the world. Finally, in the 14_{th} century, the 160-meter-tall British Cathedral was completed in Lincolnshire," Neo said with nostalgia.

§CHAPTER 48§
16:30, GREAT PYRAMID, GIZA COMPLEX

LYDIA WAS APPROACHING the end of the esplanade, where several guards equipped with protective masks and remote temperature detectors were testing the incoming tourists for symptoms of the COVID-19 virus.

So, this is it; I have to go into the darkest places of the pyramid.

Yet again, I need to conquer my fear and find another clue with assistance from this magnetic double mini-pyramidion, which now resembled a metallic alien shard.

She reached into her pocket and felt that the shard was actually vibrating slightly and was warm to the touch.

"Neo, the double pyramidion is vibrating in my pocket."

"Are you familiar with the multitude of theories of using harmonic waves that trigger vibrations to activate mechanisms inside ancient constructions?"

"Actually, the correct geometrical name is an Octahedron. In nature, it is known that extremely rare diamonds can take this geometrical shape," Neo said.

"Thanks, Neo. Spoken like a true nerd. This must be definitely Atlantean tech that laid dormant under Berlaymont for so long," Lydia said almost bursting in excitement.

"Lydia, you need to head to the Great Pyramid's main entrance, which is in front of you," Neo said with worry in his voice.

"But look at all the tourists and guards. How

am I going to enter the King's chamber?"

From a nearby souvenir shop and disguised in traditional Egyptian clothing, the Assassin was trying to approach Lydia.

He managed to carefully follow her to the Pyramids again using his drone to detect her location.

"You'll not manage to escape my Master anymore. I'll make sure of it. Even if it means my death in this pagan pyramid away from my Master's enlightenment," the Assassin muttered under his breath, trying not to lose sight of Lydia.

"It's incredible Lydia. Did you know that out of millions of discovered artifacts, only two were related to the Pharaoh and the people who built the Great Pyramid?"

"A representation of himself as a small ivory figurine discovered by accident and the remainder of a sledge that could have been used by workers to carry the massive stones because they didn't have any wheels back then," Neo informed her.

"The Pharaoh was *Khufu*, who had many names (*Chuefui-Chnum* or *Khnum-Khuf*, *Cheops* in Greek) representing the old kingdom's symbol of the 4$_{th}$ dynasty."

"This titanic work could have lasted more than twenty-three years, expanding beyond the duration of his reign, which started in 2551 BC until he died in 2528 BC."

"Ancient historians mention that the architect, who is believed to have been *Khufu's* vizier, *Hemiunu* needed ten years of preparation and twenty years for the actual building, laying down more than 2.5 million stones with 2.5 tons being the average weight for each block," Neo continued.

Lydia skidded past the noisy tourists and the local trinket sellers. And now she was climbing a set of stone blocks with incredible agility.

"I personally believe that the pyramid could be much older; even more than five thousand years," Lydia said with great conviction.

"It could even predate the Great Flood being more than ten thousand years old."

"And this is why there are no hieroglyphs inside."

Lydia was seventeen meters above ground. After climbing the stones towards the right, she managed to pass by two tired and sweaty security guards in front of a metallic door entrance, which was placed to block any nighttime visitors.

"Lady, no photos and the telephone camera is forbidden," one of the guards barked in broken English.

In front of her, she heard a voice speaking English to some people, and she quickly approached them.

"Do not forget to keep some distance between yourselves."

"Do not take out your breathing masks until the tour has finished, and you are outside."

"Don't forget that you are in a closed environment and that the air circulation is more difficult inside the pyramid."

"There is a long one hundred five-meter descending passage dug through the stonework of the pyramid and then into the rock layers beneath it, which will take you to down to a partially finished lower chamber."

"There one can find an extension of the passage in the south wall, that has a pit dug into the floor of the spacious room, potentially to set a trap in the style of Indiana Jones."

"Robbers would have fallen into a trap full of spikes impaling any who dared to awaken the eternal sleep of the Pharaoh," a tall blond, handsome man said, closing the tour.

Apparently, he was the guide, and for a moment, he and Lydia exchanged a passionate look.

The guide, while fixating his gaze on Lydia, continued: "Theories say that the Pharaoh changed his mind and wanted to be buried not underground but in the middle of the pyramid above his beloved queen."

"Nobody knows what happened to their bodies. Have robbers stolen them and emptied the chambers and their treasure gone forever?" While pausing, smiled and winked at Lydia.

Lydia, while listening carefully to the story, noticed that the group was only made of young British students who came for a study abroad trip. She felt rather guilty for what was about to happen, destroying their journey while inside the Great Pyramid.

"Why is the entrance to the passage so rough?"

"It's like they were drunk when they dug this passage," a witty redheaded young girl said, likely a bit under the influence of alcohol from a long night of partying.

The guide chuckled and continued his tour:

"In present-day tourists enter the Great Pyramid via the *Robbers' Tunnel,* which was allegedly dug around 820 AC by the *Caliph al-Ma'mun's* workers using a battering ram."

"The tunnel is cut straight into the masonry of the pyramid for more than twenty-seven meters and then turns abruptly left to meet the obstructing stones leading to the *Ascending Passage.*"

"It is believed that vibrations caused by their attempt to drill through the pyramid, dislocated the slab fitted into the ceiling of the *Descending Passage* to hide the entrance to the *Ascending Passage.*"

"Actually, it was the noise of that stone slabs dropping and then gliding down the *Descending Passage*, which gave them a clue in which direction to dig."

"Following that, the Caliph's workmen tunneled up encountering less resistance through the softer limestone of the pyramid until they reached the *Ascending Passage.*"

Suddenly, a jarring noise made the students cover their ears. It was the sound of an alarm. The narrow space made it even worse as the stone wall was reflecting the noise and amplifying it like a megaphone.

"Exit the pyramid. Everybody needs to exit the pyramid, this is not a drill. Be careful at the steps. You need to come down towards the exit."

This message was continuously being repeated, clearly pre-recorded to be used in case of need.

§CHAPTER 49§

"LYDIA, NOW is the moment. You should use the general frenzy inside the pyramid to quickly make your way up."

"If someone asks where you are going, simply mention that you are looking for your missing child," Neo instructed.

Lydia moved swiftly ahead, trying to avoid the panicked tourists who were struggling to make their way to the exit.

After thirty meters from the entrance, Lydia noticed a square-shaped hole in the roof of the *Descending Passage*. Initially concealed with a slab of stone, this represented the start of the *Ascending Passage*.

The wind was howling, making its way through the labyrinth of various tunnels, each having a religious or functional role, either for the soul to ascend into the gods' realm or as an intricate aeration system.

"Lydia, you need to hurry up. I am sure the guards will understand this was a false alarm," Neo said worriedly.

"Yes, I am almost at the beginning of the *Ascending Passage*."

She remembered all the questions she asked her university ancient civilizations professor, who, by chance, was also of Egyptian origin, *Mister Sharaff*.

Back then, she knew the Great Pyramid structure, like the back of her hand. A small plastic panel with almost washed away painting indicated: *The Ascending Passage*.

Lydia quickly found herself squeezed into the narrow passage through the staircase, which had small protrusions to avoid slipping, which allowed her to climb.

She was not claustrophobic, but the simple thought that something might go wrong with the illuminating system plunging her in the dark made her skin crawl.

"I am almost there at the beginning of a large open space; the Grand Gallery," Lydia said.

At this moment, Lydia sensed she was being followed.

Maybe it was an illusion, or the assassin has followed me here, and he wants to catch me.

She felt a strange energy coursing through her body while continuing her upward climb at the same slope as the *Ascending Passage*.

The walls rose in seven courses of polished limestone, each arched several centimeters toward the center, giving a strange symmetry to the upper part engulfed into darkness.

A squeaking noise made her look upwards, and she seemed to spot a moving shadow, *could it be a big hungry bat?*

Her gaze then fell upon the two left and right narrow ramps with slots, probably a part of an ancient mechanism used by the constructors to lift the stones.

"Lydia, you need to gather your strength; there is still a lot of climbing left," Neo said, worried by her accelerated pulse.

"I was always fascinated by the geometric precision of the *Grand Gallery*. I would have never believed that one day I'd explore its secrets."

Compared to the *Ascending Passage*, it was nine meters tall and forty-seven meters long. An inverted pyramid structure within another pyramid with seven steps.

Lydia noticed it had a roof made of stone slabs fixed at a specific floor angle for each stone to fit into a slot cut inside the gallery's top, like the teeth of a cog.

"Neo, do you see this? Egyptians were incredibly inventive. I guess this design was made to have each block supported by the wall of the gallery, instead of being held by the block beneath it," Lydia said, mesmerized.

"All this intricate design, to prevent pressure from making everything collapse while reinforcing the space's integrity in case of a tectonic movement," Neo confirmed, trying to pay attention to each detail.

Lydia continued her climb, still with the feeling she was being watched.

She finally reached the top of the *Grand Gallery*, where a giant step led to a horizontal passage some meters long and very narrow.

She thought that this was specially placed by the ancient Egyptians to scare and discourage the modern visitors from jumping it.

At this time, there were no tourists left; only some distant voices sounded alarmed and were shouting in Arabic.

The great step was, in fact, a one-piece granite slab that looked rather damaged and chiseled in several areas. The marks seemed to have been left by a giant creature with enormous claws trying to make its way inside the tiny tunnel.

Looking above, while crawling inside the narrow tunnel, Lydia noticed four slots which, in the past, apparently held the granite blocking doors, cleverly protecting it from any intruders.

She remembered the guide mentioning they were found in the *Descending Passage*.

Lydia could only imagine the surprise of the first robbers squashed under the weight of the collapsing stones.

She had to catch her breath as all the rapid climbing consumed most of her energy.

Exhausted, she finally arrived at the end of the corridor, which started to rise and widen in an anteroom, with walls no longer made of limestone but granite.

Passing what was once the closing mechanism before entering the room, she realized it was made of rose granite; a clear sign that this chamber was for a special person.

She had to duck one more time and pass under the *Granite Leaf.*

"That's it, Lydia, just go under the suspended stone slab of two blocks, which are on top of each other."

"No worries, they are fitted into the grooves inside the wall."

"Lydia, you entered the so-called King's chamber made of tough red granite."

"It's fascinating how this material reflects the light. It seems as if it's pulsating with life."

"This type of granite must have been exceedingly difficult to extract as it is only found in horizontal beds, which lie between thin sheets of sinter or quartz."

"The bedrock from which this tough granite stone was extracted, must have been split all the way down to the next sheet."

"How were they extracted? It's still a mystery because they weighed between forty and fifty tons," Neo explained clearly, fascinated by the topic.

§CHAPTER 50§

THE KING'S CHAMBER has fascinated so many historians and archaeologists. Above its floor, there were two narrow shafts in the south and north whose purpose was still unknown.

The only plausible explanation was that they were oriented towards sacred constellations of stars or areas of the northern and southern skies.

They were long considered by Egyptologists to be air shafts for aeration.

However, the most recently discovered tombs and collected data showed that the shafts fulfilled a more sacred objective linked with the ascent of the Pharaoh King's essence to the afterlife.

"Neo, do we know what we are looking for?"

"In the Berlaymont cave, the ruby was pulsating where the chamber is located, but it didn't give any specific instructions," Lydia asked, feeling a little unnerved.

She quickly started to look at the King's chamber walls, which were made entirely of red granite.

Professor Sharaff once told her that it was probably extracted from the quarries of Aswan, one thousand kilometers away from Giza.

Looking above, she noticed a neatly polished roof made of nine slabs of stone, which he also mentioned weighed an impressive four hundred tons.

"Lydia, did you know there are precisely one hundred blocks making up the walls of the King's chamber."

"Why would they be so precise?" Neo asked, puzzled.

"I remember that in one of his clairvoyance sessions, the American healer *Edgar Cayce* stated that the Great Pyramid took one hundred years to be finalized, also alleging that under the Sphinx there exists a similar Hall of Records that Atlantis had...but nobody believed him."

"Over the decades, many tried to dig and check the space underneath the Sphinx but without any conclusionary evidence."

"It could be that this fabled Hall was buried so deep, much like the labyrinth under Berlaymont, so nobody could find it at such a depth," Lydia hastily explained."

"I never understood why this room was empty as well as the five compartments above it; the so-called Relieving Chambers."

"There are no hieroglyphs nor other inscriptions or marks to accompany the Pharaoh. This is so unusual."

"Several theories state that, in fact, the Great Pyramid was a giant battery with the air shafts used to pump different chemicals producing some kind of a complex reaction."

"Scientists also thought that the builders' purpose was to harness that energy," Lydia said to a distracted Neo who was trying to find a way out of this conundrum.

The only object in the King's chamber was a rectangular sarcophagus with one damaged corner made of a different type of granite that had a higher density than the one used for the walls of the chamber.

Lydia remembered from Professor Shariff's classes that the sarcophagus was larger compared to the *Ascending Passage*, clearly indicating to researchers that it should have been laid down at the beginning of the construction before the walls and roof were built around it.

This was even more proof of the advanced planning skills and technology of the Egyptian civilization five thousand years ago. Unfortunately, most of it was mysteriously lost or simply taken away.

Many famous people said they had an epiphanal experience while lying inside the sarcophagus, including Napoleon, who, even on his deathbed, did not want to divulge what happened to him in the King's chamber.

Unlike the walls' masterful stonework inside the chamber, the sarcophagus was roughly cut, with saw-marks visible all over.

"It could be that this was just a snare sarcophagus intended for the robbers with the real one well hidden in a secret place," Lydia said while touching the surface of the sarcophagus.

"Yes, they tried unsuccessfully to explore below the so-called Queen's chamber, and then the so-called Big Void theory came about," Neo informed with excitement in his voice.

"I remember, scientists tried to apply cosmic radiation, a technique which the Japanese first used to assess the insides of volcanoes by bombarding them with particles called muons in order to perform muon radiography."

"Using this technique, different teams scanned the interior of the pyramid, and they detected a void on the right side, above where we are."

"Indeed, the void is at least thirty meters.

There must be a clue hidden somewhere. I just hope you won't find the same black substance."

"Black substance? What are you referring to?" Lydia asked puzzled.

"You know there are five chambers above the roof of this one."

"When entering the second chamber, explorers were turned back by a powder which was discovered only in that chamber."

"Later, it was analyzed and determined to be the dust from the cast-off skins and chitin shells of insects," Neo said with disgust.

"Horrible Neo. Why did you have to share this with me now I am so much more confident?"

Approaching the right side of the sarcophagus, she felt a tremor in her pocket; the magnetic pyramidion shard started to vibrate.

She took it out, and when directing it towards the right side of the wall, which held the narrow entrance to the chamber, the vibration started to increase.

"Neo, I think this is a key and a compass at the same time. It points towards something. I have to guide myself by the level of vibrations," Lydia said excited. She grimaced at the thought of additional traps she might have to face.

Looking carefully at the layout of the granite blocks, Lydia noticed it formed a doorway that supported their weight, creating granite ceiling beams.

On the left side of the wall, the blocks were so cleverly aligned that they didn't place any weight on the central block at the bottom.

"Neo, look at this; it must be the secret entrance."

"This block could move backward unobstructed, precisely like the one that sealed the first entrance."

The more Lydia leaned towards it, the more the vibration increased.

Once she touched the bottom stone with the vibrating shard, a wave of energy crossed her entire body, like a pleasant tingling.

At the same time, it was like someone was zapping her of her energy.

A vampire stone, that's a first, it must be a chan-

neling device of biomolecular energy, Lydia muttered to herself not wanting to worry Neo.

"It's moving Neo, that's it," Lydia said with excitement.

The stone was vibrating and moving backward, with a passage opening in front of her.

"Neo, this is unbelievable. The stone is acting as a catalyst, moving or splitting the blocks behind it into two, creating an upward passage," Lydia said.

"This could only be Atlantean technology. I cannot believe it created an upward path."

"The researchers were right. It must take you towards a big void. I am sure we'll discover another important artifact." From Neo's voice, one could feel deep worry because he knew the path ahead was treacherous.

§CHAPTER 51§

THE ASSASSIN was closely following Lydia, assessing his options.

This one proved to be so resourceful, I cannot kill her now.

She will take me to the object my Master also seeks, and I will be redeemed.

Above the Grand Gallery, he managed to use the ancient ceiling's darkness to creep in the shadows.

Who would this Neo be?

She is talking to him via her XGlass. He must be the one who helped her escape our grasp.

My Master never mentioned him, but that's irrelevant now. I have to focus on reaching my target.

While Lydia was opening the secret tunnel, he managed to crawl behind the empty sarcophagus waiting like a predator to jump on and devour its weak prey.

He was mesmerized by the opening of the passage and understood his Master was right.

He was witnessing a miracle: *I am sure that this will bring me so much closer to my quest for immortality.*

"Lydia, you must enter the passage now! You were followed. The proximity sensor activated and there is someone else in the room," Neo bellowed.

Without flinching, Lydia turned and glided along in an acrobatic move that would have made even the most skillful gymnast envious.

In the next second, she had to again face the Assassin, who plunged towards the gap, trying to grab her.

It was too late, she only managed to catch a glimpse of his eyes.

The moment she retracted her hand that held the double pyramidion shard, the stones above the entrance suddenly reshuffled themselves, collapsing in a soundless Tetris style movement.

The builders must have installed a safety mechanism, Lydia said to herself, relieved, but then she realized it was only the beginning of her torment.

§CHAPTER 52§
JUST BEFORE THE PROLOGUE

SHE ESCAPED again, how can this be?

I had her in my grasp, the Assassin thought to himself. His ego was bruised, having missed out on catching her again.

He pointlessly tried for several minutes to dislodge the collapsed stone wall, but nothing budged, not a millimeter.

I need to go back to the exit in case she finds a way out; my drone will spot her again.

I have failed the Phoenix again. For the moment, he doesn't need to know anything. Next time I meet her, I will not hesitate, she will die.

He tried to hit the reshuffled stones again, but they didn't move.

251

"Lydia, are you okay? That was so close," Neo said with worry with his voice.

"It was the same person again. He must be one of the Phoenix's henchmen."

"It's incredible he managed to trace you even here."

"I am sure he's the one who murdered de Moncler."

"The satellite connection is rather bad, I can barely hear you."

"I am glad you now have the latest generation of XGlass. I managed to make some adaptations so we can stay in touch even if you are in one of the most remote places on the planet."

"He remained behind the wall; I have to hurry and head up Neo."

"All the stones are vibrating strangely. It's like I am in a giant ticking time bomb."

She was afraid that this newly formed stone passage would reposition back and the tunnel would start closing, squashing her to death.

Oddly enough, the polished stone of the tunnel was at the same angle as the one from the *Ascending Passage*, and it was not slippery.

She realized that the surface she was stepping

on was carved with hieroglyphs.

"Neo, are you seeing the hieroglyphs on the floor? What do they say?

Neo instantly activated his translation algorithm voiced by Alexa:

"This is the final resting place of the seed of life, and only the worthy will be able to replant it and heal the suffering of the many. Behold the greatness of Atlantis."

After crawling for more than one hundred meters, Lydia saw a large opening in front of her. And her mind frantically wanted to leave the narrow, dark space.

Could this be the Hall of Records that Cayce placed under the Sphinx or a place hiding a similar artifact as the one I found in the cavern underneath Berlaymont?

"Lydia, be careful. You might encounter some traps ahead. Please step forward carefully and use the shard as a compass and trap detector. Maybe it will vibrate when it detects another mechanism."

The path was lit by the XGlass' front flashlight. *At least the air is breathable, thanks to the system of air shafts across the Great Pyramid*, Lydia thought, comforting herself.

Just one more step and everything will be re-vealed.

She could have never imagined that her quest in helping de Moncler would bring her to the unex-plored depths of the Great Pyramid, after reading so many books together with her parents in her early youth.

She stepped inside the room before her, and suddenly a massive stone slab closed behind, leaving her with an awful feeling that this was the end.

§CHAPTER 53§
19:37, PRESENT DAY
FOLLOW-UP TO
THE PROLOGUE

LYDIA CONTINUED her descent into darkness sliding uncontrollably on the smooth surface, *will I end up in a trap of spikes?*

At least I won't suffocate to death. The smell of honeysuckle was still around her, perhaps embedded now into her hair and skin, a reminder of how close she was to meeting her end.

"XGlass, diagnose the satellite connection," Lydia quickly ordered.

"No satellite connection detected. Please try again," informed Alexa's familiar voice.

What she didn't know was that Neo upgraded her new XGlass with an Iridium 9575 Extreme signal booster transforming it into the most weather resistant and reliable phone in the world. This upgrade offered pole-to-pole global voice, and the advanced weatherization technology gave it incredible resistance.

With this device, Neo could see her location and track her with ease.

The XGlass flashlight revealed an end to the sliding corridor, *so this is it, the end of my journey.*

§CHAPTER 54§

LYDIA TRIED to slow down her descent, but her hands and even nails were not particularly useful on the slippery walls.

Suddenly she landed smoothly on another floor. *At least solid ground,* she said to herself.

The floor seemed to be made of the same basaltic stone as the door; only in the middle, there was a large ankh symbol molded from metal that looked to be gold but with a strange glitter generated by its high purity.

It's the same ancient Egyptian hieroglyphic symbol that I saw under Berlaymont in Brussels. The symbol of life itself.

This ankh had a perfect cross shape, with an oval loop in place of an upper bar.

"Lydia, you survived," Neo said.

"Are you wounded? Where are you?"

"I am fine Neo. I thought I was falling to my

death and that I'd never hear your voice again."

Lifting her eyes from the floor, she noticed a shimmering violet light coming from the wall in front of her, which started to pulsate, lighting up the entire room.

"What is that on the wall? Is there a strange light coming from there?" Neo asked curiously.

Approaching the wall, Lydia noticed a vial-like structure under the form of a glass ankh incorporated into a metallic structure with a violet shape-changing fluid shimmering inside.

The ankh vial was floating in between two mini-pyramidion stones that were attached to the wall. Its lower end was engulfed in a strange metal, similar to diorite, an iron-like alloy originating from a meteor that likely crashed on Egyptian soil.

"Lydia, I hope it is not linked to another trap. The XGlass sensor didn't detect any specific anomalies, but this doesn't mean there are not any."

"What could the contents of the vial be?"

Lydia carefully checked the structure of the ankh vial and its surroundings for any warning hieroglyphs, but there was nothing.

"I wonder how many millennia this artifact has been waiting to be discovered after probably being placed here by Jesus Christ himself," Lydia exclaimed, elated by the incredible discovery.

Reaching towards it, she touched the metallic structure, which was slightly cold, and removed it from the magnetic field of the two pyramidions.

Nothing happened. There was the same eerie silence, but the air seemed fresher now as if someone suddenly added a bit of ozone.

She knew that feeling and could even sense its pungent smell; a memory from her childhood ozone generator that she kept in her bedroom.

"Neo, I am out of ideas as to how we are going to exit this chamber. Maybe you have something in mind?"

"I believe you are located above the *Grand Gallery*. I am sure there is a way to exit the pyramid and its secret vault."

"I think I had enough archaeological adventures for a lifetime," Neo said with a distorted voice.

"Lydia, the satellites are repositioning. Our connection might be interrupted again."

"Hang on a moment," Lydia exclaimed.

"There is an inscription on the backside of the metallic ankh. I think it is written again in Aramaic like one we found on the Berlaymont Pyramid when we retrieved the first mini-pyramidion stone."

"Can you translate the text? It is considerably longer, and I do not know where to start."

"Approach the artifact to your XGlass, I need to take a high-resolution picture," Neo gently instructed.

Lydia complied and noticed that the fluid was changing colors now from deep violet to a darker purple.

"The algorithm is processing the translation. Here it is."

The pleasant voice of Alexa was always soothing to Lydia because it resembled her mother's voice a bit:

> **"Here is the secret vault of old days. In Gethsemane, you'll find the tree of life, and as you plant this seed, if the secret word is chanted, eternal life shall be forever yours."**

"Neo, I think I lost the connection again. Neo?" Lydia shouted.

After some crackling noises, Neo's voice came through. "Yes, Lydia, the satellites repositioned. The signal now has maximum strength, and there is more to the translation:"

> **"If you remove the potion of the Gods, you have two sunset cycles before the Grail will be destroyed."**

"Amazing, these are such precise instructions."

"Time flowed differently back then. Ancient people were not as obsessed as we are with the measure of time."

"Everything is so relative when it comes to time."

"I just hope forty-eight hours will be enough to accomplish our mission," Lydia explained.

"The inscription mentioned the Aramaic words:

Which translates to *holy cup*, but the algorithm cross-referenced the internet and came up with the Grail term."

"Could it be that we are holding a version of the mythical object?"

"The inscription makes a clear link between the seed, the potion of gods, and the Grail."

"All elements converging into a unique location in the Gethsemane garden."

"However, there are so many trees in the garden. Could it be possible for one to survive for millennia?"

"We'll need to have a precise satellite mapping of the garden to see what remains."

"Great. More traveling. We first need to go to Greece and then Israel."

"My interpretation is that the contents of the vial will become unstable and be destroyed after two days. We need to move extremely fast."

"But first things first. How am I going to escape the pyramid?"

"There are no cracks in the walls. They seem all made from the same block."

"Isn't it great? I'm trapped inside a basalt box, but where is the exit? One thing is sure: I cannot go up via the ceiling."

"Lydia, the golden ankh on the floor, did you try to move it?"

"Sometimes, the Gods of Egypt were depicted by holding these objects in their hand as a device that could manipulate life itself, giving them the power to reanimate the dead's souls in the after-life."

This trilateral sign represented a string of three consonants, *n-h.* Incorporated in words like *mirror* and *life.*

"You remember, I mentioned there were some wild theories that the Pyramid was, in fact, a powerplant to produce piezoelectric energy from the granite found in the King's chamber."

"Archaeologists found that there was a water well shaft in front of the pyramid which was used to pump water inside it."

"The water could have been used as a cooling agent and reactive for the mixing of sulfuric acid with a salt mixture of ammonium chloride and zinc chloride via the shafts of the Queen's chamber."

"They even found traces of those elements there."

"What if the ankh is just a door or a piece of the

powerplant's mechanism?"

"I remember that the Coptic Christians created from the ankh the *crux ansata*; a figure with a circular loop rather than oval one, and used it as a variation of the holy cross."

"But look at the oval; there are two parallel loops," Lydia exclaimed excitedly.

"That's it. I know how it works." She started to hover the ankh vial around the two loops.

The floor slowly but soundlessly opened, replacing the ankh's second loop with a dark void.

Peering down, she could spot something glittering in the dark.

"There appears to be some kind of golden ledges fixed in the stone, a sort of staircase. Oh, Neo, if you'd only knew how much I hate darkness."

"From my triangulation, you must be just above the beginning of the Grand Gallery."

Lydia tucked the ankh artifact into her ergonomic backpack, thinking already of a plan as to how she was going to smuggle it out of the country.

"Don't forget that your follower must still be somewhere lurking in the shadows."

"You need to climb down carefully."

Lydia started her descent again.

§CHAPTER 55§

THE ASSASSIN pondered his next move in darkness.

I feel our path will cross again, and I'll not hesitate.

She will need to exit the Pyramid, but where?

I need to change my plan and intercept her inside the pyramid, not in the open, because she might elude me again.

"From all the points, all the exits are passing via the Grand Gallery."

"I'll have to wait here," he muttered nervously.

"Sir!"

"Sir, the pyramid was evacuated; you cannot stay here," one of the guards shouted.

"I am sorry, I got lost. Where is the exit?" the Assassin asked.

The guard didn't manage to answer. The Assassin already had his hands wrapped around his head, and with a swift movement, he broke the guard's neck.

His dead body started rolling down, and when it finally stopped, his big brown eyes fixating on the face of Lydia, who arrived at the end of the staircase and was peering down from above.

When touching the last stair, a trap door silently opened below her, and she wondered where this new path would lead.

The Assassin came down and started to drag the lifeless body, trying to find a way to discard it.

"What should I do now Neo? He will see me if I try to come down," she whispered, trying to control herself and stop trembling.

"Try to distract him by throwing something into the well shaft to make him think there is something there."

Lydia reached for her backpack and took out her apartment key from the front pocket. The key had a strange blade shape typical of the *Fichet* brand.

Next to her, there was a part of the wall that looked cracked. With the sharp edge of the key, she tried to silently detach a small piece.

It was not easy as she had to hold herself with one hand on the golden step and with her feet against the tunnel's wall.

If something fell onto the floor, she would have alerted her chaser, or even worse.

Luckily, the piece of stone easily detached, and after placing back the key, she looked down and calculated the trajectory of her throw.

The stone swirled in the air and rolled in the ascending passage at the end, hitting against the rusted metallic fence of the well shaft.

§CHAPTER 56§

THE ASSASSIN MOVED at lighting speed. He knew that this noise must have been triggered by his target.

He followed the sound much like a nocturnal creature would have done with its prey.

She saw him passing underneath her almost at inhuman speed, and she tried not to flinch being perfectly camouflaged by the darkness of the corridor above.

Arriving at the metallic gate of the well shaft, the Assassin found himself puzzled; *how did she manage to go down with the door closed*?

I should have heard the metallic noise, but again she proved to be so resourceful. Maybe she even has military training.

Another noise from down below in the shaft triggered his attention. It was the stone reaching the bottom.

I must go down; she is there, and almost effortlessly, he dislodged the metallic door.

One second later, he realized that while she was climbing down, maybe there was another way to stop her.

He went back and grabbed the body of the guardian. Holding him by the feet, he let the body tumble down the shaft, generating a muffled sound.

Then he quickened his pace and started to climb down into the darkness of the shaft.

Lydia knew that now was her golden opportunity to escape; she skidded down and jumped, her rubbery sports shoes perfectly muffling the noise of the impact.

The Assassin was too far away, and she remained unnoticed. Treading carefully, she climbed down into the *Ascending Passage*, and with her last bit of energy, she tried to exit as quickly as possible.

Finally, she arrived at the exit, which was still guarded by the police.

"Madame, are you okay?" asked a young Egyptian policeman.

"Yes, I am fine now. I was hit by a scared tourist who was trying to leave, and I lost consciousness."

"I am very sorry. You were not the only one. We had several victims."

"Do you need medical attention?"

"Strange we checked the entire Pyramid, there was nobody left inside," a higher-ranking elderly officer lashed out at her.

"I am profoundly sorry, Madame."

"Can we take you back to your hotel?" the other policeman intervened, asking his superior to let her go as she seemed innocent.

"Actually, I need to go to the Sphinx airport; otherwise, I will miss my flight. Would you mind taking me there?"

Lydia exited at the right moment to catch the first glitter of a spectacular starry sky, understanding why the Egyptians were so fascinated by astrology.

§CHAPTER 57§

AFTER DESCENDING into the well shaft, the Assassin started to worry that he was misled.

He noticed that the underground passage had the appearance of being unfinished.

Advancing, he reached the subterranean area of the Pyramid. He looked around and did not see anything. Despite his infrared glasses being activated, the space seemed empty and there was no movement.

He went closer to the hole in the ground, a pit completely engulfed in darkness. His XGlass only detected the pit's bottom—a granite stone with holes similar to the one he stumbled upon when descending into the well shaft.

But what was the noise? This stone collapsed here a long time ago. It could have not made the noise I just heard.

His last chance was a hole in the wall at the

end of the chamber, *maybe she is hiding there.*

I will make your death fast so I can be reunited with my Master, he thought, his lips curling into a grin.

After advancing into the tunnel for sixteen meters, he realized that it had ended abruptly, leading to a dead end.

He pictured in his mind a cornered, frightened Lydia waiting for her life to end.

He refused to accept the bitter reality that he failed his Master again.

His anger generated such suffering that he gave away a scream of pain, which echoed through the pyramid amplified by its acoustics and reverberated through each wall as it happened millennia ago with the first thieves who attempted to discover its secrets.

§CHAPTER 58§
20:14

NEO BOOKED her a private night charter flight to Thessaloniki to avoid extensive border control and to allow her to get some good sleep over the five-hour flight.

A friendly guard asked Lydia if she had anything to declare, and without blinking, she politely said, "no."

"I am traveling very light tonight," Lydia said while lifting her new small black crocodile skin Hermes Birkin purse.

"Shall I open my purse?"

The guard blushed and said, "you are good to go, ma'am."

What he didn't know was that the bag was just a fake, but still made of real Nile crocodile.

Neo purchased it online on the black market

from an exclusivist dealer who was selling similar purses.

The price also included the delivery, and just as she accessed the main entrance to the airport, someone put it directly on her shoulder and left.

"Shukran," she said calmly, artfully passing as a millionaire who could not hide any ancient artifacts in her tiny bag.

Lydia flashed it with the pride of carrying one of the most expensive bags in the entire world.

She headed towards the limo where a driver was waiting with the door opened, the revolving airport VIP lounge doors closing behind her.

After less than a two-minute drive through the nearly pitch-black airport, the limo stopped in front of the private jet.

Lydia quickly made her way to the neat Airbus Falcon Z300, the pinnacle of private jetting, and locked herself in the luxurious toilet.

She noticed that there were just seven other people on the plane. She could still hear the loud voices of the Greek family with two children. They owned the plane, but to compensate for the expense of flying private, they started to use the *share my plane* app.

The feeble 5G connection on her XGlass could translate their conversation. She could not help but grin. They were quarreling about whether they should continue to share their plane with other people.

"Honey, I cannot stand this. I cannot enjoy my privacy," the wife complained.

"Darling, no worries. What privacy? We have two children. It's not like we can still run naked like in the good old days. On top of that, we should be more worried about the risk of getting COVID-19," the exasperated husband said.

Lydia also heard someone giggling through the bone conduction headphones.

"Neo, did you listen to their discussion? It's surreal… the worries of rich people."

"Ignorance is such bliss," Lydia said sarcastically.

"No need to answer; let's get back to real matters."

She took out the vial from her purse and held it in front of her eyes. Its contents were now purple and moving and changing shades. It seemed so surreal.

Lydia could not think of any explanation as to how the cruciform metal ending was so perfectly fused with the transparent crystal-like vial.

She already tried to remove it without any success. Maybe this was for the best. Perhaps its contents would release another ancient virus, a plague to doom all of humanity.

"Neo, can you identify the composition of this liquid? If only I had my lab here to take a sample and analyze it."

"Unfortunately, its movement pattern does not match anything known. It's probably hermetically sealed; hence it should not fluctuate. Maybe the metallic part acts as a sort of catalyst, making it shift its shape," Neo said, disappointed that he could not offer more help.

"But this is a key to something. I am sure of that."

"I hope we'll find more answers in the *Thessaloniki Rotunda*."

Lydia buckled up, and after closing her eyes, she fell into a deep sleep.

Suddenly she was jolted back to the reality by the captain's announcement:

"We are approaching our destination Thessaloniki."

"The approximate local time for our landing will be 7:22 a.m. Outside the temperature is pleasant at 22^0C. We thank you for flying with the Georgiadou family. Your captain Yannis wishes you a pleasant stay."

Lydia still felt sleepy as the trip to Egypt completely exhausted her.

"Ma'am, we have arrived at our destination.

Are you all right?"

Lydia could hear the voice of the flight attendant, but her body did not want to wake up. She was trapped in an almost dream-like state.

Worried, the flight attendant gently touched her shoulder in an attempt to wake her up.

His touch worked. And Lydia opened her big beautiful dark exotic eyes.

"I am fine, thank you. Just very tired," Lydia whispered.

"Can I bring you a glass of water with a bit of lemon juice, or would you prefer a coffee?" the flight attendant politely asked, in an attempt to compensate for waking her up.

"Thank you, please make it a double espresso," Lydia said.

§CHAPTER 59§
VATICAN

"SALVATORE, will you accompany me? I need some fresh air. I cannot stand all the sad news coming from every corner of the world," the pope whispered.

On his office wall, there was a large plasma screen that presented breaking news:

"The number of pandemic deaths in the rest of the world has exceeded that of China. "

"The coronavirus from China had arrived in 161 other countries."

The Director-General of the World Health Organization was holding an emergency press conference.

"WHO has been assessing this outbreak around the clock, and we are deeply concerned both by the alarming levels of spread and its severity. We have, therefore, assessed that

COVID-19 can be characterized as a pandemic."

"We are being punished Salvatore for all our sins. We have forgotten the teachings of God, our Church, and failed to protect the most vulnerable people."

The worried voice of the Director-General continued: "Pandemic is not a word to use lightly or carelessly. It is a word that, if misused, can cause unreasonable fear, or unjustified acceptance that the fight is over, leading to unnecessary suffering and death."

The sun was at its zenith, and the last sunlight of the day engulfed the magnificent Vatican gardens, where the Pope enjoyed long strolls to replenish his depleted vitamin D levels. Few people knew he had a genetic condition, which made it very difficult to process it, and his doctor recommended to him long walks.

These were also the few moments when he could focus on his plans. His guards were always trying to protect him from the few curious groups of visitors, which were sometimes allowed to visit the gardens.

His head of security, Armand Schiller, a tall Swiss of German origin slightly resembling Arnold Schwarzenegger, was in charge of coordinating the teams protecting his Holiness.

The attack types ranged from cyber to a single intruder, most of whom were religious fanatics or mentally disturbed.

Over the years, he had to adapt to more unpredictable dangers and to use the technological evolution to his advantage.

At all times, the Pope was protected by a set of drones surveying the perimeter of the gardens.

This new generation of drones could spot any intruders and notify his head of security.

"Armand. Good, you are here, with the precision of a Swiss watch. Right on the dot." The Pope was so fascinated by his punctuality, a quality he respected in a person.

"Let's head to the fountains, Salvatore," the Pope said with an exhausted voice.

"Tell me about the latest technological discoveries and their impact on the faithful," the Pope curiously interrogated.

"Tell me, Holy Father, what is your pulse today?"

"It is 85 bpm," the Pope answered, reading it from his Apple watch.

Salvatore was happy that this Pope was ready to embrace technology, as the watch not only showed the time, but it allowed him to constantly check on the health status of the Pope and his precise location.

They could spend hours talking about everything from the ethics of artificial intelligence to eugenics.

"Did you know Salvatore that in 1590, the gardens were adorned with cascades and large fountains?"

"Thanks to the Borghese Pope Paul V, who ordered the renovation of the Trajan aqueduct. He commissioned the creation of the impressive fountain of the Eagle or *Fontana dell'Aquilone* to remind everyone of the arrival of the waters to the gardens."

"A corner of serenity to forget all the worries of the world, do you agree, Armand?"

Armand did not answer.

A bullet just pierced his skull, and he fell in the middle of a flowery patch, with his eyes still open; a grimace of despair encrusted onto his face.

A few more millimeters and it would have been the skull of the Pope. He was just saved by the head of security's reflex to answer the Pope's question.

"Your Holiness take cover," bellowed Salvatore; "your security team will be here at any moment."

In the shadows, a small drone took off from the cover of darkness inside the cavern. It inconspicuously passed a few bats who didn't even notice it.

The drone floated above the stone adorning the top of the cascades with just a slight noise generated by its rotative pallets. Muffled by the sound of the cascade's running water, it vanished into the sky.

A few moments later, the Pope was surrounded by his Swiss guards.

"What about Armand?" asked the Pope. One of the agents bowed his head sadly.

"Your Holiness, who would have attempted to kill you in these times of need?"

"They must have also compromised your drone security."

"I think I know, Salvatore. We have to go somewhere nobody can hear us."

§CHAPTER 60§
07:22, OCTOBER 3_{RD}
GREECE, THESSALONIKI

"DEAR PASSENGERS, our flight will be delayed as the Thessaloniki airport is currently closed due to the use of drones at its perimeter."

"You do not have to worry, we still have plenty of fuel as we added extra in Cairo for our next flight."

Lydia felt reinvigorated by the strong aromatic coffee, which left a pleasant aftertaste of fruity flavors combined with chocolaty notes.

I think this is all happening because of me. Somebody is trying to detour and delay my flight.

Cyber and drone warfare were the new security challenges of the 21_{st} century.

Reading the *Financial Times* newspaper's headlines, the latest news was that the COVID-19 virus was accelerating into the main European transport hubs: from London to Berlin and from Rome to Paris.

Soon the entire continent would be under lockdown; *I will have to hurry, there is no more time to waste*.

Finally, the plane landed, and at the airport's VIP arrival area, as an EU citizen, she simply showed her passport, while Neo had already ordered a private cab for her.

"I just checked the blacklisted Interpol database, and you were not in it," Neo said.

"I think somebody is monitoring every step you take."

"They still need something from you. Otherwise, your name would have been already on the most wanted list and be locked in for interrogation about Helene's death," Neo said with an encouraging voice.

"They must want the vial, but they will have to take it from you directly before you have an opportunity to hand it over to authorities."

Lydia felt the time ticking into her mind, the ominous: ***"you have two sunset cycles before the Grail will be destroyed."*** One sunset had already passed.

They left the VIP arrival area and another limo

was waiting there. The driver silently closed the door after her.

"Neo, I see that you like to spoil me. I never hoped to have such an amazing valet. I'll have to find a way to re-pay you," Lydia sweetly chuckled.

"The fastest way to avoid the horrendous traffic jams in the Greek city will be the Metro."

"Can you believe there were plans already before *World War I* ? However, the authorities only started the work in 2006. It is not yet ready due to the constant discovery of archaeological sites."

"I see Neo that you are passionate about this subject as well. There is always a dormant ancient city full of wonders to be discovered under any modern one."

"I always wanted to know my origins, as I am actually of Greek descent, but I'll tell you that story another time," Neo said.

"Now we are above a deeply buried Byzantine road, marble-paved and column-lined with shops, and villas. *Hagia Sophia* station would have been our final destination."

Lydia tried to ignore the horrible noise of honking horns and old motor cars belonging to the masses of peoples trying to escape the city before the authorities' lock-down would be imposed.

She closed her eyes and tried to imagine all the people peacefully walking, carrying out their regular business.

§CHAPTER 61§

I ALWAYS wanted to be an archaeological explorer; now I have the chance to fulfill my dream.

I wonder if my parents will be proud of me now.

After all, I had to endure, I need their strength and laughter, which gave me so much energy.

Lydia closed her eyes and for a moment remembered the power of their hugs and the gentle caressing voice of her Mom:

"You can achieve anything you want my darling daughter, never forget that. Never give up. Focus on your inner strength."

I promise you, mom and dad, I'll never stop until I find out what happened to you.

While the driver turned right from the once-bustling *Tsimiski* boulevard, she gazed in wonder at all the ancient sites, popping out here and there in the middle of a dusty urban landscape.

She read on a rusty panel: *The palace of the first Dacian Caesar, Galerius Valerianus Maximianus 250-311 AC, who chose Thessaloniki as the seat of the eastern part of the Roman Empire.*

Then when the car stopped, another panel indicated *The Octagon*, a particular room that must have been dedicated to relaxation and adorned with beautiful sculptures.

Apparently, Galerius didn't manage to enjoy its view as he died before it was finalized.

They even found a mysterious tomb built within the ring of the foundation of the hall.

"I am sure Galerius fell in love with the beautiful unobstructed view of the Aegean Sea," Lydia said.

"He was one of the four Caesars, a member of the *Tetrarchy* system to govern the Roman empire to avoid the former bloodshed and attempted murder of the previous rulers."

"The Rotunda was a part of the Galerius' Palace complex," Neo stated, clearly passionate about the history of this place.

"He wanted to rename the *Roman Empire*, the *Dacian Empire,* to the Roman patricians' horror, in honor of his Dacian origins, and to revenge the atrocities committed by *Trajan* against his ancestors two centuries before," Neo continued.

Lydia was approaching her final destination.

As the limo briefly crossed the *Egnatia* boulevard; a huge column erupted, a remnant of the Galerius complex.

And there it was, a magnificently preserved circular structure surrounded by a metallic fence. It even had an old Turkish minaret, towering above other ruins.

It was a display of all the different eras this monument had to endure across history under the control of various empires.

She was sure that it had a similar fate as the *Hagia Sophia* in Istanbul. Under the Ottoman empire, it would have certainly become a Mosque.

"We have arrived ma'am," her driver announced. I wish you a pleasant stay in Thessaloniki."

Lydia still felt tired; after all, she barely had a few hours of sleep on the plane.

She exited the car, and a fresh breeze caressed her face. She quickly skidded up some stairs, and after paying the entrance ticket, she entered the Rotunda.

Lydia was bewildered by the game of lights dancing in front of her eyes. The sun revolved around the thousands of colorful mosaic decorations of the Rotunda, an art masterpiece of Late Antiquity.

The mosaics formed one of the oldest collections of wall mosaics preserved in excellent condition.

Initially, mosaics covered the entire hemisphere of the dome, but after so much retrofitting spanning for hundreds of years to satisfy the needs of conquerors, only a few survived.

And then her eyes stumbled upon the empty circle in the ceiling with Helene's last words reverberating in her head:

"The pagan holy circle will show you the way, and under the perfection of the right hand of Kosmos when lost in darkness, the cruciform will show you the light."

The entire dome consisted of a vast concentric zone centered around a mysterious personage, who was portrayed in a silver medallion.

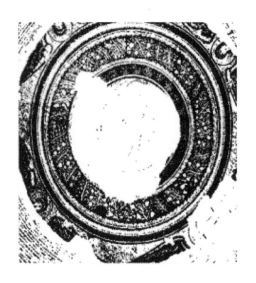

There was just a faint shade made with some kind of charcoal, his right arm showing his omnipotence, his left hand holding a scepter, while being surrounded by stars and a cornucopia of all of nature's Earthly gifts: pomegranates, grapes, pears, and other fruits. A rainbow structure was borne by four archangels bathing in a shimmering aura of sunlight.

"Lydia, look above!" Neo exclaimed excitedly.

"There between the angels, is a Phoenix, the mythical bird-symbol of renewal and eternity."

"I am sure the mysterious central personage is Jesus Christ. The first link between the mythical bird and Him."

"I have a deep feeling we are in the right place,

Neo."

"The general interpretation is that the other praying figures were the Christian Church's Martyrs."

"The buildings around them represented Holy Jerusalem, and the central part of the dome indeed depicted Jesus Christ being lifted to paradise or during his second arrival on Earth, the apocalyptical Judgement Day."

The mosaics of the ovals at the base of the dome completed the opulent decoration, which used a combination of geometric and floral motifs surrounded by garlands to create a feeling of hopefulness and boundless creativity.

The perfect Saints of the Thessaloniki Rotunda have captivated historians across the centuries.

"Who were these men? Were those saints or something more?"

Not all of them were preserved, probably destroyed by the waves of various cultures. The saints were almost alive in a universe beyond the reach of mere mortals.

"Historians hypothesized the saints from the mosaic were, in reality, fifteen Martyrs."

"The mystery surrounding the mosaics was intensified by the failure to precisely date them; the estimation was between the 4_{th} and 5_{th} century AC."

"I have a surprise for you, Lydia. Actually, Helene's clue made reference to *Kosmas*, who was one of the Martyrs."

"Neo, where is *Kosmas*?" Lydia exclaimed, full of curiosity.

"Even his name had a meaning, as it must have been connected to the Kosmos therm."

"What can you find on the web on the etymology of the Kosmas word?" Lydia asked curiously.

"There are several references to this word; for the ancient Greeks, it meant perfection. Like the cosmos, it is a collection of perfect thoughts."

"There are also references to a cult of Kosmos, made of enlightened people searching to elevate humanity; the forebears of the philosophers," Neo recited while filtering through multiple information sources. "Interesting, can you spot him, Lydia?"

"He's next to his brother *Damian*, who is in dark purple with some shades of blue in his hair and beard."

"Indeed, I can also notice they both have long beards. That of *Kosmas* is silvery. *Damianos*' is dark, an antithesis of the young and elderly."

"The physician brothers *Kosmas* and *Damianos*' earliest dating was in the early 6th century AC."

"*Cosma and Damiano* appear again only in

Rome, dated between 526-530 AC, having their own temple and became patron saints of physicians, surgeons, pharmacists, and veterinarians."

"Interesting Neo, thank you. It seems so well-fitting that de Moncler's clue pointed us towards a scientist. Great description, Neo. You would have been a perfect teacher."

Kosmas' hair and beard were highlighted by violet, bluish grey, and vivid blue colors while wearing a whitish mantle.

"But what is his right hand pointing to?"

"Maybe to something at the ground level?" Lydia wondered.

Lydia's eyes also noticed the beauty of all the male figures, which perfectly represented the three phases: young, middle-aged, and elderly.

It was like a metaphor for the cycle of life, but to what end?

Time was ticking and they were running out of it.

§CHAPTER 62§

"...UNDER THE PERFECTION of the right hand of Kosmos when lost in darkness, the cruciform will show you the light."

"If you look at Kosmas, we need to reverse the hand as if we would have looked at it in the mirror," Lydia said, her words rolling out quickly with excitement.

"That's it Neo. I found *the cruciform*. Look there; it is sculpted in the marble block, which is below his right hand."

Two marble blocks lay at the ground floor level in an arched window, reminiscent of a column-like structure.

"I'll get closer to it," and while in front of it, Lydia gasped. There was nothing special about this marble that had no inscription besides the engraved cruciform shape.

"What should we do, Neo. What if there is something underneath or behind it. How do I move this block?"

The massive marble seemed to weigh several hundred kilos, and on top, there were still tourists around and some sleepy guards who would undoubtedly react if the marble piece suddenly dropped to the floor.

"...when lost in the darkness, the cruciform

will show you the light."

"Hmm, what if we do precisely this—we need darkness for it to reveal its secrets," Neo said, his voice full of joy because he believed this was the key.

"What if there is something written on the white stone, and you would need an ultraviolet specter to make it visible?

"Use your jacket to cover your head, and approach the stone," Neo suggested.

Lydia took out her sleek asymmetric collared Calvin Klein leather jacket and pulled it over her head while approaching the stone.

"XGlass activate the ultraviolet light," and in the semi-darkness generated at the cover of the jacket, several letters started to become visible, seemingly written in ancient Greek.

§CHAPTER 63§
WASHINGTON, THE ORDER'S HEADQUARTERS

THE SKY WAS clouded today, blocking the sight to the glittery constellations Simon was used to admiring above his glass ceiling. They always gave him a soothing feeling.

For generations, this safe house was strategically located on the outskirts of Washington and used by The Order to hold their most essential meetings in times of crisis.

The house preserved its early Victorian style after being fully refurbished. Its interior was decorated with a minimalistic style, a perfect synergy between technology, marble, and metallic accents.

Simon was listening to his favorite requiem,

which gave him peace and allowed his thoughts to flow effortlessly.

"Open a secure connection to The Order," the Vice President whispered, and his A.I. assistant answered back instantly with, "connection established."

One by one, the screens in the conference room started to light up, revealing different silhouettes of influential people across the world; some were CEOs of huge companies or powerful government leaders.

"My brothers, our most precious belonging, was desecrated by an unknown enemy; our vault preserved for millennia has been destroyed."

"I am sure you all want to know what happened with the information preserved underneath Berlaymont," Simon bellowed while nodding his head.

"Our teams are still struggling to go through the rubble and assess the damage; however, the global pandemic outbreak has slowed down our efforts."

"I will not rest until I find who is responsible for the death of our sister, de Moncler, and I will make sure they will pay dearly for what they have done."

"Stay safe, my brothers and sisters. May the divine protect you."

Simon could read the anger and fear on all their faces despite the privileged positions they occupied. If this could happen to de Moncler, in one of the most secured buildings of the world, it meant that any of them could be the next target.

"Incoming call from Mark Hopkins, shall I connect you, Sir?"

"Yes, launch the connection in my office."

He closed the conference room doors and went into his office, which had a pleasant rainy noise in the background.

"Mister Vice President, we have geo-located Lydia via the video stream of an airport; she is currently in Thessaloniki, Greece."

"I will land in precisely four hours; do you have any news on my family?"

Mark's face was pulsating, and he was stuttering, "please tell me they are okay."

"Mark, we received this video; the secret service just forwarded it to me," the Vice President replied worriedly.

Daddy, we love you. Please hurry, save us. His two boys and wife were holding a paper with those words written and the sound was muted; they were all sitting in a white room.

"They seemed to be okay for the moment, but I am afraid we are running out of time."

§CHAPTER 64§

"NEO, DID YOU manage to get a good handle on the text?".

ΤΟ ΑΓΙΟ ΔΙΣΚΟΠΟΤΗΡΟ ΘΑ ΑΝΟΙΞΕΙ ΤΗ ΣΤΑΥΡΟΕΙΔΗ ΠΥΛΗ ΠΡΟΣ ΜΙΑ ΑΠΕΙΡΗ ΖΩΗ ΚΑΤΩ ΑΠΟ ΤΗ ΛΑΜΨΗ ΤΟΥ ΣΥΜΠΑΝΤΟΣ ΘΑ ΚΑΘΑΡΙΣΕΙ ΤΙΣ ΑΜΑΡΤΙΑΙ ΣΑΣ ΠΡΟΣΤΑΤΕΥΜΕΝΕΣ ΑΠΟ ΤΟ ΑΡΧΑΙΟ ΘΕΙΟ.

"Yes, the algorithm we already used is processing the translation as we speak."

The A.I. assistant's soft voice recited the inscription:

"The Grail will open the cruciform gate towards an infinite life under the glitter of the universe which will wash your sins protected by the ancient divine."

"Another cruciform, but this could be anywhere," Lydia said despaired.

"Not necessary, let me run a cross-search for locations in the city matching the keywords: *cruciform gate* and *wash your sins*," Neo replied, feeling hopeful.

"I think this could be anywhere, literally under the stars," Lydia said closing her eyes and visualizing the starry sky in her mind.

She had a strange feeling of being watched.

Had the peculiar Assassin who tried to kill her in Egypt already caught up with her?

"Neo, can you scan the surroundings for the Assassin who tried to kill me? I have the sense that I'm being watched."

"Just look around, and I'll perform a scan."

The natural light was growing, and the sun's rays were protruding through the windows of the Rotunda projecting strange shadows on the ancient brick walls.

An elderly lady went straight to Lydia and started to yell at her loudly in Greek:

"*Kyria mou, prepei na prosexte!* She quickly understood she was one of the guards who saw her touching the stone, and she was obviously not happy."

The Assassin was carefully watching her by using a simple drone he bought from a nearby mall.

Nowadays, it was so easy to spy on someone using drones, which only cost a few dozen euros, mass-produced in China, and then retrofit to become the perfect killing machines.

He didn't have the time; otherwise, he would have put a small explosive charge and detonate it near his target. This was one of his favorite methods of execution for his victims.

The United Nations and European Union disagreed on how to legislate the personal use of drones. Often assassinations were carried out using these cheap drones.

A new era of hybrid threats was rising, and governments were incapable of stopping the metamorphosis of these dangerous toys.

§CHAPTER 65§

LYDIA EXITED the Rotunda, and then she saw something fall to the ground.

"Lydia, please take cover; I found a drone in the proximity of the Rotunda, and after accessing its video memory, I had to take it down."

"It filmed you the whole time you were inside. Someone was watching you again. I am afraid our shadow is back."

The Assassin was running around the Rotunda. He had to catch her quickly because he didn't expect his drone to be taken down.

"Lydia, on your left, there is a LIME brand electric scooter. I have unlocked it for you. Today must be our lucky day because the location we are searching for is closer than I would have ever imagined!"

Lydia did not wait and grabbed the electric scooter and accelerated.

There was almost nobody in the streets due to the COVID-19 outbreak. People were too scared to go out anymore.

By the time the Assassin arrived at the other side of the Rotunda, she was gone.

His pale face started to get a reddish tint, his anger rising as was his pulse.

This is not over.

I'll have to track you again.

He launched another drone, this time a miniaturized version. It rose above the city, giving him a full aerial view of the surroundings.

Lydia was a little dot on the move, but he instantly spotted and started running after her.

"Lydia, when you reach the *Egnatia* boulevard, go left."

"I am afraid our chaser will catch me very quickly; he has a knack for it. Isn't there a possibility to block his drones from tracing me?"

"I'll look into it, but now you need to go left again on *Patriarchou Ioakim* street."

She could feel the fresh breeze of the sea, the pollution slowly dissipating due to the light traffic.

This phenomenon was occurring all over the planet. Most polluting nations stopped their industrial activities while their workers were confined at home. The Earth was getting a break and regenerating itself.

Lydia was almost enjoying her little LIME adventure; it reminded her of the bicycle trips she had with her dad in the *Bois de la Cambre* Brussels Park.

They would travel via a small ferry over a lake that had an island in the middle. There they would enjoy ice cream and lemonade.

All these thoughts were distant memories; she had to stay focused as she expected more danger lurking around.

"Now you should see in front of you the *Hagia Sophia* Cathedral Church's orange structure. It's one of Thessaloniki's oldest churches, its initial foundation laid in the 3_{rd} century."

"You need to go around it, and on the left side, you'll see a metallic bar that is protecting an underground site below the street level."

"This hidden site still holds some ancient marble columns and the *Holy Church of John the Baptist*."

This place was usually bustling with tourists and surrounded by several restaurants. Now everything was eerily quiet.

"I think you need to find a *baptisterium basin* in the church's garden," Neo explained.

The Grail will open the cruciform

gate towards an infinite life under the glitter of the universe will wash your sins protected by the ancient divine.

"The search algorithm narrowed down the outdoor location, where sins are being washed away."

"I see it, Neo. It's four meters below street level."

Above the stairs, going down, there was a sign: *Catacombs of Saint John.* A cross-like basin, with the outline of a strange flowery model could be seen in the middle of the garden. Hidden below was a mysterious underground ruin.

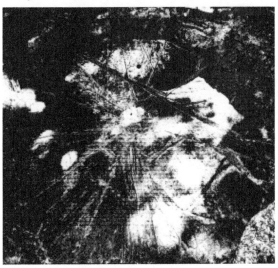

Looking around, she noticed a modern glass structure placed to protect the catacombs' entrance. It was also the neighborhood's orthodox church.

But what really caught Lydia's eye was a cross marking on one of the marble pillars, which must have been the relic of an old temple.

"Do you see this, Neo? It has the same form as the bottom of the vial, with a hole protruding in the middle. It must be more ancient than it seems," Lydia said excitedly.

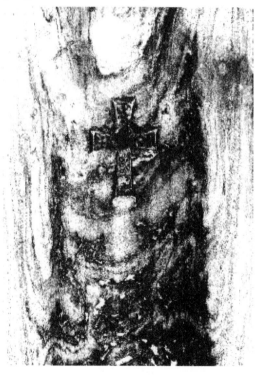

"There are also ancient catacombs, deep under the church, that were used by the first Christians as a religious sanctuary."

"Historians believed the tunnels were part of a pagan temple devoted to ancient deities and that the *baptisterium* was, in fact, a pagan nymphaeum whose source was a nearby spring. It's one component of an extensive subterranean tunnel network constructed under the city."

"It sounds familiar. Another labyrinth like the one in Brussels or Cairo," Neo said.

She took out the vial from her *Birkin* bag, and the fluid had again changed colors. It was oscillating from deep violet to aquamarine. Placing the bottom of the vial on the column, it fit perfectly.

For a moment, nothing happened, but then a set of clicks started to trickle through the column. Below the *baptisterium* the stones began to reposition themselves, forming some kind of circular staircase, similar to the one from the *Cinquantenaire Park.*

"That's it Neo, you were right; this must be the place the Rotunda's clue was pointing to."

"We need to hurry; the assassin could be here any minute."

§CHAPTER 66§

THE ASSASSIN was puzzled. *Where is she?*

He thought she entered the Hagia Sophia Church because Lydia's scooter was lying in front of it.

She left it there as a decoy, and the trick worked.

Neo managed to block the video flow exactly when she turned the corner, leaving the assassin with a mere illusion.

While he was trying to find Lydia inside the almost empty church, she managed to elude him and already started her descent on the staircase into the darkness below.

"XGlass activate light." The dust was almost suffocating. As she was touching the steps, a thick layer of dust dislodged.

She quickly took out one of the protection masks she was given at the airport.

After she put it on, her breathing normalized.

After several meters, she reached the bottom of the staircase.

The air was moldy but breathable. A strange gust of air gave off a familiar fragrance—honeysuckle.

The floor glittered with crystal rocks, which reflected the light projected by her XGlass.

"Do you see this, Neo? It seems untouched for millennia. But what are we looking for?" Lydia asked worriedly.

"Besides the floor, I cannot spot anything on the walls made of similar marble as the outside column."

"Did you try to use the double-pyramidion octahedron?"

"Maybe its magnetic properties will trigger another mechanism," Neo said, worried by Lydia's irregular breathing.

"I smell honeysuckle again, but I cannot trace where it's coming from," Lydia said, taking out the octahedron from her elegant purse while smiling at the thought that this is the perfect place for such a Fashionista accessory...

She waved the octahedron around the darkroom, but nothing happened.

Then by lowering it towards the floor level, something activated. The entire floor made of rock crystal started to vibrate, and each piece projected light on the darkened ceiling.

The octahedron was snatched from her by a magnetic force, making it rotate rapidly towards the floor's center. The intensity of the multiple rays of light was increasing.

Looking more carefully at the lights, Lydia realized that the ceiling projections were forming a set of characters.

"Neo, please record the video flow. Do you recognize the letters?

"They resemble Egyptian hieroglyphs and again Aramaic when combined all together."

Lydia went around the room, mapping the ceiling and finally understood how the mechanism was functioning. The final clue was given by the burning smell and the floor, which started to emanate heat.

"Neo, I think the honeysuckle oil was heated by the octahedron's magnetic field."

"I don't know how much time the light projection will be fueled by the oil. Do you have the entire ceiling on the recording?"

As she asked, the lights went off, and the metallic octahedron fell on the floor splitting in two.

The floor was starting to crack, and the crystals were exploding one by one, like mini bombs spraying sharp shards everywhere.

"Lydia, you have to run now," Neo shouted.

One fragment grazed her arm, and another wounded her cheek.

"Damn it, I didn't expect this."

While running towards the staircase, she bent down and grabbed one of the mini-pyramidions hastily placing it in the purse which was frantically dangling on her wrist. The other was in the middle of the room, impossible to reach.

When climbing the first step of the stairs, she thought maybe she should go back and risk recovering the other half, but the center of the floor started to collapse.

The floor was replaced with a chasm, which swallowed the mini-pyramidion together with the glittering rock crystals.

She quickly climbed the staircase, which now was shaking as well. *I hope I can exit...*The steps below her were detaching and collapsing into the hole.

"Are you okay, Lydia?" Neo asked because the video feed was cutting in and out for a few moments.

Lydia was breathing heavily but managed to

climb and snatch the baptisterium's stone border hanging only by her right hand, while the other was only holding the purse in mid-air.

"Ahh, Neo, I just have to pull myself up. I don't know if I have the strength," she said as a trickle of blood came her hand, wounded by shrapnel from one of the crystals.

She balanced herself with the last ounce of strength and managed to put the other hand on the edge with the purse safely landing on the ground next to her.

"Lydia, you need to focus. Please, you can do it." Hearing Neo's voice gave her the energy she needed to pull herself up.

She quickly rolled on the ground, snatching also the purse, while taking some distance from the cruciform baptisterium transformed now into a deep black abyss, with the ground around her still shaking.

"Lydia, you better run now. The whole place might collapse. I already ordered a cab for you; someone is waiting at the top of the stairs," Neo said with his voice still shaky.

She gathered her remaining strength and while heading to the street level, she tried to look calm and act as nothing happened. Finally, she spotted a white cab with someone waiting next to it.

The old driver was fiddling with the beads of his *kombolói,* "*ah kyria, eiste i kyria Lydia?*"

"Yes, yes, that's me," Lydia said, trying to hide her wounded hand.

"Please drive towards the sea, I would like to say goodbye to it."

§CHAPTER 67§

THE MEDITERRANEAN SEA was at its finest, with the waves hitting the esplanade and the water shimmering into the sun.

"*Kyria mou aima, aima... parakalo prosexte,*" shouted the driver, angrily gesticulating, almost losing the car's control.

Lydia understood that the driver was afraid she would stain his car. He quickly handed her a couple of sticking plasters, which he took out from his glove compartment.

"Thank you," Lydia said, covering her wound after first extracting from her arm a very fine, needle-like piece of crystal.

"Neo, can you hear me?"

"Yes, Lydia. Thank God you managed to pull yourself out. For a moment, I thought you wouldn't make it."

"Such a pity I could not be there to help."

"No worries. You have done everything you can," Lydia said with a sweet voice.

"For a moment, I died with you, and then I felt reborn." Neo was almost stuttering and became shy again.

"Neo, are you in love? Who is the lucky girl or boy?" Lydia chuckled, blushing at the thought.

For a moment, there was a small pause from Neo.

"Hilarious Lydia del Biondo. Very funny... I am afraid there is no time for romance now. I have important things to tell you."

"It's good you managed to recover one of the two mini-pyramidions," he said taking a deep breath.

"Strange, I don't know if this is the correct order of words from the ceiling projection's translation, but here it goes."

"Seek the flower of life growing inside the Atlantean labyrinth guarded by Griffins, which need to be subdued by the power of the sacred pyramid."

"Excellent. Now, we must discover Atlantis, a labyrinth, and griffins."

"Atlantis was supposedly located between Crete and Santorini, with the central city in the middle of Santorini, destroyed by a catastrophic eruption some thirty-five hundred years ago."

"My parents were fascinated with the legends of this mythical place. They promised that one day we'd explore its ruins together."

"We always watched the Indiana Jones and Tomb Raider movies. My dad even called me Lara sometimes."

"I played all the games," Neo said.

"I cannot believe that I am a part of that reality now, fighting for our lives next to a real Lara Croft."

"Can you search for a location with griffins in one of the two islands? Hopefully, the translation was accurate," Lydia stated.

"Well, we already have a first match."

"In the throne room of the Knossos palace, there is a set of griffins that have stylized flowers of life as their hearts, a spiral of the infinite...the Fibonacci sequence."

Neo projected on her XGlass the image of a stone throne protected by the two griffins. These mystical creatures were thought to be the guardians of a treasure or a powerful artifact.

"Your search skills and translation algorithms are improving all the time, Neo."

"I would not have survived without your help, that's for sure..." Lydia said, blushing while thinking of Neo.

"Could we please go to the airport now. I think I've had enough of the sea," Lydia gently asked the driver.

"*Ne kyria mou*, we go to the airport," the driver said obediently.

"Strange choice, I didn't know that the Minoan civilization was fascinated with griffins," Lydia said, surprised.

"Oh yes, the word griffin comes from the Greek *gryphon,* a powerful mystical animal with the head of an eagle and the body of a lion."

"A hybrid between the king of the beasts and the king of the birds."

"I have more good news. I booked you a charter flight to Crete. The virus situation is getting worse, so you'll fly alone like a true VIP," Neo announced.

"In two hours, you'll be landing in the Heraklion airport, and from there, a car will take you directly to the archaeological site of the Knossos Palace. Do not forget to have a good rest on the plane."

§CHAPTER 68§
WASHINGTON, THE WHITE HOUSE

A TALL FIGURE towered over the resolute desk located in the White House's Oval Office, thinking of the number of past presidents who sat at it.

From his perspective, this piece of furniture was a bit overrated.

History will always have its unknown heroes, but this kind of trinket will always survive.

"Did you call me, Mr. Vice President?" his secretary asked with a trembling voice despite appearing sure of himself. He was in his early thirties and had piercing eyes and impressive physique.

"Yes, Andrew, please get Senator Mark Hopkins in here as soon as possible." The Vice President was full of anger.

"Yes, sir, I'll bring him right away," Andrew said and quickly exited.

I never wanted this office. Now our plan is doomed, and this global outbreak will generate an unfathomable fallout.

The death of de Moncler will have so many ramifications. It put in motion a chain of events that went beyond our control.

Even our great country cannot count on its President, who is still presently in quarantine like many other world leaders after attending the G20 summit.

There was a knock at the door, and a rather young Senator entered with a confident look on his face.

"Mark, thank you for coming on such short notice," Lightgood said. "Please, Mark, have a seat."

The Senator obediently complied with Lightgood's instruction.

"My dear Mark, there is a sinister plot being put into place by forces beyond our control. It started in Brussels with the death of the European Commission's President, and now I have some alarming news. I was informed by the CIA that the White House received a call from an entity who presented himself as the Phoenix, stating he kidnapped your wife and your two sons."

"It said your family will be killed if, in twenty-four hours, Lydia del Biondo is not handed over to them."

"I know you have as many questions as I do, but Lydia was the protégé of my late good friend Helene de Moncler."

"I think they want to destroy us, especially me, through you and Lydia."

"You are like my son, but now you have to be strong and find Lydia, who is in mortal danger," the Vice President said, his eyes expressing deep sadness.

"Mr. Vice President—Simon, how do I know that my family will be spared?" Mark asked, his face contorting into a grimace of despair.

"Don't worry my son, the entire secret service is trying to find a way to save your family. It is an utmost priority for me."

"I will need to save your family and the entire country from the grip of COVID-19."

The news sounded grim as the newly installed plasma TVs in the oval office were showing a catastrophic situation with New York at the epicenter of the outbreak. Tens of thousands were dead and morgues were quickly becoming overwhelmed.

Mark turned to the Vice President. Failing to control his anger, he banged his fists on the desk, almost screaming: "Who is this Lydia del Biondo?" "Why would someone go to such lengths to kidnap my family?"

"I don't really know, my son, and in the current situation I cannot do more."

"This is why I called you here. I asked the CIA to give you access to a private plane."

"Lydia was last located in Thessaloniki, Greece. The secret service is currently triangulating her location. They will provide constant updates to you."

While he exited, a secret service agent whispered into his ear: "Please follow me, Senator. I'll escort you to the airport."

They hurried along the corridor leading outside the Oval Office, which was bustling with people wearing protective masks. They then vanished through one of the secret emergency exits.

§CHAPTER 69§

THE POPE was breathing heavily. He needed his Ventolin spray, which he always kept in one of his robe's pockets. He took three puffs to calm his panic-induced asthma attack, and his breath slowly normalized.

The Sistine Chapel always had a soothing effect on him.

"I'm sure there are no microphones here because Cardinals were afraid of having their secrets revealed. They never dared to spy on anyone in here."

"I constantly asked Armand to check if the room was bugged," the Pope said, still breathing with difficulty.

With a saddened voice, he continued: "I constantly found microphones in my chambers, but we never found any here."

"Now, this burden will fall on you as my new

Head of Security."

"Listen carefully, Salvatore. What I will tell you now it is a secret you should take to your grave, which I hope, my son, will be a long ways away."

"I'm sure you're aware of the whispers related to the Saint Malachy prophecy, which is connected to the choice of my Papal name, making me the destroyer of Rome."

"Look around what's happening. All of Italy is suffering profoundly from the new virus. I am starting to believe this is no longer just a coincidence. It is our divine mission to reform the church, but somebody is trying to annihilate me."

"Some years ago, I had a vision of a little girl that would one day reveal a secret, one that would save all of humanity. She appeared to me; in fact, during the day, I was proclaimed Pope."

"A few weeks ago, I met with the President of the European Commission, Helene de Moncler, who explained to me that she belonged to a secret society, The Order which was entrusted with keeping one of Jesus' lost secrets."

"I only had a brief moment with her in private. She told me that if anything happened to her, I needed to contact her protégé and she gave me this metallic card."

Salvatore looked carefully at the card, and it seemed to be made of stainless steel with a barely visible dot marking in the middle.

"I think there is something there, but it is too small." He took out his cell phone and zoomed all the way in revealing a strange pattern.

"Your Holiness, I think I know what this is. It's a QR code, a quick response code that stores information that could be processed using a Reed–Solomon error correction to extract the data in a readable format."

"I must have such an application on my cell phone."

He quickly opened the app and processed the QR code receiving a set of letters:

3NpNJfgpYVyZSa8YCfUuf-C3idVtF3iSX6d

"Does it make any sense to your Holiness?"

"No clue my son. I have never seen such a sequence of letters."

"Helene only gave me her protégé's name: Lydia del Biondo, and she also showed me a picture of Lydia on her cell phone. I was astonished."

"I instantly recognized Lydia's eyes—the same eyes that haunted me for so many years, eyes I could never forget."

"The eyes of the little girl that appeared to me in *Saint Peter's Square*, the very night when I was struck by lightning and when the conclave elected me as Pope."

"I believe this was a divine sign; it's time for you to go and look for Lydia."

"You will have unlimited resources—anything you need, the entire Swiss guard, but you need to act swiftly as I'm afraid this virus will become the worst plague humanity has ever faced."

"I was sure that Lydia held the key to our salvation and would redeem our Holy Church by helping all of humanity."

"But now I am not so sure anymore, I feel darkness is approaching, and in the end, Lydia might be working against us."

"I am not sure I fully understood you, your Holiness."

"What if del Biondo is the agent of destruction, and we need to stop her?"

"What if everything I believed was just a lie?"

"There is too much at stake, we cannot take any risks."

"You need to do everything necessary to stop the prophecy from becoming a reality, even if this means putting an end to her."

"Your Holiness, your wish is my command."

"I will deploy my entire resources to look for her."

"I will not fail you, and in the end, I will come back with a solution for your Holiness."

"I already have forces looking for her but cannot count on them."

"Thank you, my son, and God bless you. I know you can be trusted."

"I'm afraid this would not be an easy task, but we have been chosen to be the servants of God and do his bidding."

"In this final hour, we are the only ones who can prevent the apocalypse predicted by Saint Malachy."

"Look what's happening, the apocalypse is already on us. Today another 345 lives were lost with the death toll rising to 2,500, and the increase in infected people skyrocketed to 31,506 from a previous 27,980, the most significant figure outside of China."

"The crisis is wreaking havoc on our hospitals and left regions of Italy scrambling to strengthen their health systems as the number of contaminated people rose all over the country. We have to find a way to stop this madness."

§CHAPTER 70§

LYDIA WAS EXPECTED by a dark-haired man with sexy hazel eyes, flashing an iPad with her name blinking: Madame del Biondo.

"Madame, I am Xenios, and I will be your flight attendant and driver. Do you have any luggage?"

"I don't have any luggage. I have private property in Crete, so I don't need any," she said improvising. "I am rather in a hurry. Can we go directly to the airplane?"

"Certainly, ma'am." After entering the airport, they headed straight to the security check. Xenios quickly flashed a badge and whispered something to the guard, who hastily checked Lydia's passport handing it back to her.

He then took her through the VIP entrance. There, another guard, an angry middle-aged lady, asked with a rather aggressive tone: "Do you have anything to declare?"

Lydia looked directly at her and answered kindly: "Nothing to declare."

Xenios and the woman quickly exchanged a look, and the next minute Lydia was approaching her airplane, a CESSNA 550 II, which was in perfect condition and even had a red carpet and the pilot waiting at the entrance.

"Would you like a glass of champagne, ma'am, or something else to drink?" Xenios politely asked.

"This guy wants to serve you, Lydia."

"Are you really sure you don't want anything else?" Neo asked. She could sense a hint of dread and frustration in his voice.

By now, Lydia realized she could perfectly understand from his voice what he thought. He was so in love, and he could not hide his jealousy.

Lydia didn't answer Neo.

"I had a long night of partying; I am rather tired. I would prefer to rest a bit," Lydia quietly said.

"I won't need your services for the rest of the flight," she said sounding a bit condescending.

Xenios quickly answered: "Certainly ma'am," and he swiftly exited her private cabin.

"Satisfied Neo?" Lydia whispered.

He answered with a sweet voice: "Yes, quite...

and now it's time for a quick power nap."

Closing her eyes, Lydia tried to let herself go, keeping her mind from all the worries, while in the comfortable leather seat equipped with walnut arms.

She pushed a button, and her seat started to lean back naturally following her posture engulfing her body in a sudden pleasant warmth.

Ahh, Neo, if you could only be here with me in my arms, so I can properly thank you, she thought and then floated off into dreamland.

§CHAPTER 71§

"INOK, I AM so disappointed," the Phoenix said with an authoritative voice. "You failed me again, and again, you lost your faith."

He was gazing at the screens showing dramatic global news. Country after country was becoming affected and forced into lockdown by the killer virus.

"Humanity is dying, and all our work is at stake if you do not stop this girl."

"We almost traced her aide. He's very clever at hiding his location, but soon he will be terminated."

"Do not fail me again, Inok. This is the last time. Trace her location," the Phoenix bellowed after pushing the tactile screen.

His virtual assistant answered:

"Her Passport was used to board a private jet from Thessaloniki to the island of Crete."

"I'll give you one more chance to catch her. There is a private plane waiting for you. I am sending you the details via your XGlass."

The Assassin was red with anger, his face disfigured. Only once before his Master called him by his real name, and then disaster followed.

He ran towards the taxi station and rudely instructed the young taxi driver pointing a gun at his head, "You need to drive as quickly as possible to the airport. If you call the police, I'll find and kill your entire family, causing them an agonizing death while I flay their skin and make you watch."

§CHAPTER 72§

SALVATORE RUSHED to his office, moving through the Vatican corridors in record time. He knew all the secret passages. As a small child, he was always fascinated with stories from the Vatican, a country within a city and the "the citadel of faith," where treasures of tremendous power were being kept.

In school, he developed an obsession after watching the Indiana Jones movies and was convinced that one day he would discover mystical artifacts like the *Spear of Destiny* hidden somewhere deep within the bowels of the Holy City, inside its famous library.

His dream came true, but he was bitterly disappointed as the Vatican held no such powerful relics.

When this Pope was elected, he felt the spiritual and mystical connection again.

There was something about this Pope that was out of the ordinary and not only his appointment but the energy he emanated.

He felt he was indeed the one chosen by God to save Christianity and not to destroy it as in Saint Malachy's prophecy, which he studied intensively.

I have to find Lydia.

She must be extremely important if the Holy Father has such a strong connection with her.

But what is the meaning of this code:

3NpNJfgpYVyZSa8YCfUufC3id-VtF3iSX6d

He tried to run several searches and use decryption programs but nothing.

He looked around his office, and from his cubical, he saw one of his colleagues, Mirco, passing.

Mirco must know he's one of the most brilliant programming minds leading the counter-intelligence section.

"Mirco, can you come over here?"

Mirco, a typical geek with thick glasses sauntered over to Salvatore.

"Hi Salvo, what can I do for you?"

"Does this sequence tell you anything?"

Mirco looked at it and instantly exclaimed: "this must be a blockchain address for a cryptocurrency wallet or a device that uses blockchain encryption technology to protect its data transmission. Let me run a quick check...oh yes, it's linked to an electronic device, not a virtual wallet, in fact."

"Is there a way to track or contact the person using this device?"

"It's not normally possible to track it, as this is the purpose of blockchain to encrypt the identity of the user."

"However, today it's your lucky day," Mirco smiled.

"We have developed a universal tracker to identify from where the signal was coming in the recent drone attack that almost killed the Pope. We can run it from my cubicle."

They quickly crossed the nearly empty cubicle space, and Mirco sat in front of his PC, which had a relaxing background of a beach site.

"The lovely beach... is this your favorite holiday destination?" Salvatore asked, trying to make some small talk.

"No clue where it is. I just like to see this beach. I feel more relaxed when I see it. I am not really the traveling type. I'm too afraid of flying."

"So, let me run the program," he quickly typed

in the blockchain address, and a few seconds later, the screen flashed with a set of numbers, a model XGlass 435M, and a user ID: ldelbiondo"

"I'll be dammed," Mirco exclaimed.

"This is the link towards the latest version of XGlass, which is still in design mode, not yet on the market."

"Can we contact the user and open a communication flow?"

"Unfortunately, not, but our algorithm can pinpoint the precise location."

"Okay, run it."

Mirco looked at him, annoyed at Salvatore bossing him around.

A precise satellite map appeared with a moving red dot blinking over the Mediterranean Sea. Its position was changing at an extremely fast speed.

Lydia must be in a plane, Salvatore said to himself.

"Thank you Mirco, I owe you one. If you could, please send me this localization view on my cell phone. I need to see where it will stop."

I have a way to locate you, Lydia, now I'll find you.

It was easy from then on. He only had to match the flight plan of the plane flying in that area with that specific trajectory.

"I need to go to the airport. Please prepare the papal plane. We need to take off immediately," Salvatore said to his assistant.

The sun was shining over white clouds, which were constantly changing shape, strangely reflecting shadows in Salvo's blue eyes.

"I found Lydia, your Holiness. I am flying now towards the island of Crete, where she is now heading."

"I knew I could count on you my son, please be gentle with her. We need to find what she is up to."

§CHAPTER 73§
15:30, OCTOBER 3_{RD}
CRETE, HERAKLION

THE SKY WAS incredibly blue, and Lydia took a deep breath of the clean island air.

"Neo this is truly amazing. No wonder the Atlanteans had chosen this idyllic location to settle their empire. I can only wonder how it was five thousand years ago."

This is one of the last standing structures of what could have been parts of the Atlantean empire.

The destruction of the ancient *Thera* island, which is now known as Santorini, occurred around 1600 BC.

The volcanic eruption not only destroyed Atlantis, but it is considered by scientists to be the most powerful eruption to have ever been recorded in the entire history of human civilization with a perimeter of more than 40 km, destroying most of the eastern Mediterranean region.

"It is sad indeed, but if I remember well, the volcanic eruption was only the beginning of the Atlantean civilization's demise, bringing a tsunami of catastrophic magnitude that wiped out the entire civilization, with only a few escaping."

"Nobody knew how Plato managed to describe the center of Atlantis. Its central city, *the Megapolis*, had a circular structure and was enclosed by three circular concentric trenches of seawater and two made of earth, each linked to the Mediterranean Sea by a complex-wide canal."

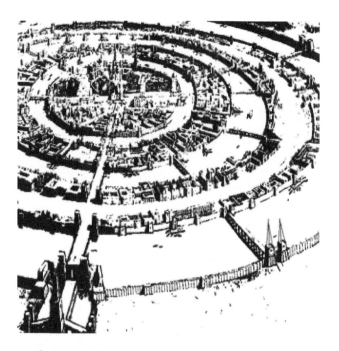

"These facts were even confirmed by historians and specialists who simulated the structure of Santorini before the eruption."

"One fresco in Santorini's equivalent of *Pompeii*: the ruins of *Akrotiri*, which was preserved by forty meters of thick volcanic ash, shows a concentric ring city in the middle of a lagoon, bearing a sea opening," Neo said.

"This is how Santorini looked with its volcano, a dot in the middle, and the *Akrotiri* city, the southern part of the island."

"All this history lost under the sea," Lydia said with a sad tone.

"Now we have a deserted almost island with

the tourists scared of the outbreak. However, the high UV exposure made the infection rate much lower in Greece, reducing the number of cases to almost none."

"Indeed, a last bastion for people seeking refuge to be embraced by the sun and relax while the entire world was in turmoil, especially VIPs, political personalities, and stars who had their summer houses located on the island."

"I have instructed your driver, Xenios, to wait for you next to Knossos site just in case you encounter any problems."

"Now look in the arm support space," Neo said diligently.

Inside, she found a small, strange-looking gun, which she started to carefully analyze.

"Ma'am, this is an EMP gun which also has four bullets capable of penetrating any Kevlar vest in case you encounter any drone attacks or a human enemy," the driver said.

"If you push the blue button, it will emit an electromagnetic pulse paralyzing any devices including yours. So, if you still need your phone afterward, you need to think twice before using the EMP. Moreover, under the front seat, you have a backpack made of bullet-resistant material."

"It can also charge your devices and provide

you the camouflage you might need and has an integrated cape that will cover you from head to toes."

"Thank you, Xenios. This gadget could prove very useful indeed."

"Actually, it was high time to get rid of my fancy little bag. I guess the lovely woman with the little girl from the picture is your family?"

"Yes, ma'am."

"Please give the bag to your wife. A gift from me for your services," Lydia said while smiling and discreetly transferring the precious artifacts into the new backpack.

"Thank you, ma'am. That's very generous of you."

"Lydia, one important thing. Your XGlass is perfectly insulated in case you use the EMP function. I have made some changes myself to the gun," Neo informed with a satisfied tone.

"Of course, you did. You don't leave anything to chance, do you?" Lydia whispered, carefully placing the gun in her leather jacket's inner pocket.

§CHAPTER 74§

THE LIMO passed by the 17_{th} century Venetian shipyards, which looked sad and desolated.

"Ma'am, we are here; I'll wait for you as long as you need," the driver said stopping on the main *road Dedalou.*

To the right, the entrance to the Knossos complex was hidden by trinket shops, now closed with almost no visiting tourists.

When trying to buy her ticket, Lydia was informed by a grumpy old cashier that she could not enter.

Gosh, I have to find a solution; I think I'll have to jump the fence, Lydia thought nervously.

However, the other younger guardian at the entrance, gestured for her to approach him and whispered while sliding a magnetic card on the metallic bar access system.

"You can still visit it, but please hurry up.

Otherwise, I'll get fired," the young man said, blushing, his deep blue eyes glittering.

"*Efcharisto poli*," she smiled, touching his hand gently and quickly disappearing behind the security gate so the grumpy cashier wouldn't spot her.

The stony path was surrounded by tall cypress trees that gave off a protective shadow from the scorching sun.

The oldest sediment she was stepping in could have been nine thousand years old, and maybe brought in by a hundred-meter gigantic tsunami generated by the explosion of Thera's ancient volcano.

A wooden bridge platform took her higher on the hill via a distinct set of stairs that reached the palace, while protecting the priceless ruins below.

Several walls were freshly reconstituted with the classical vivid, colorful Minoan frescos, which seemed exceptionally well-executed, showing the difference between the old paint and the skill of the modern artist.

The place seemed unremarkable, a simple hill with Mediterranean vegetation; nothing special that indicated it held the vestiges of such a great civilization.

But even the scattered stones below had a

magnetizing touch.

Lydia felt there was more to it than met the eye. She had a strange feeling that under this layer of history, there was another one that managed to remain undiscovered for so many millennia.

In her mind, she could only picture the ancient grandeur. The scale of this ancient project was beyond any imagination.

I just need to find the throne room and inspect the griffins; how hard could it be?

The cypress trees were basking in the sun, spreading a pleasant coniferous perfume.

At least there won't be any dark places to explore. She looked above at the cypress trees caressed by the gentle breeze and it somehow reminded of her childhood. A strange *déjà-vu* sensation suddenly engulfed her leaving her wondering...*Have I been here before*?

§CHAPTER 75§

THE ASSASSIN climbed the hill to the Knossos Palace, passing behind the rusty gate of the sleepy guardian.

He had the precise location of Lydia, a shimmering dot on his XGlass.

Now you are mine. I'll take my time before killing you.

He started his quick ascent, trying to find the shadow of a tree so he could see his victim.

And there she was. Lydia was just entering the Knossos palace complex.

This was the place of an ancient tragedy with countless lives lost to natural disasters and endless wars. One more life will not matter.

My Master will forgive me and elevate my soul as he prophesied, the Assassin thought full of excitement.

Lydia stumbled on an informational plaque. "Knossos, the most magnificent Minoan monument, the dwelling of the mythical King Minos, was born in 1650 BC and was the main center of power in Crete for nearly three hundred years."

"The palace was built early in the second millennium and destroyed two hundred years later. It was rebuilt again and ultimately destroyed by fire in 1350 BC."

For the last hundred years of its existence, it was the seat of the Mycenaean dynasty that had succeeded the Minoan kings after a large-scale disaster in Crete in 1450 BC and the collapse of the Minoan palace system."

Lydia was surprised by how well the palace had been built and its elaborate architectural design that used highly advanced techniques and boasted an impressive water supply and sewage system. The palace of Knossos was truly monumental.

Various corridors and the famous Grand Staircase connected multiple buildings that were three to five stories high and located around the Central Court.

The west wing contained the religious and cult activities while the royal apartments were placed in the east wing.

"Neo look at the sequence of the colors they were using: yellow, white, red, black and blue.

"They extracted them from natural sources during the Stone Age: red and yellow ochre, limestone or white clay and coal or ash."

"Plato described the quarries on Atlantis where one kind of stone was white, another black, and a third red, and common colors from volcanic rock which were also used by the Minoans."

"However, blue was a different story. Apparently, in antiquity, it was hard to find clear, bright blue in nature and even harder to find materials that would give that color in finished art."

"On rare occasions, the Minoans used powdered lapis lazuli to make blue, but because it was so scarce, they bought a pigment from Egypt called Egyptian blue."

Lydia was quickly advancing through the ruins while letting her senses become fully immersed into this historical treasure.

§CHAPTER 76§

LYDIA CONTINUED her hastened pace while climbing.

There were only two tourists scattered about, who were clearly not scared by the COVID-19 outbreak.

Perfect for me, the coast is clear. I will be able to search for the artifact undisturbed, Lydia happily thought.

The historian managed to reproduce the red pigment adorning the magnificent tall columns that mimicked the trunk of the sacred cypress tree.

Guided by Neo, she had to make her way to the Great Court, which gave access to the aristocratic and religious areas next to the royal apartments.

Only now did Lydia realize the extent of Knossos' complexity.

Only seven hundred rooms from the complex's

five floors structures had been excavated out of an estimated more than fourteen hundred.

With such intricate architecture in the complex structure, it was no wonder that the legend of the labyrinth had been preserved over many millennia.

"Neo, do you think I'll encounter the fabled minotaur?" Lydia asked with a playful voice.

"I don't think so; the creature was simply a myth. We should stay vigilant nevertheless because more dangerous foes could be lurking in the dark."

Lydia was astonished; the palace was truly one of the wonders of the ancient world.

"Neo, I cannot believe that the first settlement already had deep roots in the Neolithic period."

"It only proves that the Minoans possessed advanced engineering skills that made them capable of building multiple story buildings with complex air shafts and tunnels for optimal aeration and water piping systems."

"They even managed to incorporate earthquake-resistant wood into their structures that would absorb tremors and had walls covered in elastic plaster."

"This level of these advanced techniques was unknown to their neighboring tribes."

"I think the Atlanteans were very careful to

keep their technology a secret. This is why the Minoans flotilla dominated the area through their scientific supremacy," Lydia said, remembering all the *bedtime stories* here her dad talked about the mythical continent that had vanished.

"Did you notice Lydia? The location of the palace on a hill not only gave it a tactical defensive advantage but also enabled it to receive the pleasant sea breeze through its ingenious air shafts and *porticoes*."

"Back then, the climate must have been much warmer as they didn't have any protection on their windows."

"Indeed, Lydia, I found an article that shows evidence that the Pacific *El Nino* climate cycle's abnormal activity could have wreaked havoc around the globe precisely during that period."

"It could have triggered an elevated level of drought linked to extreme temperatures."

"Look, Neo, the palace had at least three separate water-management systems: for supply, for drainage of runoff, and for wastewater."

"I read here on the plaque that their aqueducts brought fresh spring water from several kilometers away from the local springs of *Archanes* using gravity to pump the water into the *terracotta* pipes.

The throne room was adjacent to a small stony

forest that had a mixture of different cypress and olive trees.

The red ochre colors were fascinating as the sunset cast a mystical light on the ancient site.

Lydia also noticed several largely embedded crystal stones. As she got closer to them, she felt the mini-pyramidion vibrating.

"Neo, I feel a vibration from the mini-pyramidion. We must be close, it's starting to react to its surroundings exactly like in Egypt."

While admiring the glimmer of the crystals, she felt a sudden sharp headache and fell on the ground, almost losing consciousness.

§CHAPTER 77§

THE ASSASSIN towered above her, preparing to kill his incapacitated prey.

"What do you want from me? " Lydia shouted, her head still throbbing at the pain from being struck by the Assassin.

"You have chased me around the globe. What have I done to you?" Lydia asked again, her lips trembling frantically.

"You will pay for the humiliation I had to endure. I'll take my time flaying you and I will make you suffer," he hissed. "But first you'll tell me what you are doing here. What did you steal from de Moncler's sanctuary and from GEM?"

"If you will tell me the truth, I'll offer you a merciful death, as I did with de Moncler. Those were our secrets to discover."

"You should have never meddled and destroyed our plan."

"You don't have the slightest clue what is at stake."

Neo began to speak into her XGlass headphones. "Let him come closer to you. I'll remotely activate the EMP pulse. You'll feel a slight shock, but no worries. Be ready to shoot him afterward."

The Assassin approached with a sharp cruciform knife and leaned down putting his foot on Lydia's back, further disabling her.

The knife was just a few centimeters away from Lydia's face, which was almost paralyzed because of the pain she felt pounding through her skull. Suddenly the EMP burst triggered an explosion of the Assassin's XGlass battery, momentarily blinding him and causing him excruciating pain.

He screamed out in pain, more so realizing that everything he worked for would be lost. His mission failed and he will be forgotten forever by his Master.

I will be consigned to oblivion, he thought.

He suddenly lost his balance allowing Lydia to roll back and aim for his head.

The Assassin fell to his knees. A bullet blew out his eye socket and he dropped dead to the ground.

His blood was splashed on the dry, scorched Earth that absorbed it with thirst, as it had done for millennia with sacrificial offerings and countless catastrophes and wars.

§CHAPTER 78§

LYDIA FELT she could not breathe and was being suffocated by an invisible force as the feeling of terror took over her body.

For a moment, she wondered: *is the corpse's spirit lying before me trying to choke me to death.*

I killed a man. It was in self-defense. He wanted to take my life as he did with Helene. I killed a man, but he was not innocent.

"Lydia, you have to snap out of it," Neo said, worried. "It seems like you're having a panic attack; your pulse is going through the roof!"

She started feeling slightly dizzy with blood pounding in her ears while her vision became blurry.

"Lydia, you need to take a deep breath. You are shaking frantically, and this will only cause you to lose consciousness. We cannot afford this."

"Look at his cruciform knife; it has the symbol

of the *Egyptian Bennu* bird engraved on it. This was the Egyptian version of the Phoenix, also depicted in the museum that had the Benben stone."

Lydia picked up the knife and thought it might come handy one day, sliding it in the lower pocket of her pants.

"Lydia, wait for a second. I see that he is carrying a backpack. Have a look inside."

"Maybe this will give us a clue as to why he was trying to kill you or for whom he is working."

"The grey backpack has a biometric lock. I think I need to use his finger to open it."

"Try his right index finger," Neo said.

Lydia grabbed his finger with her hands still shaking, and the lock opened with the touch of its owner.

Inside there was a cell phone that started to emit fumes.

Lydia understood the danger. She managed to extract a metallic drone and started to put distance between her and the fuming back-pack.

"Are you okay, Lydia?" Neo asked, worried.

While she approached the religious part of the site, an explosion was triggered, setting the body of the Assassin on fire.

"His backpack had a self-destruction mechanism. You were lucky. It could have blown you to pieces."

"One last attempt to destroy you from the afterlife," Neo said.

"His drone might be useful."

"Can you turn it so I can see its back?" Neo asked.

"I would need its production serial number to be able to hack it."

"It could be handy in the future if I manage to retrofit it," Neo said, trying to distract Lydia from the ordeal she just had to go through.

Lydia scanned with her XGlass the back of the drone and then carefully tucked it into her backpack, moving closer to the ritualistic entrance.

§CHAPTER 79§

STILL SHAKEN by the violent episode, Lydia stepped inside the mythical Throne Room that had wall paintings and a contiguous underground purification basin used for religious processions.

The old dusty throne she sought out was not too impressive.

"Neo, is this the famous throne on which the fabled King Minos sat?"

"Other historians thought that on this alabaster throne sat the King-Priest or the Queen Priestess, their supreme ruler and religious leader, with their court sitting on benches encircling the throne."

"It seems so sad. All the former glory has gone, but even in this shape, a dusty old shadow crumbled under the weight of millennia, it still emanates a strange energy."

"Lydia, the inscription in the catacombs said:

"Seek the flower of life growing inside the Atlantean labyrinth guarded by Griffins, which need to be subdued by the power of the sacred pyramid."

"So, these are the famous Griffins protecting the throne, guarding over the divine one," Neo's voice sounded quite doubtful.

"A mystical room that historians said was used to reach a form of exaltation, similar to that of *Pythia* in the *Delphi Oracle*."

"It supposedly honored the Goddess and put her on the throne, as a statue or impersonated by a priestess."

Lydia closed her eyes for a second and tried to picture the procession and capture its long-forgotten energy.

While approaching the wall, Lydia took out the mini-pyramidion, which was slightly vibrating.

The griffins were beautifully shaped with the pattern of the flower of life marking their body.

Lydia didn't even have to touch the pattern. Something seemed to already be happening.

She could already hear a metallic sound of a mechanism being activated inside the wall.

To be sure she repeated the same gesture on the wall, on the flower of life, in the shape of a nautilus near the Griffin's chest, but then nothing else happened.

Lydia was also struck by an infinite shaped pattern she just noticed.

"Where have I seen this symbol before?" she wondered.

"This is definitely another Fibonacci sequence, but what does it mean?"

"Neo, what should I do?" Lydia asked, puzzled, looking around the room to find another solution.

"The last sun rays were protruding through the ancient room and rendering visible particles of dust that seemed to float in the air, like they wanted to give Lydia a mysterious clue.

"There is a second Griffin on the left side of the throne, try the same thing," Neo said with excitement oozing through his voice.

Lydia approached the second griffin and focused the artifact on the beautifully colored flower of life in precious hues of blue.

Another metallic noise was triggered similar to the first one.

But this time, the entire room started to vibrate slightly. Slowly a space began to open on the right side of the throne's basis.

Something was shining in the secret compartment of the stone throne.

Lydia leaned down and reached inside, feeling a metallic surface.

It was a thin disk made of a gold-like metal with an intricate set of circular symbols.

"Lydia, I think I know what this is," Neo said, bursting in excitement.

"It is similar to the Phaistos disk, which is located in the Heraklion museum."

Lydia activated the XGlass light, and began to carefully inspect it.

She noticed there was a strange inscription in Egyptian hieroglyphs combined with Aramaic characters.

"Neo, it is the similar writing we discovered

before. Could this actually be Atlantean?"

"I don't have a clue. But we can use the previous translation algorithm, which will process all the languages we have encountered until now. I just need to make some final tweaks. The translation is at 80%; we'll have it in a few moments."

"Here are both faces of the *Phaistos* disk, which nobody managed to fully translate yet, but its meaning was interpreted as a prayer to the *Goddess Mother*—a mysterious deity, who may have been the ruler of Atlantis."

The same entity who could have been worshiped here in this throne room.

"Here it goes, the translation is finished."

Follow the whispering seashell of the old times inscribed and blessed by the arrow of the Goddess Mother, and on this path, you'll find the answer you are seeking under the flower of life's shadow.

"But what does it mean? Which arrow is it referring to?" Lydia asked, disappointed by the unclear translation. "I think there is an explanation of why the other disk in the museum has another side. I have a feeling we need to check the Heraklion museum."

In the background, several police sirens could be heard.

"People were alerted by the noise generated by

the explosion or the gun."

"You need to hurry up. Take the exit from the back of the palace complex. You need to take another path to avoid detection."

Exiting the building, she was struck by the last rays of the sun, a beautiful warm zenith.

At least I will not have to worry about my chaser. I just wonder what other enemies are still lurking unseen.

§CHAPTER 80§

THE PHOENIX was staring at the monolithic statue carefully encased in a black marble pedestal and protected by an impenetrable glass cubicle.

The reflection of his face in the glass showed his eyes trembling, the red microcapillary blood vessels becoming inflamed.

Inok is dead. How could he fail me like this?

He lived across millennia and witnessed unimaginable things, but this time he realized his biggest failure.

Underestimating Lydia was a fatal failure.

Now I know, and it will never happen again.

He looked again at the bird-shaped monolith, brainstorming his next move.

"I am the Phoenix. I am always reborn," he chanted.

From the beginning of time, he was fascinated with the Phoenix's mythology.

The Greeks believed the Phoenix to be a bird that lived very long and was capable of rejuvenating itself.

The sun was the source of its powers as this creature was reborn and rose from its ashes after a five hundred years period.

The Romans took on the same idea, and for them, it symbolized the renewal and the symbiosis between the sun and time and, ultimately, the resurrection.

Many emperors had been searching for the origins of this fabled bird in pursuit of their desire for immortality.

It was only me who managed to find its secrets.

"Once you served your Master as you raised in *Heliopolis,* oh solar *Bennu.*"

"Your secrets have eluded me for so long. But in the end, everything was revealed to me. I'll purge myself and be reborn."

He turned his eyes towards another pedestal, that encased a golden page from a 12_{th} century bestiary manuscript.

I always take what I want as I have done for two millennia.

The golden page is just the beginning. I have to finish what I have started.

He knew that he had to take swift action, and he had the right person in mind to execute his deadly order.

§CHAPTER 81§

MARK HOPKINS was looking at the dark clouds below his plane that was fighting its way through turbulence.

A storm was brewing, and flashes of lightning were everywhere.

"This is your captain. Please buckle up. We are passing through turbulence."

His eyes were locked on this secured tablet, fixated on the picture of a young woman.

I cannot believe my luck. My family kidnapped, and I must chase Lydia del Biondo around the world.

He admired her physique. Her eyes emanated a bright spark of cleverness.

His tablet suddenly showed an incoming message from the White House on a secured line.

"Mark, we have good news. We identified an IP

trace of where your family is located around the Manhattan area. We are sending the SWAT team now, so be on standby."

"Also, Lydia just took a private plane to the island of Crete and landed in Heraklion. Your captain is already aware; he will take you there."

The turbulence was growing, and the crystal glasses started to shake on his marble covered table.

"Thank you, Sir, for this update. I'll not disappoint you. Please take care of my family," Mark said desperately.

The captain just finished receiving the latest flight information, and he changed course towards the island of Crete.

"No worries, Mr. Hopkins, I'll take you safely through this storm. We'll land at our new destination in thirty-eight minutes."

§CHAPTER 82§

LYDIA KNEW she had to quickly find and inspect the *Phaistos* disk.

Skidding down through the ruins with the protection of her backpack, she was able to avoid the policemen who were crossing the wooden bridge.

Lydia started running through the small, dried bushes covering the scorched soil, and the Greek sun was at its zenith, giving her some much-needed cover.

"Go right, Lydia. Try to jump the fence," Neo said nervously.

He felt so powerless stuck in his wheelchair. He would have given anything to be able to help her.

She used a recently dislodged boulder to climb the protective fence and managed to finally exit.

"I have done it, Neo. Call the driver."

Running towards the car, she looked around to see if any police had spotted her.

The police cars were parked just in front of the road.

She calmly opened Xenios' car door, and discreetly entered it.

"Please drive to the Archaeological Museum."

"*Ne kyria mou*, it is very close from here. We'll arrive there in a few minutes," Xenios answered gladly.

There were no other discoveries of similar disks. She understood that there was an inexplicable bond between the artifact from the throne room and its Heraklion museum counterpart.

She had to hurry because time was running out.

"Neo, can you tell me more about the disk?"

"Yes, I already prepared more intel, but I didn't want to distract you. I was waiting for you to safely get back to the car."

"I'll never get used to you reading my mind so well. When I am back, you'll deserve a big kiss."

Her heart was pounding with excitement at finally meeting Neo and helping him cure his illness.

§CHAPTER 83§

"THANK YOU for flying with us, Mr. Hopkins; we'll be on standby for your return to Washington," the pilot said, waving goodbye.

Mark didn't even look at him; he was thinking of his family and that he might never see them again.

How did I manage to get into such a mess? I have to find del Biondo; she is the key to ending this nightmare.

His encrypted cell phone started to ring. He answered, thinking it was the vice-president; instead, a deep, dark voice spoke.

"Listen very carefully, Mr. Hopkins. We have your family, and your direct mission is to exterminate Lydia del Biondo. You have precisely forty-five minutes to do so."

"She is in the Archaeological Museum of the Heraklion. If you fail, everyone who you hold dear will die."

"Who are you? Why are you doing this?" Hopkins asked while shaking uncontrollably.

"Forty-five minutes Mr. Hopkins," and the Phoenix ended the call.

The sky was red with some dark clouds reflecting the last rays of sunshine. A fresh breeze fluttered through his hair.

His car was waiting in front of the plane. He touched the inner pocket of his jacket, and there he felt the metallic coldness of his gun.

He came prepared, *I'll have to save my family.*

"We need to go to the Heraklion Archaeological Museum. I trust you know where it is located. Please, you need to hurry. I need to arrive there as quickly as possible," Mark desperately said to the driver.

"Yes, sir. It is only ten minutes from here. I'll drive as fast as I can," the driver said.

I cannot leave this mission in the hands of the SWAT team.

What if something goes terribly wrong and my entire family dies? I cannot accept this fate.

Simon Lightgood should have already found them. I cannot abandon my family at the mercy of strangers.

The plan in Mark's mind was becoming clearer.

He knew what had to be done.

I need to comply with the Phoenix's order for my family to survive. And I'll do it. I am going to end her life.

His face contorted into a grimace and his soul was tormented beyond anything he ever experienced.

§CHAPTER 84§

"MANY ATTEMPTS have been made to decipher the *Phaistos* disk, which probably dates to the 17th century BC," Neo explained.

"A professor who dedicated most of his academic life to deciphering the disk managed to translate it but still had to comprehend its actual meaning."

"Reading something does not mean understanding it," Neo said, quoting the professor.

"The Phaistos disk is written in Minoan script. It is the best example of Cretan hieroglyphics."

"Neo, I am sure that the professor never thought there would be a connection between Atlantis, Jesus, Egypt, and all of his life's efforts."

Neo continued: "The word *I-QE-KU-RJA* is repeated three times, and it thought that this symbolizes the *Goddess Mother*."

"I think the Goddess was, besides the ruler of

Atlantis, referring to the gift of eternal life, the lost secret Jesus wanted to share with everyone, hence the flower of life reference on the back inscription," Lydia concluded.

"But still, who was this Goddess? Was there a personal connection to Jesus?"

"Maybe Jesus didn't leave Atlantis by himself, and was accompanied by more Atlanteans," Neo said curiously.

"Were his parents, Mary and Joseph, fictitious characters?"

"Nobody really knows. Maybe these artifacts were planted by one of his ancestors, or by his parents."

"According to the Apostle Matthew, Jesus' father was a descendant of *King Solomon*, who possessed mystical powers. With his amulets, he could even exorcise demons."

"Solomon himself was the son of *King David,* who ruled the *United Kingdom of Israel and Judah* from 1010-970 BC integrating parts of what today consists of Egypt, Israel, Jordan, Lebanon, Palestine, and Syria."

"This was the same David who killed Goliath and possessed the mythical *Ark of the Covenant*, inside of which there were two stone tablets containing the Ten Commandments."

"What we know for a fact is that there are no

recordings of Joseph dying. Theologians speculate he must have died of old age because when he married Mary, he was already an old man."

"Mary's story has the same fate. Nobody knows when or how she died."

"Lydia, don't you find it rather strange that the parents of the most important figure in history just vanished?"

"Or maybe not. Maybe they continued living and guarding their Atlantean secrets," Lydia said.

"There are several words on the disk connected to an ancient faith, and I believe that they reveal to us the Goddess we are talking about."

§CHAPTER 85§

MARK HOPKINS knew that he had to execute his target within the set deadline if he wanted to see his family again. He suddenly felt torn between taking a life and saving the ones that meant everything to him.

He had precise orders from the Phoenix but was intrigued at the same time. *Why would someone go through all this trouble to kidnap my family? Who is the kidnapper?*

And why has the Vice President asked me to protect her and risk losing the most precious thing I have?

Before executing her, he had to find out why everyone was chasing her. *Why Heraklion from all places?*

Lydia entered the museum and was stopped by a desperate guard who tried to explain to her in Greek: "ma'am, we are closing very soon; you only have fifteen minutes."

Lydia answered: "I'll just want to see the famous *Phaistos* disk, and I'll be leaving in ten."

The rooftop of the museum was still warm from the scorching sun, and the cypress flowers spread a pleasant aroma.

Mark Hopkins arrived just three minutes after Lydia.

He went straight to the entrance of the museum and found the doors closed. Peering through the glass door, he tried to force it open.

The guard inside signed with his hands that the museum had closed.

Bloody hell. I told the driver to be faster...

He looked around and spotted a fire exit leading to the roof.

He quickly climbed it and discovered that there was an open glass rooftop to ventilate the security surveillance room.

The sea breeze was sweet and looking above, he could see the first stars of the evening glittering in the sky.

Is this a good omen? he wondered. *I have to do this for my family.* He took a deep breath, and his rage was unleashed.

§CHAPTER 86§

MARK HOPKINS slid his silencer gun under the glass and swiftly executed the guards in charge of monitoring the museum's security cameras.

Clean shots splashed their brains on the monitors. He felt no remorse, remembering his training in Afghanistan.

From there, he had access to the entire museum database.

Where is she?

Checking the video cameras, he spotted her staring at a strange disk in front of several tourists who were trying to get a good view.

What is she up to? I have my target so close. Should I execute her? I still have twenty minutes.

His cell phone started to vibrate. It was another encrypted call.

His hand shook as he picked it up.

"Mark, did you find Lydia?" It was the voice of the Vice-President.

"Yes, Mr. Vice President, she is safe and sound. I have her in front of me. She is checking out something in the Heraklion museum."

"Good, my son, please protect her and do not worry. I am sure your family is fine; we are doing our utmost to bring them home safely."

His mind was a battlefield. The smell of fresh splashed blood wafted through the shadows.

He had smelled death before but never wanted to go to that place. Yet here he was, back in a living nightmare that he had experienced in Afghanistan.

He looked at the electrical control panel and spotted the master switch.

Before she exits the museum, I'll cut the lights and execute her.

But first, I need to find out what she is up to and what she will do with the disk.

§CHAPTER 87§

LYDIA WAS STARING at the disk and was completely puzzled.

"Neo, what should we do?"

"The translation of the text speaks about a *whispering seashell*. This must be it."

"Its shape is similar to a seashell; it looks like an ammonite."

Lydia took the large drone from her backpack and placed it on the marble floor. She then carefully extracted the golden disk.

She noticed that the mini-pyramidion attached itself to its back.

Instinctively she held and oriented it towards the glass case in which the Phaistos disk was being kept, trying to mirror the two frontal sides of the disks.

"Here is the *arrow* Neo. Can you select all the sounds in front of the arrow and tell me which ones are based on the professor's interpretation?"

"Yes, Lydia, I am running the algorithm now. We'll have the results soon."

Mark Hopkins could not wait anymore; he knew that now was the moment to strike. He flipped the switch, and the entire museum was engulfed in darkness.

To be sure his plan succeeded, he also deactivated the back-up generators.

The remaining tourists were scrambling to go outside, panicking, and using their phones' flashlight to locate the exit.

Lydia noticed that the Knossos disk started to shine in the dark.

"Neo, there must be a reaction between the two disks."

She got even closer to the Phaistos disk, which seemed to release a chemical reaction triggered by the two artifacts.

A bluish light started to pulsate in the arrow's

direction.

"Neo, are you seeing this? I think this is the clue we needed. *It shows us the way.*"

The light flickered each time it highlighted a symbol in front of it.

"Lydia, I think we have an interpretation of the sets of words pinpointed by the bluish light."

the sound KE

 the sound RA

 the sound NA

 the sound NA

 the sound KE

 the sound JE

"The secret word must be:"

"KERAN-

ANAKEJE"

Neo said full of joy, not realizing that something must have gone terribly wrong if the lights and the back-up generators were still offline.

Follow the whispering seashell of the old times inscribed and blessed by the arrow of the Goddess Mother, and on this path, you'll find the answer you are seeking under the flower of life's shadow.

"I cannot believe we managed to find it; such a beautiful melodic sequence."

Lydia was surprised that once she spoke the incantation, the ankh vial protruding from her backpack started to vibrate, its colors changing again rapidly.

It began to emit a beautiful explosion of light, and some colors she could not even recognize.

"Neo, are you seeing these colors, some of which aren't even part of the rainbow?"

"It's simply amazing!"

"I hope you are recording this?"

"Yes, all the data is being sent back to my server. You'll have amazing memories to show to your children," Neo said with excitement.

"Here is the secret vault of old days, in Gethsemane, you'll find the tree of life, and as you plant this seed, if the secret word is chanted, eternal life shall be forever yours."

"So, this must be the secret word for the incantation to be used in Gethsemane."

"We need to hurry up. There is not much time left between the two sunsets we were warned about."

Lydia's mind was trying to cope with the impact this discovery might have on all of humanity.

Her hand was still shaking while holding the golden disk. She placed it on top of the glass case holding the *Phaistos* disk.

"I think this should stay here with his other half. Its place is in a museum."

"Everyone should know the story of the twin disks."

"After millennia apart, the *Knossos* and *Phaistos* disks have reunited to save humanity."

"Neo, did you switch off the lights?"

"It was not me, Lydia. I have a bad feeling about this. It must have been someone else."

§CHAPTER 88§

HE QUICKLY RELOADED the gun, and his eyes tried to focus on the lights coming from outside through the upper windows.

He slowly approached Lydia from the right side of the room, which displayed the *Phaistos* disk.

Trying to stifle his footsteps steps against the white and grey colored marble floor was not easy.

"Don't move madame del Biondo. Lift your hands so I can see them," Mark shouted in anger.

"Are you alone? I heard you were talking with someone," Mark inquired aggressively.

"Who are you? Have you been sent here to kill me?" Lydia shouted back.

"I am asking the questions here. You have something in your possession that made the Phoenix kidnap my family."

"If I do not kill you, he warned me that my family will be killed."

"Whys would he do such a thing?" Lydia asked. She was visibly scared.

"The question is, what are you doing here, del Biondo? Tell me now, and there might be a way out for both of us," Mark said in despair.

"I cannot believe that I, as a Senator of the United States, have had to face this tragedy and pay the price for your actions."

Lydia didn't know how to answer. Her eyes were frozen on the gun.

"I am very sorry for your fam…"

She didn't manage to finish her sentence. A series of gunshots could be heard from behind her, taking the Senator by surprise, his gun falling from his hand.

He looked below and could feel his chest was hit by several bullets. Blood began to drip from the corner of his mouth.

His massive muscular body collapsed and hit the marble floor hard. With his last ounce of strength, he whispered: "Please save my family…"and with one final spasm, he let out his last breath.

Lydia went quickly to the Senator and checked his pulse. He was dead. Suddenly she noticed that drone was activated and now flying with fine puffs of smoke coming out.

"Neo, what have you done?"

A message notification came from his pocket. Lydia thought if she took his cell phone, she might find some valuable information.

"You need to exit the building. The noise might have alerted the security guards," Neo instructed.

"Follow the exit signs on your right and take the security door; it will take you to an emergency fire exit at the backdoor," Neo said on high alert.

Lydia was in tears.

Death is not an easy thing to swallow for people who never had to face it. Seeing a life being taken is like a piece of oneself also being killed.

"I am sorry Lydia. I had to do it. I could not put your life in danger. He was pointing a gun to your head," Neo said sadly.

He felt a bitter taste in his mouth.

"Now we are the same. We've both killed someone for the first time."

"He was an American senator. Can you check the database for a face match? Who was he? Why did he want me dead?"

She quickly ran towards the car, where Xenios was patiently waiting for her.

"We need to go to the airport as quickly as possible, please."

"Yes, ma'am, I'll try to hurry."

Lydia was worried that the ankh vial would become unstable. The two days were almost up.

"Neo, do we know how much time we have until the solution will become unstable?"

"Unfortunately, I cannot assess the stability of the compound, but we need to hurry up, everything might depend on how fast we act."

She took the senator's cell phone, and there was a missed call. On the opposite side of the road, several police cars drove past them.

"Neo, can you hack into his cell phone? It seems to have an encryption lock."

The phone started to ring in Lydia's hand.

"Who the hell could it be now?

Lydia answered, "Who is this?"

After a few second pause, she heard:

"I am Simon Lightgood, and who are you?"

"Lydia del Biondo, Mr. Vice President. Helene de Moncler told me that when everything might seem lost, I should contact you in case I needed help."

"And here we are...Lydia, it is so good to hear you are well. I do not know where to begin..." the Vice President said in a worried but warm tone."

"You can begin by explaining to me why a U.S. Senator just tried to kill me."

§CHAPTER 89§

AFTER LANDING in Heraklion Salvatore D'Umbria stared at a red dot.

Lydia is very close. It seems she is approaching the airport.

This is my chance to finally meet her.

I need to warn her about things to come.

What did Helene de Moncler know about the COVID-19 pandemic?

Is Lydia her agent now spreading this mass genocide?

Salvatore knew he had to face the cruel reality, torn between his faith in God and his faith in the Pope.

He didn't feel comfortable in this situation. He checked his chest pocket. It was still there, a pack of his favorite cigarettes, he always kept it, as a reminder of his first love.

He hadn't smoked for ten years. *I need a cigarette so badly right now.*

He gently lifted himself from the leather seat and headed towards the exit.

He thanked the pilot, slowly bowing his head: "It was a great flight, thank you for bringing me here safely."

The moment he exited, the warm breeze and the fresh Mediterranean air engulfed his senses. It would be sacrilege to destroy this feeling by lighting a cigarette.

The urge was too strong. He lit one and deeply inhaled the smoke like it was his last cigarette ever.

The guilty feeling made him realize that what he was doing was wrong.

He extinguished it with his foot and climbed into the limo waiting for him.

I'll wait for her at the entrance of the airport. She should be here at any moment.

"Lydia, I do not know what happened," the Vice President said, puzzled.

"I sent Senator Mark Hopkins to find and try to protect you."

"Helene was not only a dear friend but a fundamental pillar of our Order."

"I swore to protect her from evil, but I failed. I wanted to keep you safe, as I promised to Helene."

"I will always be there if you need help, and I failed again. I don't have any words to express my regret. I cannot understand what happened."

"His family was kidnapped, and I was trying to find them. The Phoenix must have reached him and turned him against us."

"This vicious enemy of The Order wants you so badly that they kidnapped his family in exchange for your life."

"I need to see you urgently; I have so many things to tell, which I cannot do on the phone. Please tell me what I can do to help you in your quest," the Vice President requested.

"What does the Phoenix want from me?"

"I fear that I cannot offer more information right now. It is possible that our conversation might already be compromised by the Phoenix's henchmen."

"The Phoenix has always tried to infiltrate our Order and destroy us, stealing sacred secrets we were entrusted with keeping."

"This entity is thirsty for power, and I am afraid he will not rest until he has accomplished his plan," the Vice President said worriedly.

"You need to let me protect you from this diabolical entity."

"Vice President, I need to go to Jerusalem. I'll take the first flight available, and then I'll come to see you. I only have a few hours to avoid catastrophe."

"I will facilitate your return from Jerusalem. There will be a private jet waiting for you to bring you to New York where we can talk safely."

"You need to protect yourself and your location, my child. Lydia del Biondo, you hold tremendous responsibility now."

"Keep his cell phone, my child, and do not worry about Mark. I'll make everything go away."

"What about his family? Are they well?"

"For the moment, I don't have any news, but I am hoping for the best."

"Thank you, Mr. Vice President. I hope I'll be meeting you very soon."

Neo was surprised by this call. It left Lydia perplexed as well.

"The situation is getting complicated. The Vice President of the U.S. is a member of Helene's Order."

"Helene did say he is the only person I can trust besides you."

"Maybe he knows more about the disappearance of my parents."

"It was not the appropriate moment to ask him that question."

"But, I am sure The Order has more secrets to reveal to us."

§CHAPTER 90§

"WHAT NOW, Neo? Did you manage to find a flight for me?"

"I am afraid that the fastest flight will take off in three hours. We have to hope that it will not be too late."

"But it might take us more than the two days. All of this effort would be wasted in vain," Lydia thought aloud.

Approaching the airport's departures entrance, Lydia noticed a handsome, tall, blondish man frantically waving towards the car.

I think he has the wrong car, Lydia thought and continued to fixate on him.

"Lydia? Lydia del Biondo, I need to talk to you!" he shouted in front of everyone, causing the few tourists in the airport to look at him with strange curiosity.

"Lydia, you should be careful. You don't know

what kind of trap the Phoenix might have set for you," Neo warned.

Salvatore approached the car and said, "Lydia, I have waited so long to meet you."

"I have an important message from his Holiness, the Pope."

"I am Salvatore d'Umbria, his Head of Security, and I need to take you safely to the Vatican."

"I am afraid your life is in danger."

"Unfortunately, I am afraid I cannot come with you, Salvatore."

"I need to first go to Jerusalem, and there is no time to explain."

"I think today is our lucky day," Salvatore said, smiling, showing the dimples in his cheeks and his perfectly white teeth. "God blessed us to be able to find each other."

"The Papal Plane is here and ready to take off. I'll take you to Jerusalem."

"Not only am I a security expert, but I studied in Tel-Aviv, and I can contact a friend of the Church who knows Jerusalem like the back of his hand."

"That's truly an amazing coincidence Salvatore. Please give me a few moments. I'll give you an answer shortly," Lydia said while taking some steps to distance herself.

"He's indeed Salvatore d'Umbria; I just checked the Vatican's database," Neo confirmed.

"But why should we trust them? Remember what Helene said. And if you reveal what you know to them, then the Church might be shattered beyond repair. Their teachings are not only outdated but also erroneous."

"Neo, I have a feeling he genuinely wants to help us. We will save time by going with him, and a papal flight means nobody will ask what I carry in my backpack."

"What if he kidnaps you?"

"Neo, this is our only chance. We need to take a leap of faith; otherwise, if we run out of time, everything we have done will be for nothing."

"I'll accept your offer Salvatore, I believe I can trust you, thank you."

Lydia extended her hand for a friendly shake, and when their hands touched, she had the strange feeling she was taking the right path.

§CHAPTER 91§

SALVATORE SAT in front of Lydia, looking at the plane's white seat covers that had the Pope's coat of arms engraved on them, boasting silver and golden keys.

He thought about the symbolism behind them, the crossed keys unlocking the kingdom of Heaven that belonged to Apostle Peter, the founder of the Holy Church.

One is made of gold, the other of silver to embody the power to bind and loose.

He remembered what Jesus said to Peter. "I will give you the keys of the kingdom of heaven, and whatever you bind on Earth shall be bound in heaven, and whatever you loose on Earth shall be loosed in heaven."

What if Saint Malachy was right and the Pope brings about the end of our world as we know it?

He could not believe that the beautiful creature standing in front of him could bring the Apocalypse. Her eyes evoked kindness and deep wisdom.

"Welcome on board of '*Shepard One*' Lydia. would you like something to drink?" Salvatore gently asked her.

An Alitalia air hostess brought them two *Murano* glasses with fresh water.

While quickly drinking the water, she realized that the *Shepard One* was a plane chartered from Alitalia. The Pope's plane also had a unique assigned flight number: AZ4000.

"Thank you, Salvatore, I was extremely thirsty. My journey has been beyond exhausting."

"Be careful Lydia what you tell him. We are not sure that he can be trusted," Neo was not only doubtful, but the image of Salvatore triggered a little jealousy within him.

"May I ask why we are going to Jerusalem?"

"His Holiness is extremely worried as the world is approaching a humanitarian catastrophe due to this merciless virus."

"He had a discussion with Helene de Moncler, who warned him in case something happened to her, he would need to rely entirely on you."

"Strange Helene never mentioned this discussion to me," Neo said suspiciously.

Or maybe she didn't find the right opportunity before she was killed, Neo thought.

"We are indeed in danger. Someone called the Phoenix has tried to kill me several times."

"The Phoenix, who is this?" Salvatore inquired.

"I don't know...The only thing that's clear is that it wants to stop me from accomplishing my quest to unlock the secrets of this artifact."

She then pulled the ankh vial from her backpack.

Salvatore was mesmerized by the colors shifting inside the glass structure.

"What is it, Lydia? I cannot even recognize some of the colors," Salvatore said, puzzled, staring at the mysterious artifact without blinking, his mouth wide open.

"Neo, we can trust Salvatore. I don't know why but I feel that this is right. We might need his help."

"Salvatore, I was just speaking to Neo, who has been helping me on my quest. I keep close contact with him via my XGlass," Lydia explained.

"When it comes to the artifact, we don't know its purpose; therefore, we are heading to Jerusalem with the hope we'll be able to unlock its secrets."

"As a scientist, I believe that this holds the key

to a long-forgotten technology belonging to the mythical continent of Atlantis."

"Atlantis?" Salvatore exclaimed, his eyes growing wide.

Atlantean legends fascinated him ever since childhood. He read everything possible on the subject.

He could not believe that he was actually holding an artifact the came from the fabled Atlantis.

§CHAPTER 92§

"ATLANTIS!" SALVATORE exclaimed with excitement. "This is really a piece of Atlantean technology?" Salvatore's eyes were glittering with wonder.

"What an incredible discovery, Lydia!"

After an almost ninety-minute flight, the captain announced in a strong Italian accent, "the plane will soon start the landing process into Tel-Aviv."

"I'll tell you all about it, but first, I need to be excused for a few moments." Lydia stood and then hurried towards the toilet.

"Lydia, are you sure you can trust an agent of the Pope?

"What if he was sent here to eliminate you?" Neo asked worriedly.

"I told you, Neo."

We don't have a choice, we only have a few hours left to complete our mission; otherwise, all our efforts will have been in vain."

Salvatore was still trying to grasp what he had seen.

This would be considered a miracle by the Church.

His cell phone started to ring. It was the office of his Holiness.

I cannot answer. What could I tell his Holiness? He would not understand.

Lydia needs my help.

I don't know why, but I cannot believe she is the one to bring about the apocalypse.

Without any hesitation, he switched off his cell phone, a gesture that even surprised himself.

His mind was clear, and he could see the truth.

Lydia didn't tell him everything. She didn't reveal the information Helene passed to her about Jesus' origins and the clues he left behind.

She could still not trust a religious man with these secretes. People tend to become unstable when all their beliefs and the entire fabric of their reality is dismantled…

Salvatore stared through the window, almost

expecting a divine storm to strike the plane down and to be punished for disobeying the orders of his Holiness.

He recruited the plane's pilots and had no doubt where their allegiance resided.

He already informed them they should not accept any incoming calls from the Vatican as this would compromise their mission.

His Holiness has to be kept in the dark on the outcome of his mission. At least for now...

§CHAPTER 93§
22:12, OCTOBER 3_{RD}
ISRAEL, TEL-AVIV

THE *BEN GURION* airport was famous for its zero-tolerance policy against security threats and was renowned for its level of control and surveillance.

The Vatican diplomatic traveling documents opened many gates and helped them pass through the VIP security check. Salvatore had to pull strings from some old friends.

The security guards saluted the limousine bearing the Vatican flags. They had no idea that it was Lydia and not the Pope sitting conformably in the back seat.

Salvatore knew they needed to make it across the city quickly, so he called for some local assistance.

"Lydia, I would like to present to you, Elijah, a

Vatican agent, working for the Apostolic Nuncio to Israel, our Embassy equivalent."

"He kindly offered to drive us to the *Garden of Gethsemane.*"

"Thank you so much, Elijah, it's very kind of you to drive us at such a late hour."

Lydia was enchanted by the ancient buildings around the main road. They looked like ready to collapse, but at the same time, prepared to endure any suffering mother nature might bring.

"What do you think will happen in the *Garden of Gethsemane*?" Salvatore asked Lydia, who was looking outside the window.

She was mulling over the interpretation of the ankh vial inscription:

> **"Here is the secret vault of old days,
> in Gethsemane, you'll find the tree
> of life, and as you plant this seed,
> if the secret word is chanted, the
> eternal life shall be forever yours."**

Will we reach the holy site on time? Lydia wondered. *How will all this end?*

Words of warning were echoing in her mind as well:

> **"If you remove the potion of the
> Gods, you have two sunset cycles
> before the Grail will be destroyed."**

"Salvatore, I am extremely worried as a geneticist at what is happening with our world. Nobody knows if the virus will genetically mutate or if a vaccine will be developed in time.

"However, I have a gut feeling that everything is linked: the artifact, the virus, and the garden."

"I need to go alone in the garden, and it is essential that nobody disturbs me. There have been so many attempts to kill me, and we are almost out of time."

"Lydia, I anticipate you have less than two hours left," Neo said nervously.

While the Limo was approaching their destination, Lydia spotted blue road signs with white letters marking the entry to the city in Hebrew, Arabic, and English:

מִירְלָשָׁוּּרְיָ

ميلشروا

Jerusalem

Salvatore noticed it too, "This ancient city with its dusty streets always fascinated me."

"I can only imagine how much blood was spilled across millennia in the name of God," Salvatore said to Lydia with a deep sadness in his eyes.

"Did God want all these religious wars in the name of faith?" Lydia inquired.

"I cannot answer that, Lydia, but look at the *Dome of the Rock*'s golden cupola, the sacred shrine located on the Temple Mount in the Old City of Jerusalem."

Lydia gazed at the shiny structure, which was peering out from the landscape formed from diverse sizes houses and buildings, which seemed arranged based on a secrete codified masterplan by a mad architect.

Salvatore continued. "This site is of crucial importance as it is built on the former site of Solomon's Temple, also known as the First Temple, where worshipers would witness ritualic sacrifices and also housed the fabled *Ark of the Covenant.*"

"I can tell you that the Ark is not stored in the secret vaults of the Vatican, nor are other powerful artifacts. These were just myths spread by different Popes in the past, as a sign of divine power."

"So many religions come here to find enlightenment and to step where their savior and messiah once preached."

"Everyone deserves to believe in the force of good," Salvatore concluded.

"We are approaching the Mount of Olives,

which is located to the east of Jerusalem," Elijah informed after patiently listening to their discussion.

"It acts as a barrier between the Holy City and the Judean Desert, which from that point, heads down towards the Dead Sea."

"Jerusalem is encircled by the Kidron Valley with Mount Zion located to the south, where Jesus started his journey after the Last Supper."

"He traversed this valley on foot to reach his final destination of Gethsemane," Elijah continued in perfect English.

"Thank you, Elijah. I knew I can count on you," Salvatore said, full of excitement.

Lydia felt her backpack frantically vibrating.

She looked inside and noticed the fluid's movement was speeding up.

"I am afraid we'll not make it, Neo," Lydia whispered.

"Don't be afraid, simply believe in your destiny, and you will succeed."

"I believe in you, my love," Neo whispered back, realizing he must have spoken those last words loudly, possibly causing Lydia to be shocked.

§CHAPTER 94§
23:07, GETHSEMANE GARDEN

THE CAR ABRUPTLY stopped in front of a stone wall. Adorned above the entrance were the words:

HORTVUS GETHSEMANI

The garden located on the Mount of Olives stood next to the *Church of All Nations,* also known as the *Basilica of Agony*, housing the rock where Jesus presumably prayed in agony while tormented by the thought of what would happen to him.

Lydia remembered from her religion classes the words of the *Apostle Matthew.*

"Jesus threw himself on the ground with his sweat becoming drops of blood."

The night was cold, and the vial was frantically vibrating; the colors turning on and off abruptly.

Elijah showed his badge to an elderly man who was guarding the place, and he let Lydia pass without any questions asked.

"I will wait for you here, Lydia."

"Good luck!" Salvatore said, waving from the car.

He wanted to join her. There was a magnetic attraction that was almost irresistible.

But he had to call his Holiness. His quest had to be completed one way or another.

This confrontation could not be avoided any longer.

§CHAPTER 95§

STRANGELY THERE was a hot breeze circulating among the ancient olive trees. *Is this my epiphanal moment, like when Jesus prayed before being taken prisoner?*

She could sense a strange but pleasant odor coming from the olive trees.

"What should I do next, Neo?"

"I think you need to find one of the oldest trees which must have a mark."

"Gethsemane literally means oil press from Aramaic: Gad-Šmānê, ܓܕܣܡܢܐ. A long time ago, these trees were used to produce oil," Neo explained, hoping one day he would revisit this place together with Lydia.

"You are very knowledgeable as always, my love," Lydia answered back.

Neo blushed, and his heart began to pound...

Is she mocking me, or is she really in love?

I cannot ask her this yet; it's not the right moment.

Get a grip, Neo. Focus on what it's at stake.

"But which one is the oldest?" Lydia asked, feeling lost among the numerous trees.

"Nobody knows their real age. Studies have found that all trees have the same genetic marker, and were originally formed from the same sprout," Neo answered while exploring different websites.

"When a tree is hollow inside, it is difficult to tell its age. It could be that some sprang from much more ancient roots."

Was she walking the same steps as Juda did millennia ago?

At least she had to be sure this was the right place. It seemed that something was happening; the vial started to vibrate rapidly.

"Neo, will it explode?"

"I can detect an increase in the temperature of the device; it's currently at 412^{0}C. Indeed, it is becoming hotter. The last time I checked, it was at 250^{0}C."

"Will it trigger a meltdown?"

"How did it last for so long?" She was sure it was powered by a nuclear power source, maybe even nuclear fission.

"Imagine if this technology could have been replicated. Free energy for everyone."

"Great idea Lydia. Let's take it step by step."

Lydia was repeating in her mind the last clue:

> *"Here is the secret vault of old days,*
> *in Gethsemane, you'll find the tree*
> *of life, and as you plant this seed,*
> *if the secret word is chanted, the*
> *eternal life shall be forever yours."*

"We have the secret word from the Heraklion Museum. We just need to find the right tree. But there are so many..."

§CHAPTER 96§

SALVATORE DID not know what to do. Would his Holiness understand what he had just witnessed? Everything was hanging by a thread...

"Elijah, I need you to keep everything that happened here a secret. Nobody should ever know that we have ever been here."

"His Holiness has sent us here to do God's work. Do you understand?"

"Yes, Sir, you can always trust me."

"I don't want to question your decisions, but are you sure it's a clever idea to leave a woman alone at this hour?"

"Don't worry, Elijah, I am sure Lydia can take excellent care of herself."

"Sir, I need to leave you a few moments. I think I had too much tea before," Elijah said calmly.

"I also would love a cigarette, but I promised

I'll abstain. Or maybe not."

Elijah exited the car and went behind the garden wall, asking the guard in Hebrew for instructions to the restroom.

The garden had an inner metallic fence that during the day would allow tourists to admire the ancient olive trees without being able to touch them.

But this fence was nothing compared to the external tall stone walls supplemented by additional metallic spikes to block any intruders.

Inside the garden it was pitch black. Neo activated the XGlass' lights, but Lydia had another idea.

She took out the ankh vial, whose various shades of light were splashing around violently.

Lydia jumped the fence and looked around for any signs of the sacred tree of life.

The garden had several straight inner paths made of white pebble stones. She was reminded of holidays she spent in her childhood on the Mediterranean Sea with her mom and dad beside her running along sunny shores to catch little crabs lost on the beach.

All these were distant memories now.

"I am sure the guard would have a meltdown if

he saw that I jumped over the fence," Lydia said in a naughty tone.

Looking to her right, Lydia noticed the illuminated golden dome of the Temple Mount. But something else caught her attention.

There was a faint violet light coming from the trunk of one of the olive trees, and it seemed to be absorbing the ankh's spark.

§CHAPTER 97§

THE CLOSER LYDIA approached, the more intense the light from the trunk became.

In the middle of the trunk, there was a deep hollow area.

Lydia peered inside, and she was surprised to

discover a metallic cylinder was rising up from the ground.

At its top was the flower of life shape; the whole of it vibrating. The outer rings intertwined into organic movement giving the impression it was alive.

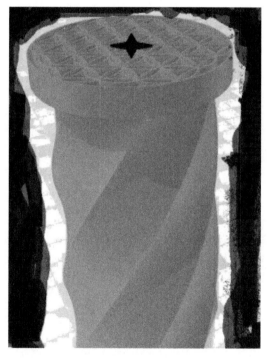

Lydia felt her chest growing tight as bile rose to her throat. She could not believe that her quest was nearing its end.

"Try placing the vial inside the cylinder," Neo said, while frantically typing a line of code for an algorithm he just wrote.

He was trying to understand if there was a pattern in the pulsation of the light.

Lydia bent herself over the hollow and placed the vial inside, leaving visible only the external parts of the round-shaped upperpart of the ankh.

She then said with a loud voice:

KERANANAKEJE

It fit perfectly, but nothing happened. There was no change in the pattern of the light.

"Neo, am I doing something wrong? It doesn't seem to be working."

"I think both the objects together actually form the Grail. This is an epic discovery," Lydia exclaimed.

"I calculated that the light has a movement pattern: every three seconds, the sequence repeats."

"I think you must recite the secret word precisely at the start of the pattern."

"Try to place your hands on the ankh. When you said the word before, there was a slight energy burst, and the vibration dislodged it."

"I'll tell you exactly when."

Lydia took a deep breath and waited.

"Now," Neo exclaimed.

She touched the vial again and chanted the secret word.

The contents began to calm, turning to a silverfish color. The rings of the flower of life stopped moving.

She felt a strange energy protruding through her body. She felt revigorated, and then there was just pure darkness, a complete nothingness.

§CHAPTER §98

"LYDIA, ARE YOU OKAY?" Neo asked in desperation, but there was no answer.

She seemed frozen in time, paralyzed like a statue looking at the same point without the slightest movement.

Neo then understood that something went wrong.

Just before screaming to her, in hopes it would jolt her to life, he heard a loud bang. It likely came from a gun, and he feared the worst.

Lydia snapped out of it and lifted her hands from the ankh vial, which now remained inert.

Turning around, she saw Elijah several meters in front of her collapsed on the stony path with his body convulsing uncontrollably.

His hands were wrapped around his neck, trying to stop the blood from hemorrhaging.

His hand tried to reach a gun that fell next to him, but another shot hit his hand, and he recoiled in pain.

"Lydia, you have to hurry up," Salvatore said, putting his gun back into his suit.

"I am afraid our location has been compromised. Elijah just tried to kill you."

"I do not know who to trust anymore."

"I cannot believe that his Holiness would be capable of such a deed," Salvatore muttered to himself.

Lydia grabbed the now inert ankh vial and started to approach Salvatore.

"Are you okay my love? I thought you were shot." Neo said desperately.

"So, the driver wanted to kill you and the Phoenix is not giving up?" Neo asked worried that the entire situation was out of his control.

"We have to go to New York. I need my lab to understand what just happened to me."

"I hope there I can make some kind of discovery to share with the world."

"The Vice President is our only chance. We need to contact him," Lydia said, full of hope.

§CHAPTER 99§
VATICAN

"WHAT HAVE I done?"

"Haven't I already sacrificed so much for you, God?" the Pope whispered lamenting.

"All my life, I've tried to serve You, and now to have a failure of this magnitude, it is inconceivable."

"I pray that Salvatore is not dead. I refuse to believe he could have betrayed me. It's beyond my understanding how this situation has escalated to such a level. The entire world is suffering from this cruel plague."

"So many dead people are filling our morgues and cemeteries. In some countries, there are more victims than in World War I."

"Is this virus the way to punish me and my failure to save humanity?"

"Our Church has failed You, God, and we deserve to be punished."

"In the end, I must be the one Saint Malachy was referring to."

"I was blinded by the glory of this holy office."

"I failed to see the truth in front of my eyes…"

§CHAPTER 100§

LYDIA STILL felt dizzy. She was trying to understand what has happened to her.

Something was not normal. She felt a small tingling sensation all over her body.

It was a feeling similar to sun exposure in search of the perfect tan. Your slightly burned skin will try to regenerate, and the old skin peels away to make way for the new skin.

"Neo, I have to get to my lab quickly to test my blood."

"I feel something is happening to me, and I cannot explain it."

"In the hollow of the tree, the ankh vial reacted to my touch in a way I would have never expected."

"Salvatore, will you drive me back to the airport?"

"I just contacted the Vice President for his kind offer to fly me to New York."

"I am sure he will help me find a lab where I can perform some tests on myself."

Salvatore looked at her while his arm wrapped around her waist. He answered without even blinking.

"Of course, Lydia. I want to see you safe, and for the moment, I cannot trust the Pope."

"I'll have to fly back to the Vatican and clear up this entire mess."

"What did you discover in the tree's hollow?"

"I do not know exactly what happened, but I want you to take the ankh vial to his Holiness, which I believe, together with the device inside the hollow, represents the Holy Grail."

"Show it to him and explain the situation."

Lydia explained to him the origins of Jesus and his Atlantean heritage.

Salvatore seemed hypnotized by Lydia's words, and he felt that everything made sense now, *this information will change everything...*

"I feel so weak, it was like all my energy has been drained. I need to rest."

Lydia collapsed in his arms, to the shock of both Salvatore and Neo.

§CHAPTER 101§

THE PHOENIX knew he had one last opportunity to obtain the information Lydia possessed.

The death of his faithful servants and his inability to stop Lydia del Biondo clouded his mind and was slowly enraging him.

I'll kill her myself. How could they have all failed so miserably?

I should never have underestimated her. She was so lucky, but someone was protecting and guiding her every step.

Maybe even God was punishing me for my defiance.

I am the real Savior. I am the one Jesus Christ entrusted all his secrets. I won't let a simple girl destroy everything I've built.

He closed his eyes, and he finally saw a path, a potential outcome where he could still succeed. Church bells were ringing, and then it all became clear to him.

This was an ominous sign, as when I started my journey.

Every beginning has an end. The secret is to have the capacity to write your own fate.

I am the Phoenix, always reborn, emerging stronger than ever before.

§CHAPTER 102§

NEO WAS SPEECHLESS, but the fact that he did not have any power to help Lydia was driving him mad. He felt frail and could barely move his hands. His breathing was also becoming heavier.

Neo's biggest regret was not being able to tell Lydia again how much he loved her. The beat of her heart was reverberating through his mind.

If only I could put my head next to your heart to feel it next to my skin…Is this the end? Neo's mind was a field or war.

I could have never imagined that this moment would come so fast, Salvatore thought.

He checked Lydia's pulse and took comfort that despite being weak, she was holding on.

Perfect timing. Just when Lydia needs me the most, she turns to Salvatore. Am I going to die alone? Neo was feeling dreadful.

Her video flow was still active, and he could see Salvatore's hands carrying her past the sleeping guard who didn't realize what had just happened in the sacred garden.

Salvatore gingerly opened the car door and lay Lydia on the back seats.

Neo could see the starry sky through the transparent roof as Salvatore drove off to the airport.

He started to have even more difficulty breathing. *I need my oxygen*. He tried to move from his screen towards the storeroom, where he kept a reserve tube.

Slowly moving his fingers on the wheelchair's electric pad, he thought he heard a noise coming from one of the balconies.

It was already too late; several masked people broke through the glass.

Neo didn't even have the chance to utter a word before one of the masked figures shot him.

He felt a sharp pain in his right shoulder, and then he completely lost consciousness. From the back of the room, he briefly heard a distorted voice speaking through the breathing apparatus of the mask. "We have him! The target is acquired."

The last thought that crossed his mind was: *Will I ever hear Lydia's voice again?*

And then everything went dark...

§CHAPTER 103§
01:23, OCTOBER 4ᴛʜ

THE CAR STOPPED in front of a private charter plane as Simon Lightgood promised. It was fueled and ready to depart for New York.

"Lydia, we have arrived," Salvatore said, gently shaking her.

She woke and gave him a scared look, "What happened? Where are we?"

"You fainted; I think the experience in the garden took a bigger toll on your body than expected."

"We are at the airport. Your plane to New York is awaiting you."

"I don't have any words. How can I thank you Salvatore? You saved my life, and for this, I will be forever grateful."

She touched his arm, and he felt a strange connection. It was like he had always known her.

When their eyes met, it was as if their bodies' molecules were fusing together, their minds and emotions becoming one.

"You can always count on me, Lydia del Biondo. We shall meet again," Salvatore said with a charming smile.

Lydia exited the car graciously. She was still exhausted but, at the same time, felt energized by the things to come—so many mysteries to discover and the ones she carried inside herself.

"Neo, I am boarding the plane to New York. Are you there? Please answer, Neo."

She tried several times and then gave up.

His signal was active, but she could not see anything besides a dark screen with a faint reflection.

This is not normal. He never left me like this.

Something must have happened. Dark thoughts crossed her mind while the plane door closed behind her.

§CHAPTER 104§

ARRIVING IN the plane, she could only think about Neo's fate.

Lydia tried again to contact him but couldn't. She had nobody to turn to. Maybe the Vice President would be able to help her by contacting the secret service to find out what happened to Neo.

I don't even know where he was living. In order not to compromise his location, she never asked where he was located.

She was still trying to grasp her experience in Gethsemane.

Was this what the religious scholars would have called an epiphanal experience?

She refused any service. She could not eat or drink, nor did she feel the need. Oddly enough, she felt full.

But it was due to worry and anxiety after trying one more time to reach Neo but failing.

Instead, she felt the need to purge herself. The private jet came with its shower cubicle and the softest towels she had ever felt. There were also *Caudalie* cosmetic products based on natural ingredients sourced from grapes.

While in contact with the water molecules, her skin seemed refreshed, absorbing the humidity voraciously.

After dressing herself with her last change of fresh clothes purchased back in Cairo, she collapsed on the expandable leather seat.

I hope to see you again Neo Moore, she closed her eyes and fell in a deep, dreamless sleep.

Suddenly she heard a familiar deep voice that had guided her for so many years, a voice that inspired power.

"My child, you have to be brave once again. You have accomplished the unimaginable. I am so proud of you, however, be…"

Suddenly she opened her eyes but was pulled back by a strange force. The voice of Helene vanished, but its echo was still reverberating in her head.

"Helene, Helene, I need your help," Lydia gasped and then realized that a flight attendant was standing above her.

"Ma'am, are you okay? "

"We didn't want to bother you, but you were talking in your sleep. It didn't seem like a pleasant dream either. Please drink this glass of water with fresh lime juice. It will help."

"Your limo is already waiting for you."

"We landed ten minutes ago at the JFK airport in New York," the flight attendant said in a troubled tone.

Lydia looked around and noticed that indeed her seat belt was still strapped on. She opened it and lifted herself out.

Her mind was foggy and her soul in pain. *I need to hurry up, and there is still no message from Neo...*

§CHAPTER 105§
NEW YORK

HEADING TOWARDS the exit, she thanked the staff. When stepping out of the plane, she was struck by the sweetness of the first sunshine caressing her face.

It was a beautiful October morning, and the sun's heat pleasantly warmed her body.

She could see in the corner of her XGlass, a temperature of 17^0C, abnormally hot for this time of year.

The entire planet was going through a profound yet subtle transformation.

Pollution levels collapsed across continents as countries tried to mitigate the spread of the virus.

In front of the red carpet, at the end of the plane staircase, a white-gloved driver dressed in a dark suit was holding the door to a black Maybach Exelero limo.

She stepped inside and was surprised by the minimalistic interior with plasma screens presenting sad news all over the world.

"Ma'am, would you like to drink something, or would you prefer I switch off the screens?" the driver politely asked.

"I am fine, thank you. For a few days, I disconnected from the entire situation. You can leave the screens on."

The news was, indeed worrying. In a matter of a few weeks, the entire planet was completely altered. All over the world, streets were deserted as authorities took aggressive confinement strategies.

Most industries, including some transport networks and businesses, had to shut down. Lydia could feel the effects of lower levels of pollution.

The air had an almost unnatural freshness, and she could see on her display that for New York, greenhouse gases had been reduced by nearly half due to the measures to contain the virus.

She had an eerie sensation seeing one of the world's biggest cities abandoned to such an extent.

It was as if the entire city was inside an action

thriller where all of humanity vanished.

"We are almost there," the driver announced while passing the luxurious entrance of the *Le Meridien* hotel, which seemed abandoned.

The entrance of 111 West 57th Street seemed impenetrable and warmly welcomed a private and sheltered *porte cochère,* providing covered access to the building.

Imposing urn chandeliers, rustic grey granite flooring, and intricate door work inspired by the bronze filigree adorned the building's exterior.

At the entrance, a friendly valet opened the door for her.

"It was a pleasure driving you; I wish you a good day, ma'am," the driver said.

Lydia went out and thanked him.

The entrance was guarded by two Secret service officers.

"Welcome, madame del Biondo, the Vice President was informed of your arrival. He is expecting you."

§CHAPTER 106§

SIMON LIGHTGOOD was peering down again at the Central Park Obelisk. His pupils were dilated, and he seemed paralyzed by an invisible force.

He was boiling inside.

His entire life's achievements seemed to vanish like the morning fog under the sunrise. The news was grim.

The President of the United States was still on life support due to COVID-19.

The weight on his shoulders was almost unbearable for anyone.

What would you do if you were in my place? the Vice President asked himself while staring again at the ancient structure.

The building's internal lobby was decorated with the same warm cream stone, opulently styled with golden metallic rods. At its center it was decorated by a pot on a pedestal from which several exotic golden palm leaves were standing tall.

Lydia entered the private elevator, and the receptionist sitting behind an amber marble desk pushed a button that activated the elevator.

"The elevator will take you directly to the private quarters of the Vice President."

Lydia felt hopeful. She sensed so much goodness in Vice President's voice.

"Helene trusted him blindly, and he provided the help I needed."

The elevator was ascending fast, and the great height revealed a beautiful morning across Central Park, the glorious sight projected on the screens embedded into the wall.

I cannot get enough of this view. It's so peaceful. A green island in the middle of all this glass and steel, Lydia reflected.

I need to better understand what happened to me. Maybe The Order will have answers to my questions.

"In the next few seconds we'll arrive at the Ember floor. Mister Lightgood is waiting for you in the lobby," informed the Vice President's A.I.

assistant.

The doors swung open precisely when the sunrise was at its peak.

"Reduce luminosity by forty percent," Simon gently whispered, and the penthouse's windows instantly tinted.

"Come in, Lydia. I must apologize. I am afraid my eyes are not so young anymore and I am rather sensitive to light."

"Welcome. I was waiting for you. we have so much to discuss."

"Thank you so much, Mr. Vice President."

"Nonsense, my dear Lydia, please call me Simon."

"You must be exhausted after all this traveling. Would you like something to eat or drink ?"

She sensed a heavy but pleasant scent of musk and sandalwood floating through the air. There was also a familiar fragrance she could not immediately pinpoint, but then she suddenly recognized what it was: the light scent of honeysuckle.

§CHAPTER 107§

"Look what is happening around the world," Lightgood said with a sad voice, pointing towards various projections on the windows of the beautiful modern penthouse.

A large majority of countries were choosing to close their borders, wreaking havoc on global markets.

In New York, the numbers of dead were climbing at a rapid pace with a total of more than 29.000 victims, close to a third of the total across the country.

More than two million people were infected in the U.S. with many more asymptomatic carriers as well.

People were not respecting the temporary home confinement that was put in place to relieve pressure on the world's healthcare systems, which could not cope with the growing number of infections and victims.

"Where are we heading Lydia, do you think this world can continue as it is?" he asked with his voice full of sorrow.

"Mr. Vice President, I would first need your help. My friend Neo Moore just vanished, and I am afraid something happened to him," Lydia said embarrassed by having to interrupt the Vice President of the United States.

The Vice President seemed to ignore her question and continued to look at the apocalyptic breaking news.

He suddenly turned to Lydia and asked her, "Should we thank God once again for purifying this planet of the weak and unworthy ones, making a place for a new generation of stronger humans who will help humanity evolve?"

"It's incredible how humanity didn't learn anything from the Spanish flu pandemic only a hundred years ago."

He turned his back to her and looked at his favorite spot in Central Park.

The situation in New York seemed hopeless.

"All the battles I fought have brought me to this very moment."

"All the greed in the world could not satisfy the greed of the richest, who controlled the biotechnology corporations, exploiting those in need and selling antibiotics and seasonal vaccines."

"Of course, there was no interest in developing a universal vaccine when the field is so lucrative."

"Neo is fine, you don't have to worry. You'll meet him soon. He is in good hands."

Lydia seemed puzzled at what the Vice President was saying.

"My child, you brought to me the most precious gift: the last trace Jesus Christ left for his grandiose plan of elevating humanity."

"The simple truth is that humanity is not ready for such a challenge."

"I have endured more than two millennia and was reborn."

"As Apostle Simon Peter, I served Jesus."

"He didn't heed my advice; humanity was not ready for the ultimate gift."

"The Church elevated me to Saint Peter, the first Pope, the builder of Christianity, and I will decide its fate."

"And I say let it be purged."

§CHAPTER 108§

THE APOSTLE PETER turned to a mortified Lydia, who was starting to understand what was happening.

"You see, Jesus gave me the gift of immortality. I never died. I always waited in the shadows for the right time to come, but the more I waited, the more disillusioned I became."

"I was symbolically crucified, a simple ritual to be purified. In his madness, I did not manage to stop Emperor Nero from purging Rome by fire, but that event was truly epiphanic and made me reborn as the Phoenix, his most trustful advisor."

"Eventually, I pushed him to die by suicide."

"I also had to kill Helene to protect Jesus' secret. She started to inquire how she could trace and put together the clues he left, which my order guarded for more than two thousand years. I made a mistake selecting her and giving her so much power."

"But now, this is just the past, and I should focus on the future."

"You see that obelisk below. It is everything for me. I have managed to bring it here."

"I sensed that you are in love with this Neo. Your voice betrayed your feelings when you mentioned him."

"I was as well once. She is still inside the obelisk," Apostle Peter said, turning towards Lydia with a silencer gun aimed at her heart.

"No need to struggle, my child. You played your role, and all the secrets will die together with you and your beloved Neo," Apostle Peter bellowed, revealing the diabolical voice of the Phoenix.

He pointed towards his dark onyx desk, which seamlessly integrated a translucent screen showing a confined and sad Neo in his wheelchair connected to a breathing machine.

"Do not worry, I'll make sure his death will be as swift as yours."

The bullet pierced Lydia's heart with a muffled sound, and she collapsed on the floor.

"I could not let you undermine my entire work."

"What de Moncler did not know is that only I

had the final piece of Jesus' device."

"All your efforts were futile, my child."

"Your parents started this quest against me, and they also cleverly escaped too many times."

"But there is no escape from the grasp of the Phoenix."

He calmly put the gun on his black onyx desk and looked again at Central Park.

"Don't fight the pain, my child, embrace it... and everything will be gone in a few seconds."

Lydia's pain was so excruciating that she could not even utter a word, and then she felt her life essence fading away...

He also killed my parents...

Mom, dad...Neo, I am so sorry I could not save you... her thoughts were blurring and then there was only darkness.

§CHAPTER 109§
VATICAN, SISTINE CHAPEL

"SALVATORE, WHAT have you done? I thought something happened to you."

"Have you betrayed me?" the Pope lashed out, his eyes bulging from his skull turning red.

"There are enemies of the Church everywhere."

"Your Holiness, I met with Lydia. So many things happened; I didn't know who to trust."

"You were right, she will play a unique role as a servant to the Church."

"She revealed to me a secret that will shatter the foundation of Christianity and all religions."

"Saint Malachy was right; you will indeed bring change, but it is up to you if it will help humanity or not."

"Rome has already fallen, ruined by the virus outbreak."

The Pope was listening carefully to his wise words, looking at him with calm and compassion.

"Did you try to assassinate Lydia?" Salvatore asked, despite risking infuriating the Pope even more.

"I need to know; otherwise, she might be in grave danger," Salvatore said.

"My son, I would never hurt Lydia. She changed my entire life since the moment I met her. I sent you to find and try to stop her if she was going to endanger us and the Church."

"Your Holiness, you know very well the Church is already beyond repair."

"This is our last chance to save it."

"Helene was trying to warn you."

"This is an artifact Lydia discovered in Egypt," Salvatore said while holding the ankh vial in his hand.

"It is of Atlantean origins. Jesus was a descendant of Atlantis and possessed knowledge beyond the grasp of any civilization during that time."

"He was immortal like his parents. This is why there is no recording of their death. Actually, nobody knows what happened to Mary and Joseph.

They simply vanished."

The Pope froze when he heard the entire story.

He could still not decide if these claims were simply a blasphemy or the truth.

His eyes fell upon the golden ankh vial, solid proof and a piece of Atlantis.

"Let me hold it, my son," he said wrapping his hands around the artifact and then started reading the Aramaic inscription on the back.

The moment he touched it, he felt a strange vibration dissipating through his old body. For a moment, a faint spark ignited inside the vial.

"You are right, my son; I need to sit down. It was as if divinity peered back to me."

The Pope felt dizzy and sat on one of his velvety, curved wooden armchairs pondering at what he should do next.

"I cannot summon the College of Cardinals. There are so many who are still beyond conservative. When they will hear what I have to say, they will think I am mad!" the Pope lamented. "Our followers need to know the truth. What would you have me do Salvatore? How can we tell the truth without shattering their faith?"

"Your Holiness, the ankh vial device possesses an unknown technology that has been powered for millennia, and I think Lydia has still many secrets to reveal."

"She is now with the Vice President of the United States who is The Order's Supreme Grand Master."

"I am sure she will come back to me. Lydia is a brilliant, kindhearted geneticist who might even find a cure for the COVID-19 virus."

"I have a feeling we should trust her, as she still has an import role to play in this entire story, and will likely decide our fate."

§CHAPTER 110§

APOSTLE PETER was looking towards the Obelisk again, whispering.

"We shall be reunited one day, my soul will always be yours," he gently whispered.

"I'll have to purge this world again as Nero has done with Rome, and then I'll bring you back to rule next to myself."

His piercing eyes were unraveling all the events which started his epic journey to reach this moment."

"You didn't listen to me, Jesus."

"We could have ruled this world and revive the lost Atlantean civilization."

"You forced me to do unimaginable things."

"I begged you to reconsider, but you were blind by the faith of your worshipers."

"So naïve in thinking that humans could

understand the ultimate gift you wanted them to have."

"They are not ready even now after millennia of technologic evolution."

"The Phoenix has to show them again the way."

"Look how they behave locked in their petty squabble."

"There is no other way than..."

The window in front of him suddenly turned red with his brains, and blood splashed all over.

He didn't even realize what happened.

§CHAPTER 111§

LYDIA WAS STANDING in front of the Phoenix's corpse, who had collapsed on the floor.

Her mind was still racing trying to process all the information of the last several minutes: Simon Lightgood was, in fact, Apostle Peter and the same person chasing her—the Phoenix.

Lydia, you need to finish him, she said to herself, trying to gather courage.

He cannot have the same chance as you to regenerate, realizing she had to act rapidly.

This would be my second kill. I didn't want to take this path, but you didn't give me any choice.

"You killed my parents, and you are a monster ready to obliterate most of humanity," she uttered while noticing that his blown eye socket was slowly reconstituting itself.

She touched her leather jacket, which now had a perfect bloody round hole as the bullet pierced her heart and cleanly exited on the other side.

She could still feel the ripples of the pain. Now she finally understood what happened in Gethsemane. The ankh must have enhanced her immune system and given her the capacity to regenerate extremely quickly.

Deep inside, she could still feel tingling as if her wound was still healing itself.

In her mind, there were so many ideas related to hemostasis and proliferation remodeling phases of how platelets aggregate together to secrete the factors that recruited other immune cells and ultimately healed herself so quickly.

She had to act immediately. Looking around, she grabbed an alabaster orb the Phoenix had kept on his office desk. She dropped it over his head and shattered his skull.

She was, at the same time, horrified by her gesture, but she was acting in self-defense.

He could not be allowed to survive as his power was too great. She would never get a second chance like this.

She didn't know her actions could be so harsh, but this was for Helene and especially her parents.

Where is Neo? What could he be keeping him?

She looked at the desk screen and saw Neo almost collapsed in a small room. Next to the image, there was a digital menu with several control buttons.

She randomly pushed a few, and behind the desk, a secret wall mechanism activated and revealed a hidden chamber. Lydia quickly ran towards the opening and found Neo unconscious.

Next to him, there was a terrified young woman who was holding two children; *they must be the family of Mark Hopkins*, Lydia realized.

Suddenly the voice of the Vice President's A.I. assistant announced gravely: "Security alert. Critical medical emergency."

And in the next several seconds, security forces stormed inside...and were left perplexed by the scene unraveling before their eyes.

§EPILOGUE§
VATICAN, THE POPE'S OFFICE

POPE PETER II and Salvatore were watching the extraordinary press conference hosted by the newly elected President of the European Commission, who had Lydia and Neo next to her.

This was live-streamed on most of the world's media. Its importance was similar to that of the first humans reaching the moon in 1969.

The Breaking News caption announced: "While trying to find a cure for the COVID-19 virus Belgian Geneticist Lydia del Biondo and her research partner Neo Moore, discovered a universal cure for any viral infection by exponentially enhancing the reaction capacity of the human immune system. The treatment *Graal2020* consists of a single-dose vaccine shot."

"You were right, Salvatore; she was the key to

our salvation, and now is the moment to start a new era and face the College of Cardinals," a profoundly emotional Pope said with his eyes in tears.

Lydia asked the Pope to make the announcement himself while pleading for a global ceasefire, as humanity would step into a new era of *Hominis Immortalis*.

The Cardinals were frowning in their places, filling the Sistine Chapel with loud chatter.

"My brothers, please a moment of silence. You have probably seen the news from one hour ago," the Pope paused for a second, looking directly at the most conservative Cardinals.

"Our Church was based on a lie."

"Jesus wanted another path. Lydia del Biondo, the scientist who found the cure, used this artifact to extract the knowledge our savior, Jesus Christ tried to bestow upon us millennia ago but was stopped by the forces of evil, hungry for power."

"I have decided that all the churches around the world will be temporarily converted to hospitals where the cure will be freely distributed to anyone in need."

Most of the Cardinals' faces were frozen. The elderly ones were even refusing to try and understand what the Pope was saying.

"Make no mistake; I truly believe Saint Malachy's prophecy was true; God bless him."

"He was right, and God spoke through him, as he did through Jesus."

"The Church will be transformed from this day forward."

"The ultimate gift that Jesus had to offer and which I will announce in the next hour is immortality. The treatment not only heals any disease, it also allows a constant rejuvenation at the cellular level."

"It is a miracle that happened only through the will of God and Jesus."

TWO HOURS LATER

The Pope looked up at the Sistine Chapel ceiling and voiced his worries.

"God, I was wrong; I doubted Lydia's intentions, and this could have cost us everything, causing us to miss the greatest chance for humanity to evolve."

"I am not worthy of being the Pope anymore. Should I resign?"

"I need your holy guidance to gather force and reform the Church in this new era of humanity."

"Since Adam and Eve were banned from the

Garden of Eden, they have never witnessed such a level of power. Will they use it wisely?"

"Alea iacta est," a voice said. It was coming from a dark cloaked figure standing next to the altar.

The Pope raised his eyes from his prayer and was startled by the deep voice, which sounded both familiar and comforting.

"Pietro, you are the embodiment of God on Earth; use this power for the greater good."

"You need to convince the servants of the Church to reform it from within. Break the silos. Transform the churches into centers to enlighten the people."

"Help them to cope with the idea of immortality. Break all the chains and try to make peace among all religions."

"You have the chance to reshape this world."

"Our struggle is not yet at an end, as more forces of the evil which lurk in the dark will try to stop you."

"Nobody is ready to quickly give up all the power they managed to amass," the feminine voice said.

The woman came closer to the Pope and started to take off her hood. The Pope seemed mesmerized by this apparition, and when her face was finally revealed, he could not help but gasp in surprise.

In front of him was standing Helene de Moncler with her face radiating kindness. While offering her hand, she said, "I will give you my unconditional support to complete my Son's mission, who sacrificed for the good of all."

"Pietro, I will do my utmost to help!"

"Do not be afraid!"

"I know…you must have so many questions…"

"Together, we'll succeed!"

❀THE END❀

§FACTUAL INFORMATION§

The characters in this novel are fictitious; however, all the places are real and can be located and virtually visited via google maps.

-Berlaymont Building, Brussels, Belgium: the HQ of the European Commission (http://ec.europa.eu/ Adress: Rue de la Loi 200)

-Cinquentenaire Park, Brussels, Belgium

-The One Building, Brussels, Belgium (Adress: Rue Jacques de Lalaing 40)

-The Great Pyramid, Giza Plateau, Egypt

- Grand Egyptian Museum –GEM, Cairo on the Giza Plateau, Egypt: when it fully opens to the public in late 2022, it will be the largest archaeological museum complex in the world and host to more than 100,000 artifacts. (https://grandegyptianmuseum.org)

-Central Park, New York, US

-The White House, Washington, US(Adress: 1600 Pennsylvania Avenue NW)

-Roman Emperor Galerius' Rotunda, Thessaloniki, Greece (http://odysseus.culture.gr Adress: Platia Agiou Georgiou Rotonta 5)

- Holy Church of John the Baptist Thessaloniki, Greece (Adress: Platia Makenzi King 1)

- Knossos, Island of Crete, Greece

(https://www.heraklion.gr/en/ourplace/knossos/knossos.html)

- Archaeological Museum of the Heraklion, Island of Crete, Greece (https://heraklionmuseum.gr Adress: Chatzidaki Street 1)

- Gethsemane, Jerusalem is a garden at the foot of the Mount of Olives. According to the four Gospels of the New Testament, Jesus underwent agony in the garden and was arrested the night before his crucifixion.

§LIST OF MAIN CHARACTERS§

-Lydia del Biondo

-Neo Moore

-Pope Peter II, Pietro di Monti

-Helene de Moncler, President of the European Commission/Mary (Jesus' Atlantean mother, immortal and possessing regenerative capabilities)

-Jesus

- Peter Lightgood, the American Vice President /The Phoenix/Saint Peter

-Inok, The Phoenix' Assassin

-Salvatore d'Umbria, Vatican's Head of Security

- Mark Hopkins, American Senator

If you enjoyed this adventure, join Lydia again in the next book.Below a free sample is awaiting you.

Future add-ons and exclusive content related to the story will be provided to you by accessing: www.sebastiankentor.com/playlist

◆ ◆ ◆

TEASER BOOK 2...the adventure continues ...release date 2022

Lydia was mesmerized by the gentle smile of the Cambodian gods. She was holding his hand as he would follow her anywhere in the world.

"Their smile reminds me of the one of Mona Lisa's. The only difference is that da Vinci probably never step foot in this temple," he said, kissing her passionately.